BLUE, GRAY AND BLACK BLOOD

PRAISE FOR BLUE, GRAY AND BLACK BLOOD

Anne Simon's new historical novel, BLUE, GRAY AND BLACK BLOOD, not only depicts episodes of the Civil War as it was fought across the bayou country of South Louisiana but tells a narrative that explores contrasts between American cultures. As soldiers of Massachusetts find themselves marching and fighting in a South just beginning to see the end of the plantation system, they explore their own family structures and political systems. Their experiences and musings lead them to the commonality of all human beings-—their capacity for brutality and their ability to love and have compassion for others. BLUE, GRAY AND BLACK BLOOD combines good history and good storytelling.

Ann B. Dobie, Author and Educator
—Professor Emerita, University of Louisiana, Lafayette

BLUE, GRAY AND BLACK BLOOD

A Novel about the Civil War in the Bayou Country

Anne L. Simon

Border Press Books, Sewanee, TN
2023

Cover and maps:
Project Director: Rose Anne Raphael
Graphic Design/Production: Kate Ferry
Bayou Teche area map reprinted with permission from
The Battle in the Bayou Country by Morris Raphael, copyright 1975

ISBN-13: 978-1-7346802-7-0

www.borderpressbooks.com
Border Press Books
PO Box 3124
Sewanee, Tennessee 37375
borderpress@gmail.com

Library of Control Number: 2023912709

Printed in the United States

Dedicated to Phebe Hayes, PhD, whose passion for uncovering the hidden past has inspired a movement in the Bayou Country

TABLE OF CONTENTS

PART IV: GATHERING CONTRABAND, HUMANS AND GOODS

PART V: THE SIEGE OF PORT HUDSON—THE TRIP HOME

FOREWORD

Two historical circumstances came to my attention and launched my imagination into the story you are about to read.

First, while researching for pleasure the history of the Louisiana Bayou Teche country during the Civil War, I learned that the Fifty-second Regiment, Massachusetts Volunteers, that served in Louisiana in 1863 was largely made up of farm boys from Franklin and Hampton counties of western Massachusetts. As a transplant from New England, I am familiar with that area of the Berkshires and had an acquaintance with a few families who spoke the Acadian French of their ancestors displaced from Quebec.

Fortunately, the Chaplain of the Fifty-second Regiment wrote home daily to his wife, who preserved his letters and, after the war, collected letters the men of the Fifty-second Regiment sent home to their families as well. These letters provide details of their thoughts and experiences in Louisiana as they matured in understanding the war, the enslaved, and themselves.

In a second fortunate circumstance, my friend Dr. Phebe Hayes, President of the African-American Historical Society of Iberia Parish, shared the fruits of her genealogical research with me. She learned that her ancestors were barely literate French speakers enslaved in St. Martin Parish, who fled their plantations and followed Union soldiers to freedom. Dr. Hayes provided me with a copy of the Pension Record of one ancestor who joined the U.S. Colored Infantry. This official document is a storehouse of information in the form of sworn affidavits by the soldier, his family, and his fellow soldiers describing their life in slavery, in service with the Union Army, and their postwar life in this area where their descendants live today.

From these two situations, I imagined a nexus: a meeting and a relationship between two French-speaking Union soldiers from Massachusetts and a Louisiana enslaved family who followed them to freedom.

This is a work of historical fiction. As can be seen from the Sources Consulted, it is written within a framework of historical events and recent scholarship. Any similarity to actual persons and details of events is coincidental.

PART I: WAR ANXIETY IN THE NORTH

CHAPTER ONE

William Wells kept step to his own whistling of Yankee Doodle as he rounded the back porch of the Wells farmhouse and headed for the stable. His favorite mount, Madeleine, neighed when she heard him coming. Battered by a week of disagreements between his dominating father and his impetuous younger brother, Aaron, William looked forward to a fast ride through the foothills of the Berkshires on his Chestnut mare and then relaxing over Sunday dinner and a leisurely afternoon visit with the family of his fiancé, their older daughter Elizabeth. Conversation on the Samuel Putnam farm would center on arrangements for the upcoming marriage, the one topic able to drive underground the specter of war hanging over the nation.

One month ago, the militia of the seceded State of South Carolina fired on a Union ship coming into Charleston Harbor to bring needed food to federal forces holed up in Fort Sumter. The ship returned fire. Foiled, the Union felt it necessary to withdraw their troops from the fort. President Lincoln issued a call for the mobilization of the state militias and an order for a naval blockade of the southern ports. Would the steps taken by President Lincoln be sufficient to cause the State of South Carolina to pull back from its threat to consider Union ships entering the Charleston Harbor an act of war? Would other Southern states pause in their moves to secession? Or would there be an uptick in the rebellion? What would these events mean for a peaceful life on the farms of western Massachusetts? Today, William hoped he would not need to worry about such matters.

Drawing in the familiar smells of the stable, William adjusted the saddle on Madeleine. He tightened her girth strap and tossed his lightest pack across her withers. He placed his left boot in the stirrup, swung his long right leg over the saddle, and settled his seat while soothing her with the voice she knew well.

"We're quite fortunate with the weather for our ride this morning, Madeleine. I see a few clouds over the high peaks of the mountains but nothing to cause worry. Mountains make their own weather but rarely share with the valley."

Anyone observing the mare's nods and snorts in response would not be delusional to believe she understood every word William spoke.

William closed and secured the pack. "No reason to carry much with us today. All we'll need this morning is a few treats and a swallow or two of water. In about an hour, we'll see our dear Lizzy. I'm sure she'll have something just for you tucked into the pocket of her dress."

William tapped the mare's shoulder with the loop of the reins he held in his left hand and signaled the stable hand to close the gate behind them with his right. A slight pull told Madeleine to circle to the front of the Wells home. On the road down to the town of Deerfield, William pulled his straw hat down to shield his eyes from the rising sun. He urged his mount into the rocking rhythm of an easy canter with the motion of his body.

"That's my good girl, Madeleine," he said, leaning forward and patting the arch of her neck.

William could have chosen to ride directly to the north through the foothills of the Berkshire Mountains from his family farm to that of his fiancé. To do so would require his mount to pick her path across the half dozen farms in between. William knew all the owners, and everyone would be happy to make it possible for him to cross their fields. But that route would require him to factor in one delay after another: a friendly conversation with his neighbors, dismounting to open and close gates, fording the many streams that run down from the peaks. He knew from over a year of courting Elizabeth that a cantor traversing two sides of a triangle—down the gravel road to Deerfield, a left turn, then another cantor up the road to the Putnam's farm—would be the fastest way to go.

The spring breeze on his face was exactly the tonic William needed this morning to blow away any vestiges of a week of contentious days and restless nights. When William turned Madeleine's head to the Putnam farm, Madeleine felt a different surface under her hooves. She twitched her ear for confirmation of the signal.

"That's right, my girl. We're going to see Elizabeth."

~~~

For the past week, every evening at the dinner table, William's younger brother Aaron tried to persuade their father to permit him to join the Massachusetts militia. The fire of the discussion crackled louder each night. William's father's voice rose until Madeleine could have heard him back in the barn.

"No, no, no. You don't know what you're saying, Aaron. You are not of an age to make such a serious decision. If we have war, the militia will be the first to be called."

Aaron responded through tight lips. "Good! Wells men have always served their country. Your father fought at Valley Forge, and his grandfather died defending the town of Deerfield from the Indians in the Great Massacre of 1704! We were little boys when you told us about those early frontiersmen, some much younger than I am."

"Enough! Now if William—"

Aaron interrupted his father, never a wise move. "William, William. Always William! His best friend Nat Bradford is going to join the militia. He's younger than William."

"By a few months. And he has had different experiences. Every year of life makes a world of difference in understanding, my boy."

"Your boy! There you go calling me a boy. Everyone thinks William and I are twins. My friend Henry Arnold is going to cross over the state line to New York to join their militia."

"Probably because his family will not permit him to join the Massachusetts militia either. They also believe he is too young to serve. That is enough, Aaron. We will have no more discussion of the topic."

Incredibly, Diana interrupted her husband. "Perhaps we *should* have more discussion, Father. Aaron doesn't understand why you are so adamant. Perhaps you could explain.

"Diana! I cannot believe—" Father interrupted. "The militia is a serious military unit, Aaron, not frontiersmen with muskets. Your mother loves you and wants you to have anything you desire. But if there is one quality that is a prerequisite for military service, it is to accept orders without question. You and your entire unit are at higher risk if you do not. Whether you have that quality is for the head of the household to decide. We will talk about this matter at another time."

William looked around the table. His father was red-faced and steaming, and his mother was on the verge of tears. Aaron pushed out of his chair to flee. Surprisingly, that no one slept well after that dinner table exchange.

~~~

In the morning, the sky over the town of Deerfield was clear and bright, as was the smile on William's face. In three weeks, Elizabeth Putnam would be his wife. The patterns of the yearlong engagement would come to an end. God willing, he and Lizzy would be living together in the elm-shaded cottage they had found just off the Deerfield Town Square. They would have a backyard large enough for a kennel, a small stable, and a corral for Madeleine and any other animals William might bring home from the Wells farm.

According to their plan, most mornings during the week, William would ride from their cottage in town to the Wells farm to handle the operations that were his prime responsibility—the horses and cattle. At day's end, he would make the trip in the opposite direction. Elizabeth would spend her days at the Deerfield schoolhouse a half block from the cottage. She would teach children during the school year and, in the summertime, tutor adults just learning to read and write.

On Sundays, one or both of their families would join them at the Congregationalist Church on the Deerfield Square for the following service and fellowship. Most Sundays, they would spend the remainder of the day with her family or his. Today, after a wagon ride from the Putnam farm to church and back, William had an invitation for Sunday dinner with Elizabeth's family. Roast leg of lamb, of course. The Putnam farm raised the finest flock of sheep in Franklin County. William took a deep breath and imagined the rich aroma of the roast. He felt better already. But he could still hear his brother Aaron's words ringing in his ears. "Something exciting is finally reaching us here in the western mountains, and Father won't let me be any part of it!"

~~~

A succulent leg of lamb it was. After dessert, as soon as good manners allowed, Elizabeth's two younger brothers asked to be excused from the dinner table. No chores were required on Sunday. They ducked their chins and scampered to the barn for their fishing gear. The boys planned to join friends at one of the fast-moving mountain streams to cast their lines. Snowmelt made spring the best season to catch brown trout. The ladies of the Putnam family—William's fiancé Elizabeth, her sister Abigail, and their mother Martha—retired to the kitchen to discuss wedding reception plans with the cook.

William and his soon to be father-in-law found comfortable rockers in the shade on the south porch. Samuel Putnam stroked his full ginger beard, lit a cigar, and set his chair in motion. William declined the smoke. He tipped back his chair and propped his boots on the railing. He looked forward to an hour of easy conversation as they watched sheep slowly grazing on the spring green slope of the pasture. A record number of lambs joined the flock this spring.

"I love watching my sheep from afar, William. From afar, that is. Closed up in a barn with them is another matter." Mr. Putnam took a quick intake of breath, wrinkled his nose, and passed a forefinger across his upper lip. "If you're close enough to hear them bleat, you'll wish you weren't!"

"From here, the scene could illustrate a fairy tale, Mr. Putnam. Snow white clouds shift shapes on the lea. I know why you have wide porches all around your house. Pastures of sheep make the most beautiful farms."

William didn't tell him his own father thought sheep hopelessly stupid. He preferred to raise horses and cattle on the Wells farm. He had only a small flock of sheep. When rain threatened, his hands swore to him they had to move quickly to put the sheep under cover. The animals were too lazy to walk over to a water trough if thirsty. They would stand right where they were, open their mouths, turn their heads skyward for a drink—and drown!

After a spell, William dropped his feet to the porch floor and sat forward in his chair. "My father gave me some important advice last week," he said to Mr. Putnam.

"And what was that, William?"

"He said the words that should spring first to my lips over the next three weeks were: *Whatever you would like, my dear Elizabeth.*"

Mr. Putnam grabbed the cigar out of his mouth so his sputter of laughter didn't propel it onto the porch floor. "Wise advice! I do believe I heard you say those very words a half dozen times at the dinner table today."

"Seriously. Mr. Putnam, I don't plan to get involved in wedding details. I'm content to leave all those matters to the Putnam ladies. I've suggested to my mother that she do the same."

"To my knowledge, she has—which surprises me. With no daughters of her own, I thought your mother might want to put her own mother-of-the-bride dreams in the mix. I'm convinced little girls and their mothers start practicing the wedding march when their toddling daughters take their first steps." Mr. Putnam smiled at his own joke.

"I guess you know two little girls came into our family, one before I was born and another between me and Aaron. Sadly, both died before they were two years old."

Mr. Putnam stopped rocking. "No. I didn't know. That might complicate matters when Elizabeth becomes her daughter-in-law."

"Oh, I don't think our family losses matter at all. She and Elizabeth get along beautifully."

Mr. Putnam raised his eyebrows, parted his lips as if to speak, but closed them again. He waited a half minute before resuming his rocking.

William returned to the subject of being involved in wedding plans.

"Just so you understand, sir, if there's anything you need me to weigh in on, I'm willing. Just say the word. My reluctance to express an opinion is because I'm being noble. I have no idea whether the flower bouquets on the ends of the pews should have two sprigs of baby's breath or three—I'm told an odd number is more pleasing to the eye—or whether the sandwiches at the reception in town after the ceremony should be cut in triangles or rolled!"

Mr. Putnam chuckled. "I think we can relax with my daughter Elizabeth as our bride. As you have probably already learned, Elizabeth doesn't hesitate to express her opinion if something is important to her, but she has limited interest in obsessing about small matters. Now, if her younger sister Abigail were to be the bride..." Mr. Putnam rolled his eyes. "She and her mother can worry every little detail to death. Abigail will probably have a dozen attendants rather than just one. That multiplies the number of particulars to consider."

"Just so you know, sir, I will help where you want me to. Say the word and I'll do what I can."

"Thank you, William. I doubt I'll need your help, but I appreciate your offer."

William still sat forward in his chair.

"Something else on your mind, son?" Mr. Putnam asked.

"There is a matter I would like to ask your opinion about, Mr. Putnam."

"Go right ahead."

The talk about war."

Mr. Putnam sighed. "Ah, yes. A worry. Do you have a specific question?"

"Yes, sir. Should our plans take the possibility of war into account? I know you are active in political circles. Do you have any prediction to make?" His voice trailed off.

Pulling on his beard, Mr. Putnam paused before responding. "South Carolina lit the fuse at Fort Sumter by firing on our ship. In fairness, they had made it quite clear they would consider our bringing a Union ship into Charleston Harbor an act of war. But how else could we get food to our soldiers manning the fort? In response, our Governor Andrew has ordered the Massachusetts militia to be combat ready—to replace anyone not fighting fit with someone who could leave when needed. Our legislature has made plans for the financial support our state must provide, perhaps to be reimbursed."

"So, we are already planning for war?" William asked.

"No. We are not. We are taking steps to deter war. Our state has a proud history."

"I know. Every boy child is fed the importance of our role in the Revolution and the formation of our government with his first solid food."

"I like that! Massachusetts was indeed instrumental in the formation of our country. We have a unique and quite marvelous form of government. Massachusetts will not sit by and watch the United States break apart. If necessary, I expect we will be at the heart of preserving the Union."

Mr. Putnam continued. "Our President has ordered a naval blockade of all southern ports. Our fleet far outnumbers the ships under the control of the slave states. Most people believe a blockade will be sufficient to bring thoughts of secession from the Union to an end. The southern states need to get their cotton and sugar to the mills here and abroad. Their economy depends on it."

"As does ours, sir. Here in western Massachusetts, we need cotton to operate the new mills around Northfield and Springfield. So, you believe, Mr. Putnam, that the southern states will think better of rebellion?"

"Let me say I believe we have good reason to hope. There are many difficult decisions ahead. Slavery is wrong, but vexatious problems bedevil the means to eliminate it. Maintaining the Union is critical. Compromises about slavery may be necessary to keep the border states in the fold. You know, only seven states have seceded. There are eight states in which slavery is legal remaining in the Union. Then, there is the issue of extending slavery to new states. We have strong and impatient abolitionists among us. John Brown stirred up a nest of hornets attempting to foment a slave revolt. If we learned one thing from his ill-fated efforts, we know rebellion is not a simple matter. The enslaved don't easily flee from the security of food and shelter. Let me say this. I would not like to sit in President Lincoln's chair right now."

"You do have faith in President Lincoln, don't you?"

"As much as I have in anyone. But no one, not even Abraham Lincoln, knows the answers to the difficult issues. He's doing some serious thinking right now. We should be thinking as well. Our friends in Boston are abuzz with the topic."

"That's not the case around here, Mr. Putnam."

"You are correct. As a rule, I find concern about anything to be proportionate to the proximity of immediate danger or the effect on the pocketbook. Being directly affected focuses attention. The Atlantic coast and Cape Cod are much more exposed to attack than we are. The easterners believe they are vulnerable and poorly defended. The militia we have assembled comes from around Boston, and the call for three-year volunteers is going out in the same area. Here in the western part of the state, people change the subject when the topic of war comes up." A smile crept across Mr. Putnam's face. "How about your father, William? What is his opinion? He has spent more time than I have with the Republican powers that be. I do believe your father has even attended a Saturday afternoon dinner at the Bird Club. I'm sure the possibility of war was on the table."

"Ha!" William tossed his head and ran his hand through his dark forelock. "Yes, father went to one of the Bird Club dinners with our representative, George Davis. Representative Davis thought he could help Father gain support for a tunnel through the mountains to get our products over to the Hudson River and out to markets in the rest of the country. I know very little about politics, but even I've heard that Frank Bird is the power behind Governor Andrew! Just one meeting. Father is hardly in the inner circle of Republican politicians. Representative Davis is a long-time friend. Father even calls him Thaddeus, his middle name."

"If your father has a project in mind, especially one that involves a legislative appropriation and may affect commerce with other states, he may have to work himself into that inner circle. Not much happens in Massachusetts that doesn't have Frank Bird's blessing." The smile disappeared from Mr. Putnam's face. "Does your father think we need to plan for war right now?"

"He has told me basically what you have just expressed, sir. We should be working on how to avoid it. Everyone pays a tremendous price for war. But he is frustrated by the lack of concern about the issue in the western part of our state. He says when a ship goes down, port and starboard sink together. He thinks we should be studying our alternatives while we have time. There are a lot of decisions to be made."

"I agree. But in our defense, we are not very well informed here in the west. The news is stale when the *Greenfield Gazette* learns of something and puts it in the paper. We don't get the Boston newspapers here and cannot read the columnists in the Capitol and the New York press for weeks."

Mr. Putnam continued. "Bringing the issue right down to our wedding, does your father think we should be going ahead, or should we postpone the event until some of the decisions are made?"

"My father only talked to me about a possible postponement one time. He thinks that is the wiser course, but my mother would not hear of it."

"Then you understand that I have even less chance of convincing Elizabeth and her mother to delay the wedding. No force on earth can deter a mother of the bride from putting into effect wedding arrangements a year in the making."

Lines appeared on the faces of both men. They sighed and grew quiet. After a few moments of silence, William spoke up as if they had never mentioned delaying the wedding.

"If it comes to war, Mr. Putnam, the Union will win, right?"

"Absolutely, we would win. Preservation of the Union is essential. I know Massachusetts, and, as I say, I have faith in our President. William, I think if the President would stop his generals from dithering and force them to take decisive action, we could push those Rebel forces in Virginia back home to Richmond in jig-time. But I'm told the President thinks his job is to appoint trained generals and leave strategy to the experts. As a result, we all wait, including the President."

"Have you ever been to the South or any slave state?" William asked Mr. Putnam.

"No. I haven't. My father made a steamboat trip down the Mississippi River to Louisiana many years ago—just to see New Orleans. He loved the food—and the music. My mother kept his letters, and I have read them. New Orleans is an anomaly. They even speak French there— Parisian French, not the French of the Acadian exiles spoken in other parts of Louisiana and some parts of New England. And, unlike the remainder of the South, half the negroes in New Orleans are not enslaved. They are free men. *Gens de couleur libre,* they are called. My father never talked about plantation life."

"All I know about the South is what I read in *The Greenfield Gazette* or hear from the abolitionists. Maybe I'll try to learn—."

Mr. Putnam interrupted. "Hold up a minute, William. I think I hear the ladies coming outside to join us. Let me add some advice to that you received from your father. I suggest we both avoid the possibility of war in the presence of the ladies for the next three weeks, even if we have to participate in a spirited discussion about how many sprigs of baby's breath to attach to the ends of the church pews."

~~~

Anyone with connections to Franklin County, whether through family, politics, or commerce, wanted to see and be seen at the wedding of Elizabeth Putnam and William Wells. The uniting of Deerfield's two most prominent families brought out a crowd. Everyone dressed in Sunday best. The men polished their boots to a high shine. Hoops ballooned the women's skirts, so every cart was pressed into service. Every face wore a broad smile.

The young pastor of the Congregationalist Church of Deerfield had been in the pulpit for less than a year. Handling an important social event presented a challenge for the young man. He called for help from Rev. John F. Moors, Pastor of the Congregationalist Church in the larger town of Greenfield just a few miles up the Connecticut River. Rev. Moors came first to help with the planning and again to assist with the rehearsal and the service. He supplied three soloists from the Greenfield church to add professional voices to the choir and gave words of advice to the young pastor.

"Practice the service with the organist," he said. "He gives you your cues. And no sermon should be longer than fifteen minutes." William and Elizabeth enjoyed meeting Rev. Moors. With an expert on the scene, Martha Putnam stopped fretting. She felt confident the service would come off without a hitch.

The ladies of the congregation outdid themselves. Spring gardens bloomed at their peak at this time of year. On the wedding day, there was not a plant within 25 miles of Deerfield that still bore white blossoms. In the preceding days, every flower had been cut and brought to the church to be contorted into bouquets for the bride and her sole attendant, her sister Abigail, and for decorations at the church, the Deerfield Community Center, and the Putnam farm.

When the pews were almost full, and more guests still waited to be seated, the ushers set up chairs along the side aisles. The head usher sent word to the wedding party in the church hall next door to delay their appearance; people were still squeezing in. Fifteen minutes later, everyone rose with the first note of the Wedding March. Elizabeth, on her father's arm, appeared a vision of shimmering cream-colored silk. Her green eyes sparkled. Tall and handsome as a storybook prince, William awaited her at the altar with his Best Man, his childhood friend Nathaniel Bradford of Conway, a town to the north between Deerfield and Greenfield. Nathaniel stood as tall as William. He wore an identical dress suit. He could have passed for a fraternal twin: slimmer and with blond curls rather than dark locks swept back from his forehead. His eyes were luminescent blue rather than deep brown.

Mr. Putnam kissed Elizabeth's cheek and placed her right hand in William's. William smoothly included in his clasp her left hand with which she held her quivering bouquet.

Three-quarters of an hour later, the pastor pronounced William and Elizabeth husband and wife. Applause overpowered the pealing of the church bells.

Walking back down the aisle with his bride on his arm, William paused to express his gratitude to her parents. "Yes, William, everything was perfect," Mr. Putnam responded. Then, with a twinkle in his eyes, Mr. Putnam leaned toward his new son-in-law and whispered, "Perhaps we could have used another couple of sprigs of baby's breath on the ends of the pews."

Close behind the newly married couple, sister Abigail held the arm of Nathaniel Bradford.

Mr. Putnam had a question for his wife, Martha. "Did you plan the matching act for William and Nathaniel, identically clad right down to the *boutonnières*?"

"Abigail's plan." Martha rolled her eyes. "Inspired, I'd say. Would we be so fortunate to have another wedding soon with the couples in reverse order? Abigail gets dreamy-eyed looking at Nathaniel's blue eyes and blond curls!"

"They are both fine men, Martha. Nathaniel is more serious than William. I prefer William's lighter outlook on life."

Mr. Putnam said a silent prayer that the two childhood friends would not soon be wearing matching uniforms of Union blue.

~~~

The first reception took place in the Deerfield Community Center, a half block from the church. The bride and groom welcomed the guests over punch and sandwiches—cut in triangles and rolled. No politician missed the opportunity to mingle with the citizens who mattered in Franklin County. One after another raised a glass in an effusive toast to the bride and groom. After two hours of meet and greet in the Town Square, a procession of wagons brought more than a hundred invited family and close friends to the Putnam farm. The champagne flowed. The dining room table creaked under the weight of a banquet. After the bride and groom finished the first dance, Nathaniel Bradford spun Elizabeth's sister Abigail. He did so many times that night as accordions and fiddles enticed dancers to take a turn on the porches. Another couple that caught everyone's eye was Aaron dancing with Nathaniel's oldest sister Susanna, guided in Acadian dances by the Wells ranch manager Pierre.

A thought crossed William's mind, but he didn't speak aloud. Perhaps Susanna, the liveliest one in Nathaniel's family, could spark Aaron's interest and keep him more content to remain on the farm.

Later in the evening, Elizabeth had a question for her new husband. "Who is the handsome man in uniform floating on the edges of the crowd? I see him occasionally speaking confidentially with Nathaniel. We were introduced, but I cannot remember his name."

"I've also forgotten the name, but he's the commanding officer of Nathaniel's militia. I asked Nathaniel if the commander had any information about plans for the unit, but Nathaniel said we wouldn't think about that tonight. I know they have purged everyone who is not fighting fit and recruited able replacements. I saw concern on Nathaniel's face. I'll talk to him as soon as I have an opportunity."

Sometime after midnight, William put his arm around Elizabeth's shoulders, kissed her on her forehead, and whispered in her ear. "Now, Lizzie, my love, I need no more champagne and dancing. I'm ready to go home."

"You have read my mind, Will, my love. I am ready to shed these hoops and slip into your arms."

William found his ranch manager Pierre and asked him to bring around the wagon to take them to their cottage in town.

~~~

Midmorning, sunlight streaked through the east windows of the cottage on Deerfield Square. William propped himself on one elbow, the better to see Elizabeth's flushed face on the pillow beside him. Her eyelids fluttered open, revealing the green jewels. "Ah-h-h. Now that's a perfect picture!" he said. After a brief and sleepy conversation, William and Elizabeth realized neither wanted to spend a weeklong honeymoon in Boston. They agreed to change their plans and cancel their reservation at the Parker House Hotel. Days of lazy trail riding through the green-forested foothills and quiet nights in country inns appealed to them more than putting themselves into the bustle of the city. William was relieved not to be exposed to the talk of war that gripped the East.

They rolled over together. They didn't make it to the remains of the wedding cake Pierre had left on the kitchen table until well after noon.

CHAPTER TWO

S ix weeks later, at the end of the day, William led Madeleine through the rear gate behind the cottage on Deerfield Square. From her rocking chair on the back porch, Elizabeth watched her husband lift the saddle off Madeleine, hang it on the rack inside the stable, and lead the mare around the corral to cool down, talking tenderly to her all the time. With long, firm strokes, he brushed her well. He gave her food and water and moved her into a stall for the night.

The final routine of the workday usually brought ease to William's shoulders and a soft smile to his lips. Not tonight. William's boots rapped like a woodpecker as he mounted the stairs to the porch. A kiss for Elizabeth was much briefer than usual, and he sat down in the rocker beside her. He asked if her day went well. She told a story about one of her students and asked about his day. "Just fine," he mumbled in response. He didn't elaborate. Unusual. He must have something on his mind.

Elizabeth knew her husband preferred to share his concerns in his own way, and at the moment, he might choose to do so. She didn't question him. She waited. She advanced a few topics to see if one opened the door to his thoughts. No luck. Opportunity to intrude came after they had finished the chicken and dumplings and most of the dessert, and she noticed William working his spoon to corner and capture a last bite of Indian Pudding.

"Ah, ha! You trapped it," she said. "I believe you enjoyed the dessert, Will. I thought I might see you pick up your bowl and lick the last morsel as you did when you were a little boy."

"Oh, my." He raised his napkin to feign covering his face. "I apologize for being distracted. Licking the dessert plate is a story my mother loves to tell on me to watch me turn red. How did you know about that?"

"I confess I have inside information. I've always loved Indian Pudding, and your mother told me you do also. She gave me her recipe. I'm trying to prepare food you enjoy."

"You are succeeding, my love. If Madeleine could talk, I'm sure she would tell you I'm gaining weight. I can't stop my mother from putting the pots on the fire every morning when she sees me ride into the corral. I send most of the food home to the Acadian village with Pierre, but I have to eat a bit. More food than I need!"

"I'm pleased you liked the pudding tonight, love. The only reason I'm sorry we didn't have our honeymoon week in Boston—far outweighed by the many reasons I'm glad we chose to spend a peaceful sojourn in the mountains—is that we would have been able to check out the dessert at Durgin-Park Restaurant. I'd like to know if I'm getting close to duplicating the original dessert."

"A pointless exercise, my dear. Close to the Durgin-Park version or not, your Indian Pudding is delicious, with just the right balance of molasses and spice." He paused. "But I need to tell you that I may soon have an opportunity to sample the original pudding for myself. Let's put up these dishes and go back out onto the porch for a bit. I have something to tell you about."

When they were settled on the rocking chairs with a good view of the sun slipping down the western sky to meet the peaks of the mountains, Elizabeth took her husband's hand. Having been invited to hear about *something*, she felt free to prod in a roundabout way. "So, tell me, Will, what will enable you to check out the original Indian Pudding?"

William took a deep breath before he answered.

"Today, I was working with a couple of horses Pierre and I hope to have ready to take to the Northampton sale at the end of the summer. Pierre came out to the corral to tell me my father wanted me to come to the house. Father had company—George Davis from Greenfield. I believe you know who he is: the Franklin County State Representative in The General Court."

"Yes, I know Representative Davis. I met him at our wedding. But you speak of The General Court. Is he also a lawyer?"

William chuckled. "No, no, my dear. The General Court is the official name of the Massachusetts State Legislature."

Elizabeth pinched her lips together and shook her head. "Civics!

Schools think girls have no reason to know about such things. If we should have a daughter... Sorry, William. I apologize for the interruption. Please go on."

"A good interruption, my dear. You should know I will help with the education of our girls! And I hope we have a few of them!"

Elizabeth squeezed her husband's hand. He continued.

"We were close to the end of the day. I left Pierre in the corral to complete the evening chores. Out of consideration for a visitor who might not be accustomed to the aroma of the stable the way Father and I are, I asked Pierre if I had time to clean up a bit. Pierre suggested I delay only long enough to take off my boots."

Elizabeth stiffened. "Oh, dear. Pierre must have thought the meeting urgent."

"My first thought, Lizzy, and it gave me *un frisson*. We don't have a big problem, just something that takes some thinking and planning around. I went into the house and joined them. I learned the reason Father asked Pierre to summon me in five minutes. Representative Davis wants Father and me to help him wake up the western part of the state to the difficulties facing the Union."

Elizabeth's eyes popped wide open.

"And how does he propose you do that?"

"First step: He wants us to go to Boston to the Republican Party State Convention. All the important politicians will speak about the issues confronting the Union. Second step: when we return home, he wants us to have some meetings here in the western part of the state to discuss the issues, possible solutions, and how the west can be involved in the decision-making."

"Boston? Can your father manage a trip to Boston? The last time he went there, he said the ride had become too hard for him. And now he has a sore left shoulder to contend with, or at least he said he did last Sunday when he left the dinner table without dessert. He must have had a speedy recovery."

"No, he has not recovered. On the contrary, the shoulder seems just as troublesome as it has been for the past two weeks. Probably more so because he's discouraged. Yesterday, Dr. Thomas came from Greenfield to see him. He told Father the shoulder bones were out of place, but that surgery was too great a risk for him to undergo. The only safe solution is to eliminate strenuous work for a few months to see if the shoulder will heal. Father was not happy to hear that. He will have to ask Aaron and me to do extra work with the cattle. Of course, I'm willing, but Father doesn't want to give up his favorite tasks. And Aaron? Who knows about him?"

"And yet, your father is thinking of traveling to Boston?"

Elizabeth pinched her eyebrows, looking as if her father-in-law's pain was her own.

"He can't ride to Boston, but if I will come with him, he believes he can make the trip by railway. There's a new connection from Greenfield to Fitchburg to meet the direct line to the city. And when we get to Boston, he wants me to join him and Representative Davis at the Republican Party Convention. He and Representative Davis think it's time everyone in the Western part of the state wakes up to the serious issues the North is facing. They think I can help reach the younger people."

Elizabeth raised her eyebrows. "Everyone? I bet I know who isn't included in "*everyone*.""

William pantomimed a check in the air. "Point well made, my dear. Not ladies, of course." William continued, "I believe Representative Davis thinks my father is not as sharp as he was and needs my help with the political issues."

"Really? Do you see that he's not as sharp?"

"No, I don't. I think the pain he is in now makes him tire easily. He doesn't want to talk with his old buddy, Thaddeus, all evening. He prefers a short exchange of thoughts, one stiff drink, and then straight to bed. Dr. Thomas says when the pain subsides, and it will, he'll be fine."

"Tell me, did your father have a particular accident that started the shoulder problem?" Elizabeth asked.

"He doesn't remember any particular event, but you know how he is. Physically, he's as headstrong as Aaron. And as reckless. He always has scrapes and bruises he can't explain. He loves to break horses and throw around bales of hay. He helps at the birth of every animal on the farm. He's a good twelve years older than your father, Lizzy."

"I cannot believe his age when I see him work. That's where you get your broad shoulders and strength." She reached out and caressed her husband's upper arm.

"Whatever the cause of his sore shoulder may be, Mother and I both think it's time he gave up the heavy work on the farm. Now it's the shoulder, but soon it will be something else. He's fighting the very idea of accepting his age."

"You and your three brothers can give him a lot of help, William. All of you except Aaron like farming as much as he does. The problem is your father is happiest saddling up and making rounds to check on his farm."

"Not right now. Pierre tells me he hasn't been on a horse for over two weeks! Thank goodness he hurt his left shoulder. He'd be in a bind if he couldn't use his right arm. This will pass, but if we could find any method to speed up the process, I'd like to help make it available to him. Which gets me to the *lagniappe* built into this proposed trip to Boston."

"What is that?"

"Thaddeus has a cousin who is on staff at Massachusetts General Hospital. He teaches anatomy in the medical school. Thaddeus thinks his cousin could look at the shoulder and tell him if anything else could be done."

Elizabeth's eyes widened. "That is reason enough to go to Boston! We should do anything we can to make your father more comfortable," Elizabeth continued. "But, the Republican Convention, William? You have never shown much interest in politics. Why now? My father says the problems the Union faces are very difficult."

"Your father is correct, but perhaps it's time I became better informed. I'm embarrassed to be almost twenty-five years old and still asking my father how I should vote."

Elizabeth was quiet for a few moments. "What you do about politics is entirely up to you, William. I can't even vote, you know. I'm relieved a trip to Boston was the reason for Representative Davis' visit. I thought you would to tell me he brought news of more difficulties between the north and south."

"No news that I know of, good or bad, but you know how we stay in the dark out here in the west."

Elizabeth looked far from relieved. William gave her hand another squeeze. "My dear, let me share my idea. I know you miss your sister. What if you invite her to visit while I'm away? The two of you could take a trip to Greenfield or Northampton to shop. I wish you could come with me to Boston, but—"

"No, no!" Elizabeth interrupted. "Your father needs you with him at all times in the city. I would be in the way. We should do everything we can to help him. As for a visit from Abigail, you know I would love to have time with her. I hoped to have the cottage a bit more settled before

she came, but summer is best for us to be away from home for a couple
of weeks. My teaching duties are flexible, and Abigail doesn't have to
keep up with the tutoring of my brothers. I thought the possibility of war
had put worry lines between your brows."

"No, no, love. As far as I've heard, all is quiet, but we get very little
news in the western part of the state. Father says he's realized that if
western Massachusetts wants to get support for a tunnel through the
mountains, he will have to persuade the powers that be of the wisdom of
the project. He wants my help doing that. I want to help my father,
but..."

William took a deep breath and scratched his chin. "I have a lot to
learn. First, I've never been able to keep the political parties in
Massachusetts straight. People talk about the Liberty Party, the Know-
Nothings, the Free Soilers, the Nativists, the Constitutionalists, the
Whigs, the Democrats, and the Republicans. Despite the labels, it always
seems the old-line Bostonians are still in control at the end of the day.
They hardly know we exist out here in the west. Thaddeus says they
think the sun rises over Chelsea, hovers over State Street at noon, and
sinks in the waters of the Back Bay in the evening."

Elizabeth chuckled. "Although ladies are not permitted to vote, I do
know we are both Republicans at heart. From what I hear, Democrats
want to accommodate slavery. I think that's wrong. And I believe in our
Republican President."

"There are a lot of thorny problems involved in eliminating slavery,
my love."

"They can be worked out."

"We can say that when we are not ourselves responsible to the citizens
for the *working it out* part! We Republicans have some impatient
abolitionists in our number, some of whom, like old John Brown, think a
worthy end justifies dangerous means."

"A lot of people say John Brown was mad, William. Maybe, but from
the little I've heard about him, I don't think he knew very much about
the enslaved he expected to follow him. He talked to God but not to the
people he thought would flock to his cause! Not that I know much more.
I've never been south of Springfield. All I know of slavery is what I've
read or heard talked about. You've never been to the South either, have
you?"

"No, I haven't. I know of people who've gone to New Orleans. Your
father says your grandfather went once. But the city is different from the

cotton and sugarcane plantations we hear about from the abolitionists. Some negroes in the city are free. Many in the city speak French! Pierre and I would like that. Seriously, I would not mind being better informed. Now I have an opportunity and couldn't have two better teachers than my father and Representative Davis."

Elizabeth sat forward on her chair. "We have a Republican President and a Republican Governor. Western Massachusetts supported both. They might even pay some attention to us to reward a base of their support."

William raised his free hand. "Good thinking, my dear! I believe you'd be better at politics than I am. Representative Davis expressed the same thought." He continued, "On another subject, I hope I'll have an opportunity to see Nathaniel while I'm in Boston. I wonder if he knows more than we do about the military plans."

"That is a meeting I am sorry to miss. Abigail tells me he hasn't been home for a good while. She says his father tells her the militia training is intense. They seem to be on a fast track to readiness. He gets into Boston now and then. There are those, especially in the Capitol, who think the President should command the northern army to march on to Richmond right now and end the rebellion before the South can raise an army! If we should do that, we need to be prepared to know how to deal with the problems that will arise. I don't know that anyone, not even President Lincoln, understands what's ahead."

William and Elizabeth discussed the Union's issues until the sun disappeared behind the mountains.

The following evening, Elizabeth read to her husband the letter she had composed to send to her sister.

Deerfield, June 30, 1861

My Dear Sister Abigail,
I knew I would miss you when I moved from the farm to town but caught up in all the excitement of falling in love with William, planning and having a wedding, and then moving into our cottage in Deerfield, I didn't realize that no longer being close to my little sister every day of my life would leave such a big hole. Especially when William might be away. And now he will be!

Before the end of the month William and his father will be going to Boston to the Republican Convention. William may be gone for at least a week. No more suspense; I'll get right to my big request. Would it be possible for you to come for a visit while William is away?

Of course, William wants me to stay at the Wells farm and, when she hears of the trip, Mama will want me to go home for a visit. But I have so many unfinished projects here at the cottage I shouldn't leave. Frankly, the projects defeat me. I don't have to tell you that I've never been very good at the domestic arts! Mama used to try to get me to take an interest when she was sewing curtains or putting up the summer produce. She said one day I'd be sorry that I was always running off to a quiet corner to read a book. Well, she was right. Now I need help!

A few days ago, I found myself asking Pierre what color to have the kitchen painted and what material to use to cover the windows! Isn't that ridiculous? Imagine asking William's ranch manager to give me advice about decorating?

Dear sister, I could definitely use the help of someone like you who has skill in such matters. William thinks you might know where we should go to find supplies for curtains and such. North to Greenfield? South to Northampton? I hope we would not have to go all the way to Springfield, but we could. William says he could arrange for Pierre to take us. He delivers our animals to the markets there and knows safe rooming houses where we could stay.

This is an opportune time. My students will not be back in school for another month, and you probably won't have to supervise lessons for our brothers until the fall. Please, please tell me if you will take it under consideration and we can proceed to make plans.

Much love to you, dear sister.

Elizabeth

P.S. I confess that I would love to talk to you about all the rumors of war. Most people think the South will think better of secession and, if they do not, the Union will make short work of their rebellion. Is that what our father still thinks? You see, I need to know about paint colors and fabrics, but I'm interested in lots of other things as well. I miss our long conversations. E.

CHAPTER THREE

Williams's mother and Pierre, the ranch manager, tried their best to turn the finest wagon on the Wells farm into a comfortable conveyance for the trip to meet the railway to Boston. Pierre greased the axles of the wooden wheels, and Mrs. Wells lined the wagon bed with blankets and sheepskins. John Wells climbed aboard expecting a reasonably comfortable ride to Deerfield to pick up William. The blankets they spread in the wagon cushioned the ride they took around the farm for a test drive. But alas, when the wooden wheels of the wagon encountered the potholes on the road from the Wells farm down to the Deerfield Village Square, Mr. Wells pinched his lips; every bump stabbed a twinge across his face. Pierre's expression mirrored his boss's pain.

"I'm sorry, sir," Pierre said time and again.

To Pierre, Mr. Wells was far more than an employer. Pierre's father had been the original ranch manager of the Wells farm. An only child, the same age as the boss's son William, Pierre often came to the farm to be William's playmate.

Pierre's father and his mother both died of fever when he was just four years old. From that time, Pierre did not miss a daily visit; Aaron joined them when he turned four. Mr. Wells included Pierre in his sons' lessons with the tutor in the morning and the operations of the farm in the afternoons. William and Pierre concentrated on raising and training horses; Aaron worked with the other animals and the crops. Both Wells boys spoke with Pierre and to the animals in Pierre's Acadian French. By the time of the visit to Boston for the Convention and the visiting doctor, Pierre and William had been birthing, breaking, and training horses together for over a dozen years.

Elizabeth added another layer of cushioning to the wagon at the cottage in Deerfield. She brought a picnic basket and stowed it under the seat with their other gear.

Elizabeth repeatedly asked her father-in-law if there was anything they could do to make him more comfortable.

Mr. Wells waved his hand to dismiss her fretting. He patted the breast pocket of his shirt and tried, but failed, to catch his son William's eye. Finally, he sighed and said, "Let's just get the wagon on the road."

When the wagon left the cottage behind, Mr. Wells drew a silver flask from his breast pocket. He raised it to his lips and took in a generous draft. He swallowed and exhaled. "Ah, ah, ah..." He closed his eyes, leaned back into the blankets, and smiled. The amber liquid suffused his chest with soothing balm. In less than an hour, Pierre pulled the wagon up to the new railroad depot in the center of the town of Greenfield.

The stationmaster delivered a pleasant surprise. Following instructions from Representative Davis, he had reconfigured two bench seats in the railcar scheduled to travel north to Fitchburg. The seats faced one another and supported a thick pad on which Mr. Wells stretched out. Fortunately, he was not as tall as his son.

When the rail car pulled from the Greenfield station and headed for Fitchburg, Pierre stood on the dock, shading his eyes. He peered down the tracks to watch father and son disappear.

"I believe Pierre would have loved to be included in this trip," William said to his father.

There were to be many times over the next ten days when William had the same wish.

At Fitchburg, the engineer unhooked the car they had ridden in from Greenfield and attached it to the last car on the train headed east to Boston. This maneuver added benefit for the Deerfield passengers; the car was farthest from the snorting, the soot, and the noxious fumes belching from the steam engine pulling the train. With another draft from the silver flask, Mr. Wells sank deep into oblivion. He missed the many stops on the route to Boston. Hours later, the conductor's voice brought him back to consciousness.

"Haymarket Street Station! Last stop. All passengers must depart the train."

Another accommodation from Representative Davis awaited them. He had sent his carriage. A skilled driver threaded through the evening crowds of the city to the Parker House Hotel.

"Extra! Extra! Read all about it," a newsboy at the hotel door cried, thrusting a copy of *The Boston Daily Journal* in their direction. "First reports from the battlefield at Bull Run!"

"Get a paper for us, William," Mr. Wells instructed. "And a tip for the wagon driver while you're at it." William dug in his pocket for some change.

William had received his first lesson in managing in a crowded city: be prepared for the frequent distribution of coins.

Imposing red brick buildings lined the busy streets. Unfortunately, soot from a cluster of smokestacks only a few blocks away left a layer of black powder on every surface except the glass doors with gold lettering adorning the entrance to the Parker House Hotel. A liveried bellman stood polishing the doors all day long. William took a deep breath and wrinkled up his face; he had missed the clear mountain air of the west.

William picked up a message for his father at the front desk. Representative Davis suggested they have dinner in the hotel and get a good night's rest. He'd be at the hotel dining room at nine o'clock in the morning for breakfast and to make plans for their presence at the Republican Party Convention. The note said the chairman would gavel the general session to order at 1:00 PM. Representative Davis further reported that he had contacted his cousin at Massachusetts General Hospital. The doctor said he would make the Wells' room at the Parker House his first house call the following day to look at John Wells' shoulder.

A uniformed bellman pointed out the dining room, showed father and son to their room, and gave William instruction on how to light the light the lamps—another tip required. Before he had completed the lesson, Mr. Wells pulled off his boots and stretched out on the bed without removing his clothes. A deep snore accompanied his next breath.

William shook his head at the décor: heavy draperies and dark wood furniture upholstered in red velvet. He wrinkled his nose. He and Elizabeth passed up this for the spare, rustic furnishings of country inns in the mountains they visited on their honeymoon. They had made a good decision.

William's invitation to his father to join him for dinner downstairs only momentarily interrupted the rhythm of the older man's snoring. His eyelids fluttered but did not open. William dined alone.

An hour later, William returned to the room after savoring a fine cod expertly deboned by the headwaiter decked out as a member of George Washington's Continental Army. He turned up the lamp and read *The Boston Daily Journal*. A banner headline, letters two inches tall, stretched across the top of the front page. BLUE AND GREY POISED FOR BATTLE AT BULL RUN. The supporting article carried the byline of three special reporters and their location: *a hillside in Manassas, Virginia, thirty-five miles outside the Capitol.*

Through field binoculars, the reporters observed two armies taking positions opposite one another not more than 100 feet away on the far side of the stream known to the residents as Bull Run. The reporters expected to watch whatever action occurred between the two forces and send couriers back to the Capitol. From there, they would transmit reports throughout the Union by telegraph, the recently installed communication system. Unfortunately, the telegraph did not yet reach western Massachusetts.

William considered whether to wake his father. Mr. Wells would be delighted to learn that the commander of the Union Army planned to engage the enemy. He knew there was no guarantee of success, but, in his mind, he believed the Union Army would send the Rebels packing. His father slept deeply; William decided against disturbing him. There was, as yet, no real news. Tomorrow would be time enough for his father to learn the armies were in place. Anticipating a good report before the end of the following day, William slept well. By tomorrow night, the secessionists might have thought better of the whole idea of rebellion!

~~~

John Wells rose at the farmer's customary early hour, cleaned up, and dressed. He and William went downstairs to the dining room to meet Representative Davis for breakfast. To the casual observer, Mr. Wells looked splendid in his well-tailored suit, tall, starched collar, and cravat. His father's appearance didn't fool William. He detected a twinge knifing his father's expression as he walked across the dining room floor to their table, and another twinge as his left shoulder touched the back of his chair. His coffee cup rattled on its saucer. His fork pushed bacon and eggs around his plate; only a few bites traveled to his mouth.

John Wells proposed a revised plan for the day.

"Thaddeus, I'm not up for hours on a hard chair enduring the oratory of our long-winded colleagues. My carriage will call for William to take him to the convention hall. "I will instruct him to ask for the usher called Robert. Robert will make sure he is seated. William will then be able to manage on his own. I'll rest today and be ready to greet the doctor in my room."

Like a leaf tossed about by a nor'easter, the crowd buffeted William in a forest of red, white, and blue banners at the entry doors to the building hall where the Republican Convention would take place. William took his hat off and clutched it to his chest. Following instructions, William showed his ticket to the first usher he encountered. He asked for Robert. In a flash, another usher, one with double the number of badges and banners on a sash across his chest, came scurrying. This usher unloosed a burst of words.

"Good day, Mr. Wells. My name is Robert, Mr. Wells. I hope you are feeling well. I am instructed to show you and your father to your seats. Is your father coming along behind you?"

"Unfortunately, he is not. William responded. "He will not be able to be here."

"So, you will be alone? I'm sorry about that, sir. I hope he is not unwell. Just follow me. I believe Representative Davis is in a committee meeting—the transportation committee. Then, he must take his place on the stage. He asked me to seat you and tell you he will come to you at the first break in the proceedings. He hopes you will find the location of your seat satisfactory. If there is anything you need, ask any usher to find Robert. That's my name. Robert. Please follow me, sir."

Robert showed William to a choice seat in the rapidly filling hall, ten rows from the edge of the dais, no more than twenty feet from the podium. William's impression: Representative Davis mattered around here.

William introduced himself to the occupants of the neighboring chairs. Their eyes rested on him for only two seconds as they mumbled their names in response. Clipping off their words like native Bostonians, they resumed their conversations with each other, which now required them to lean forward and back to communicate around the obstacle created by the tall stranger in their midst.

William spotted Representative Davis in the crowd of bearded men, many in morning coats, taking place on the stage. He recognized no one else.

Fifteen minutes later, one of the men on the stage rose and stood at the podium. He banged a gavel, called the meeting to order, and introduced the first speaker, Governor John Andrew. Less than a year previously, at his father's direction, William had given the Governor his vote.

William had trouble following the Governor's rhetoric. He could not extract any firm opinion about the issues. *On the one hand… On the other hand.* What did the Governor think should be the party position on the return of runaway slaves to their masters, abolition of slavery with or without compensation to slave owners who stood to lose their most valuable assets, or the expansion of slavery in the new states? What would be the future of liberated slaves or any of the many other issues William's father thought they should consider? Most importantly, did the Governor believe it was time to bring on conflict with the rebellious states and risk defection by the border states and opposition from European countries?

William learned nothing and grew increasingly irritated at his neighbors. Their running commentary made it difficult for him to hear a firm opinion should one be expressed.

The Governor summed up his position. "We are here today to consider our course—and the ramifications of whatever positions we might choose to take. Those who have made known their desire to address this assembly are asked to limit their remarks to fewer than fifteen minutes so that all who wish to speak may be accommodated. Each issue raised will be referred to the appropriate committee for consideration and report to the Party's next meeting."

Now William understood what the Governor considered his role: not to give answers but to present positions to *consider*. The Governor did follow his direction to limit remarks to fifteen minutes. William's second impression? If this is what politics is like, it may take more patience than he possessed.

William did not recognize the names nor know the positions of the speakers who followed the Governor. For that reason, he didn't know whose opinion mattered and whose was destined to be ignored, even if wise. He decided the best use of his attention would be to try to digest the point each speaker made and, in that way, familiarize himself with the many matters at issue. He would not try to come to any conclusions, to figure out what the decisions of the body might eventually be, or if he agreed with them.

Talk, talk, talk. Shortly, one bold question rang through the room. "Has the time come to end appeasement of those seeking to accommodate slavery?"

Answers exploded as if grapeshot had been fired into the crowd. "Yes!

Yes!" "Abolition now!" William's neighbors called out in the affirmative. The Governor returned to the podium to gavel the crowd to order. Five minutes passed before he could restore the attention of the audience.

Next, a man identified as "the Senator from Lowell" rose to take the podium. He argued that the Constitution is the paramount law of the land. Since the Constitution recognizes slavery, slavery is bedrock of Constitutional Law. Any endorsement of abolition would be to respond to the secessionist perfidy with another perfidy—because abolition would be unconstitutional!

Several speakers jumped to their feet to pound that opinion into oblivion. The winner of the shouting match brought down the house with his response. "Absolutely not. No law of man, not even the Constitution of the United States, can require that we take positions contrary to the law of God or the dictates of our own conscience. Slavery is evil. Slavery must end!"

When the crowd settled, the next speaker began an analogy based on Solomon's solution when two women argued over the parentage of a baby. The speaker suggested that we permit hostilities to break out; he predicted one or both sides would then come to the table to talk.

"Really?" William mumbled rhetorically to his neighbors. "I think the speaker has strangled on his Biblical reference. Neither side of our disagreement shows any sign of backing down. They would each happily put the baby on a pole and take turns carrying him into battle!"

His neighbors laughed. William cast kindlier looks in their direction. At least the proud people of eastern Massachusetts had a passing acquaintance with Biblical reference and a sense of humor.

Next, William heard a proposal he liked: all the political parties, including the assembled Republicans, should suspend political activity for the duration of the threat to the Union and devote full energy and resources to the pursuit of victory, militarily if necessary.

The idea appealed to William. He needed time to understand the issues. No one could deny that eliminating the threat to the Union was a priority. After Fort Sumpter, with secession votes scheduled throughout the South, President Lincoln had been reluctant to be aggressive. When Virginia voted for secession, the direction of events became clear. The President should take note and prod his dithering generals to get down to business. On to Richmond!

Then William realized what the speaker had proposed meant immediate war without any plan for dealing with the inevitable consequences. He had been swept along. At least he hadn't spoken out loud! The same realization and a hush swept through the crowd.

The next speaker proposed they do no more than issue a statement disapproving of slavery. Damn! Another plan to do nothing!

Charles Sumner, whom William knew to be the highly respected Massachusetts Senator in Washington, rose and spoke eloquently for the firmer statement to a respectfully silent crowd. A striking figure, ramrod straight, locks of hair curling over his ears, a slight limp the only effect he had from the injuries he suffered from the near-fatal caning he received four years previously on the floor of Congress. Preston Brooks, a congressman from South Carolina, had taken offense at an antislavery speech Sumner made, which Brooks thought attached the label of sexual exploiter to Brooks' slave-owning cousin.

"Pure Bird Club talk, and I like it," commented one of William's neighbors after Sumner's remarks. William was pleased he recognized the name Charles Bird and knew, whether one agreed or not, that Bird's opinion mattered.

A known radical abolitionist followed Senator Sumner with the thesis that since every state's Secession Resolution contained the statement that the seceding state did so to preserve slavery, one could not deny that these states had begun hostile action for the right to hold persons in perpetual bondage! Eventually the North would be driven to the opposite position. Why not espouse the elimination of slavery right now and occupy the moral high ground?

The man who had identified himself as the Senator from Lowell opposed that view. "And break up the Union by losing the border states and prompting the European powers to pour money and resources into the South to ensure the cotton supply for their mills? No! We first need a post-abolition plan in place for the thousands of freed slaves without the means to live in freedom. One columnist in the *New York Daily Tribune* claimed President Lincoln believed freed slaves should be returned to Africa for resettlement. We need to know now what the President has in mind, opined the columnist."

A man William thought wise followed the abolitionist and suggested they appoint a committee to list the pros, cons, and costs that could be expected from each proposal about slaves that had been brought before the Convention. A way to delay a decision! Refer the matter to committee! William liked the idea of postponing action. Surely, they would have good news from the confrontation at Bull Run in a few days, maybe even by tomorrow.

The speeches were turning to consider the problems that might arise from abolition when Governor Andrew stood up in the assemblage of dignitaries on the dais and stepped forward to reclaim the podium. He abruptly announced a recess of the Convention proceedings. He did not explain despite the chorus of demands for one.

William caught sight of a grey object bobbing up and down toward him on a path from the stage. Representative Davis's grey head! It looked like a ship running for port through choppy seas.

"Well, young man, what did you think of all that?" Representative Davis asked William when he reached him.

"My head is spinning, sir. Hearing Senator Sumner was a privilege indeed. He is impressive. Usually, when I read the news from the Capitol, I can't keep straight all those men whose two-syllable names start with an "S": Sumner, Stanton, Seward. Now, I'll no longer confuse Senator Sumner with anyone else. All this is very complicated, sir. It will be a long time before I express an opinion on any of these issues. I have much to learn."

"I understand. But do you agree it's time you took over your father's worries?"

William blinked hard. "Take over? My father doesn't want to give up anything. I'm fascinated, but is *taking over* the only option?"

Representative Davis's face broke into a smile. "I guess there are less drastic positions. Your father may soon be back to good health. But William, we have another matter to deal with right now." He drew William away from his neighbors to a quiet spot at the side of the dais.

"Governor Andrew has just now called for a recess of the Convention. In a few moments, he will shut down the Convention completely!"

"What? Shut it down? Why is that? There are still several men in line to speak."

"He has received a messenger from Bull Run. The news from the battlefield is not good. It is dreadful. The paper tonight will have a full report."

"What? We are not defeating the Rebels?"

"Worse than that. We have been chased from the battlefield with tremendous losses."

"My God! That can't be true!"

"I'm afraid it is."

"That changes everything!"

"No need to panic, William. Not everything, but the transportation committee is scheduled to consider the tunnel through the mountains this afternoon. No one will care about a tunnel right now. Have Robert call my carriage to take you back to the Parker House. Ask the desk to send newspapers to your room as soon as they are on the street. I'll come over around seven to have dinner with you two."

William picked up a copy of *The Boston Daily Journal* at the door of his hotel. A four-inch headline proclaimed: UNION ARMY IN RETREAT. With eyes on the newspaper in his hand, William stumbled up the stairs to their room.

Dispatches to the paper came from reporters who observed the battle at Manassas, Virginia, from a hillside 35 miles from the Capitol on the Washington side of the Bull Run stream. Early in the day, confident that Union forces would drive back the Rebels, citizens of Washington packed blankets and picnic baskets and joined the reporters. They were in a holiday mood. Through opera glasses, the picnickers had a near perfect vantage point from which to witness the spectacle of two armies setting up for battle.

The troops fixed bayonets and formed two lines facing one another in the fashion of combat taught to the commanders of both armies during their training at West Point. Anticipating an easy victory and a march to to the Confederate capitol at Richmond, the partisan Union crowd on the hill whooped and hollered with excitement. They hissed scorn at the Rebel yells from the troops in grey. Below them, rifles at the ready, blue and grey uniforms moved toward one another. Gunshots rang out.

Cheering in the Union ranks and celebrations on the hillside did not last. The hurrahs morphed into groans as the reality of the slaughter in both armies became apparent. The spectators saw bodies fall and blood flow. Men in blue and grey dropped like toy soldiers swept off their feet by an invisible hand. Screams of the wounded replaced the cheers of the previous hours. Reserves for both sides moved in, climbing over the fallen bodies to gain footing—only to become part of the bloody pathway for the next wave as a reserve line on each side stepped up to take a position to fire again.

Still reading the newspaper, William reached their room at the top of the stairs. He entered, found his father asleep, and headed for the chair closest to a lamp. He took a deep breath and resumed reading the paper.

On the hillside, the din of celebration morphed into groans and shrieks of alarm as the reality of the slaughter in both armies became apparent. Shouts began again when they saw a phalanx of Confederate reinforcements arriving from the west.

Whether the tide turned against the blue because of the arrival of Confederate forces under General Joseph E. Johnson, who had learned of Union plans through interception of what was thought to be a secret communication, or because it was on this battlefield that the forces of Confederate General Thomas Jackson earned for him the nickname of "Stonewall," or because of the lack of commitment from Union troops nearing the end of their period of enlistment, the Rebels soon gained the upper hand.

The sound of bugle calls rose above the noise.

Union commanders who were still mounted shouted, "Withdraw!" The men in blue turned from the carnage and streaked toward the capitol in disorderly flight. The reporters ran with the retreating soldiers, anxious to transmit telegraph reports of the disaster to their readers throughout the Union.

For a reason unknown to the reporters, the Confederate troops did not pursue the retreating Union forces. The reporters speculated that had they done so, the Rebels could have taken the Capitol.

William's hands trembled as he read the article to the end. This time, he woke his father and read him the newspaper account from the beginning to the end—twice.

An hour later, Representative Davis came for a somber dinner. He left quickly. William went to bed and attempted to fall asleep. Scenes of the slaughter and sounds of men in blue and gray moaning in the bloody pile ran before his eyes as nightmares haunted his dreams.

CHAPTER FOUR

At 8:00 in the morning, William answered a knock on the door. A slim white man with fair, thinning hair and a kindly expression stood in the hallway. He wore a long white coat. At his side, one step to the rear stood a tall negro with a short white coat that struggled to span the well-defined musculature of his chest and upper arms.

"Good morning, sir. I am Dr. Franklin Richards, and this is my assistant, Ezra. We have come to see John Wells. Are you perhaps his son?"

"Yes, sir. Please come in. My father is waiting for you."

After an exchanging pleasantries—Ezra spoke his greeting with the lilt of the British West Indies—they sat down. With a gentle voice, Dr. Richards asked Mr. Wells a few questions about his general health and the circumstances of his shoulder injury. Ezra took notes.

Dr. Richards then asked Mr. Wells to remove his shirt and trousers, skip the troublesome shoulder area, and lie on the bed for an examination. Starting at the top of the head, Dr. Richards kneaded the fingers of his large hands on the topside of Mr. Wells. He asked Mr. Wells to turn over. When Mr. Wells struggled to do so, Ezra reached under his body and turned him as easily as if he were a China doll. Dr. Richards repeated the examination on the patient's back. Dr. Richards dictated his observations to Dr. Martin throughout.

"Thank you, Mr. Wells. You have been very cooperative. Take some deep breaths and make yourself as comfortable as you are able. You will be happy to know that to this point I detect no structural problems in your body. I will examine your shoulder in just a moment. For now, please rest a bit. I will do the same."

William asked Dr. Richards and Ezra if they wanted a cup of tea. The doctor and his assistant smiled broadly and accepted, taking seats next to William on the red velvet settee behind a tea tray table.

"Very thoughtful of you, young Mr. Wells, to realize that someone who has just spent almost three years in England would have acquired a preference for tea. My cousin speaks highly of your family, and his admiration is well-placed."

"Thank you, sir. My father and your cousin, Representative Davis, are good friends. I hope one day you will visit us in the mountains. Are you a native of Massachusetts?"

"Yes. I was born in Lowell and trained at Massachusetts General Hospital."

"And you Ezra?"

"I came to New Orleans from the British West Indies, where I was born. A medical education was impossible for me in Jamaica or the Southern United States. Through the good offices of the Free Men of Color organization in New Orleans, I was fortunate to befriend a doctor from Massachusetts who arranged for me to go to London for medical training. I will pursue the same program as Dr. Richards."

After additional social conversation, Dr. Richards returned to his examination. He asked Mr. Wells to sit on the edge of the bed. Ezra helped him and took a position behind him, supporting his back. His thick arms encircled the patient's waist, holding him in a vice. The fingers of Dr. Richards went to work palpating the shoulder, front and back. Mr. Wells' face twinged at each touch, but he did not move his body. He couldn't. Movement was impossible. He did not cry out. Watching the twinges of his father's face, William came close to asking the doctor to stop. He closed his eyes and gripped the arm of the settee until his fingers were white.

"I'm sorry to be causing you pain, Mr. Wells," the doctor said to his patient. "I know every millimeter of this area suffers at my touch. I am locating the bones. Try to take your mind elsewhere and endure. I will be through in just a few minutes."

And he was, except that he asked his assistant to re-examine one spot. Mr. Wells reacted as if Ezra had inserted a hot poker into his flesh. The two men conferred. They gave the patient a moment to gain his composure, congratulated him on his tolerance for pain, and then Dr. Richards delivered their assessment.

"Again, my apologies, Mr. Wells. First, let me tell you I agree with Dr. Thomas of Greenfield. We both believe you have torn a muscle, and

I guess you know the exact spot. I also agree that surgery holds more risks than rewards. An operation requires the administration of ether or chloroform for the pain. Perhaps if you were thirty years younger…. However, the good news is that complete inactivity for a fairly long period will bring recovery."

"Complete inactivity?"

"Yes, sir."

"Not just staying off my horse?"

"No, sir. Resting on a sofa or in bed."

"For how long?"

"Several months, and then you will be limited to light work for a good while longer."

Mr. Wells closed his eyes and mumbled, "A very long time indeed."

"I realize. But it is necessary."

William dropped his head into his hands. "Oh, my poor mother."

Dr. Richards smiled. "Yes, it will be a challenge for all the family."

"My father was in considerable pain on the trip here. How long before the return trip might be more comfortable?"

"I am afraid comfort for your father is well down the road. You must wait two weeks before he can travel. Even then, he will have to be wedged in with cushions to minimize the effects of the rocking of the railway car."

William smothered a laugh. "Perhaps Ezra would come along and put him in a grip for the journey?"

"Unfortunately, Ezra must return to his studies."

"Of course, sir. I was making a joke to keep from screaming. My father is not known for his patience. He is a dreadful patient."

"I understand. I could arrange for an orderly to help you here, travel with you, and return to Boston when you can send him back."

"Please, please, sir."

Boston, July 22, 1861
My Dear Elizabeth,
Dr. Richards and his assistant came to our room at the Parker House this morning to examine my father. Dr. Richards immediately concurred with the opinion of Dr. Thomas that surgery presents more risks than rewards. He also agrees with Dr. Thomas that with strict immobility for a fairly long period of time he will recover. Dr. Richards will send an orderly to help us here and travel home with us in a few weeks. I hope and pray the trip home will be more comfortable for

Father. We will have to wedge him in with pillows to minimize the effect of the rocking of the train.

Nat came by for a visit tonight. He and his commander are in Boston talking to the Governor's office about the militia. They will be going to Washington soon for meetings about war strategy—yes, that is the term he used. He answered a few of our questions about what is ahead.

He believes the chances for a speedy end to our confrontation with the Armies of Virginia are diminished. We must reassess the time necessary to defeat the Rebels and the number of troops we will need to do so, but he remains confident we will succeed. Fortunately, winter is just around the corner. We probably need not expect any major offensive right now. When spring comes, we will have to replenish our forces, and President Lincoln must take more initiative with his generals.

Fortunately, our militia is not yet under the command of the Union Army, which might send Nathaniel anywhere.

A silver lining: I have arranged with Durgin-Park for delivery to our room of several servings of Indian Pudding!!

Much love to you, my darling Lizzy. I will be home soon, and I will tell you more.

William

~~~

Pierre and the wagon from the Wells farm were waiting at the Greenfield Station when the train car from Boston pulled in. Before they left to take Mr. Wells on the last leg of the journey home, Pierre drew William aside to make a request. "I hate to ask this of you on your first day home, but I have something urgent to discuss. If possible, I'd like to help your father settle at the farm and return to you after I do so. I'll ride back down to Deerfield as quickly as I can."

William put his hand over his face and shook his head. "Something more about my brother Aaron, I suppose. I haven't heard a word about him all the while we've been gone."

Pierre laughed aloud. "A good guess, but not this time. Aaron told everyone he oversaw the farm in his father's absence, so I was worried about what that might mean, but I rarely saw him, not that I went looking. I hope he was not caught up in any mischief. I do not know. I want to talk about something entirely different. With just you, William."

An hour later, Pierre and William sat on the back porch of the cottage. Elizabeth had not been included. Pierre introduced his concern.

"William, with you and your father both away, I slept in the stable to keep watch on the animals. I hadn't spent the night on straw for years. It felt wonderful. The night noises brought back memories. But …"

He dropped his voice to a whisper. "Last night, late, Black Prince, one of the dogs I brought to the stable, kept turning and turning on his blanket. I figured he had dreams like me. But then he went to the back door and whined. He sensed some activity out near the maple trees, towards the mountains. It was a dark night with no moon or stars. I told him to stay and sauntered back there. When I got close to the stream, I was sure I saw movement."

Pierre looked around furtively as if someone might be watching or listening right then.

"I told myself it was probably some night animal, but you know how it is. Once the thought or feeling gets in your head that someone is watching, you can't will it away. When my eyes became accustomed to the dark, I walked about twenty-five feet along the stream. Six huge white eyeballs slowly appeared above the rock and looked right at me. Two negro men and a woman were on the other side of the stream. They saw me and whispered in that broken way they talk."

"We be goin'. Don't turn us in. Please, Massa. Don't turn us in."

"They kept repeating the same words, and I kept urging them to be quiet."

"We lost. We lost to Canada. We be gone before first light, sooner if you show us due north."

"I came closer to the rock and warned them again to be quiet. They repeated that they were on their way north to Vermont or Canada and lost the way. Now I'd figured out what they were up to."

"Pierre, I think I know, too."

"I thought of just pulling out of there, saying nothing, pretending I didn't see them, even to you. But I knew that was wrong. Your father left me in charge, so I've got to tell him what happened on his farm. They were on his property. But I'm scared, William. You know the law. We're not supposed to help them. And I did."

"How did you help them, Pierre?"

"I gave them food and water and told them about a church over the border that helps escaped slaves. They thanked me and ran like chickens to the feed tray to where I told them they could cross. I also told them about some Acadian families I know who help, too. You know, it was only a few generations ago when we were fleeing the British. The Brits believed in beating us but nothing like the torture of the whip. One of the men showed me his back. Purple welts looked like a half dozen purple snakes hanging there like they were sunning on a rock. He said this time the slave catcher had instructions to kill him on sight because he'd run twice before."

"Have they gone now?" Pierre asked.

"I think so. I checked before I went to meet your train, and there was no one around."

William thought for a few moments. "Pierre, I think we must tell my father. I could say I found them, and I would if I thought father would punish you for helping. But I don't think he will. Something else. We need to get word to the *conductor*. That's what they call the one in charge of each station on what they call the underground railroad. He needs to have them turn north sooner."

"I'm ahead of you on that one, William. I asked one of the men if he could go back to the last station and tell the *conductor* they are too far west. There's no point being over here. They'll never get through the mountains to New York."

"So, you think they're gone?"

William thought for a minute. "Yes, I do. I think they're gone, but you know there could be others out there anywhere along the border. I'll come with you to talk with Father first thing tomorrow."

In the morning, William and Pierre told Mr. Wells about their visitors. After the initial shock, Mr. Wells understood Pierre's anxiety. And he admitted he would have done the same thing. "Keep watch, Pierre, without appearing to do so," he said.

~~~

After two weeks with no sign of activity, Pierre told Mr. Wells he thought they could relax. Mr. Wells said he believed they could assume the conductor got the word, but they should be vigilant. "Maybe check once every other night," he told Pierre. "I'll be holding my breath. I do not plan to tell any of my neighbors."

"That statement is a relief to me, Father," William said. "I was prepared to urge you not to breathe a word to a couple of neighbors I know support the Union but have no sympathy for the slaves."

William could not forget the terrified eyes he saw that night. He kept an emergency package of food and water in the stable, just in case. Surely the railway wouldn't run during the deep winter. But when he thought about those eyes, he knew you couldn't expect calm reason from someone who would be shot on sight.

Four weeks after William brought his father back from Boston, William's mother sent word they were ready for a regular Sunday family dinner. After attending church on the Deerfield town square, William and Elizabeth took the wagon out to the Wells farm. They found Mr. Wells in the parlor. William dipped his chin to his father—the usual code report of *all clear on the northern border.* Mr. Wells smiled and exhaled deeper in response. The underground slave route had probably gone into hibernation for the winter and, William hoped, taken his nightmares into the same cave.

Elizabeth clapped her hands together at the sight of her father-in-law waiting for them in the parlor.

"Now, don't you look the picture of health, Mr. Wells! When you stopped by the cottage on your way home from Boston, I thought months would pass before roses returned to your cheeks."

William had seen his father almost daily, so he didn't realize how much better he appeared. To William, he still looked pale.

"See this?" Mr. Wells raised his left arm to demonstrate his mobility. "I'm still not strong, but I will be. I'm coming along splendidly. I'm impatient, of course." His bushy eyebrows lifted a good inch. "Wouldn't you agree, Mother?"

She responded with one hand on her hip. "You will continue to come along splendidly as long as you behave, John."

"Elizabeth, save me! My wife is my jailer! For one week, she wouldn't let anyone into the house who wasn't immediate family. Then, she only allowed one visitor at a time. Now, we're up to three! Do you think you might go to four visitors next week, Diana?"

"Stop that, John. One would think you were Odysseus returning from the ten-year journey home from Troy! Everyone within a day's ride of the farm feels a need to welcome you. Once I allowed the first one of your friends to stay and visit for a half hour, they all thought they were entitled."

"I'm tired of the four walls of this parlor, my love. I want to see the animals and breathe fresh air."

"Exactly what I'm afraid of. You enjoy having company, especially when you join them in repeated toasts to your good health. But then you and your visitors want me gone. I hate to leave the room for fear you'll talk one of them into taking you out and about the farm."

"Exactly where I want to go, my dear."

"John, remember what you went through. When William and Pierre carried you in here, you didn't open your eyes for twenty-four hours. You admitted the trip had been dreadful. Just how do you expect to travel around the farm? You are specifically prohibited from riding a horse. You may not remember, but you said you never wanted to put your hindquarters into a wagon again!"

"That was then."

"Patience, my dear. Just a little longer. The worst is behind us. Let's not take risks."

"Yes, Diana." He saluted, with his right hand, of course.

"See what I mean? She does love to give orders."

Diana Wells turned to her daughter-in-law. "Dinner will be ready soon, Elizabeth. Come with me and help put together the serving dishes. Have a seat, William, and keep Father company for a few minutes. Just shoo a dog off any chair you want to sit on. Your father will tell you about the visitors he'll be expecting on Wednesday. I think you know them."

Big dogs, no two exactly alike but all showing visible evidence they were related to one another, sprawled on every soft surface in the parlor. The hanging tits on one of them revealed the source of the additions to the herd. Half the cushions sat off kilter. In her effort to keep her husband distracted, William's mother must have agreed to relax many of her customary rules about animals in the parlor. The furniture had suffered. William smiled, thinking his father would soon be complaining about the expense of the reupholstering she would undertake following his recovery.

Mr. Wells interrupted, "Wait a minute, Diana. "I haven't seen Aaron. Is he here?"

"He'll be here in a minute, John."

"Well, where is he? He knows when lunch is. He has to report on the operations of the farm."

"He's getting cleaned up, John. We can give him a minute to wash. You just talk with William for a minute."

John Wells did not look happy.

When William had located a cushioned chair, he could share with one of the smaller canines, he sat down. "So, tell me, Father, who's coming to visit you next week?"

"Ah, ha! Representative George Davis and Representative Henry North for sure. They've also invited Representative Cole from Pittsfield to come but do not yet have an answer."

"Now, that's interesting. They're the political powers of western Massachusetts. Those men don't waste time on strictly social calls. My guess is they have a project in mind."

"I agree, and I believe I know what they're up to."

"Tell me."

"Thaddeus came to see me when I first arrived home. He asked me a lot of questions about my experience in Boston. Even though I had not actually been admitted to the hospital, he wanted a full report on Massachusetts General—the facility itself. He wanted to know how many operating rooms they had, how many patients the hospital could handle at once, how much property they needed, and so forth."

"Curious. Did you figure out why those details interested him? Surely, he doesn't think we could have anything like Mass. General out here."

"I believe he thought we could. He had a location in mind and had drawn plans for a building in his head. I'm afraid I burst his bubble when I told him I thought the physical plant was the least important of the requirements for a hospital. Massachusetts General has a medical school for students and teachers! I had an international expert looking at my shoulder. Out here in the west, I think we have a greater chance of getting support for a rehabilitation facility for slower recoveries than a real hospital."

"I've never heard talk of the Union needing a rehabilitation facility."

"Nor I. Before the war, we probably didn't need one. Now, I see a dire need. The medical facilities in Washington are overrun with casualties coming in from the Peninsula. They're converting hotels. Mass. General Hospital is willing to keep those patients who need skilled medical services, but they want, in turn, to send on those for whom longer-term but less critical care is more appropriate. After initial treatment, learning to accommodate to life with a missing limb can take months and more but doesn't require advanced medical services. I think good mountain air would be a welcome cure."

William scratched his head and smiled. "Now, there's a good project for you, Father. The Governor is clearly not enthusiastic about a tunnel through the mountains. We have every reason to expect an increase in fighting in the spring. I hope we can soon put an end to it, but even when we do, eastern Massachusetts will oppose sending our products to the rest of the country by way of the Hudson River rather than Boston Harbor. Let's look hard at a rehab hospital. A facility for wounded soldiers would bring development, especially if money came from Washington for the building and operations. Then, when our difficulties with the business of secession are over, we will inherit a fine facility here in the west."

Mr. Wells slapped his thigh. "You're sharpening your political instincts, my son. Money coming in keeps politicians in office by "bringing home the bacon."

"And I note that a month of inactivity hasn't diminished your nose for a successful project one little bit."

"I'd appreciate it if you could come to the meeting. Representative Davis asked me to have you present."

"I will come, Father."

~~~

Mr. Wells retook his place at the head of the table. Just as he did so, Aaron came into the dining room, kissed his mother, and greeted everyone else. He shook his father's hand and took his seat. John Wells grasped the arms of the chair as he sat, then raised his glass to his assembled family.

"Make a wish, everyone. I've been confined for my recovery, but Diana has cracked open the door and let me venture out to walk from the parlor to the dining table. Let me say a few words—"

Diana Wells rolled her eyes. "Just ask the blessing, dear."

"Of course. But I will slip in my thanksgiving for the return to the way life on the Wells farm has always been."

Aaron raised his eyebrows at that remark. Life on the Wells farm was not as it had always been! Mrs. Wells placed the roast to be carved in front of Aaron. Aaron answered the questions about the general farm operations, including those asked by his father. To his credit, Aaron barely mentioned the physical aspects of the operations. No one at the table wanted Mr. Wells to resume.

William felt optimistic. Maybe Aaron didn't get into mischief while they were in Boston, and maybe he had developed some sensitivity about bringing up ideas that hadn't been thought through.

No. He had not changed. Aaron had a gift for the gaffe. He

immediately introduced a new way to step on his father's toes.

"Father, I've been thinking we could be making sugar."

"Sugar?"

"Yes, producing sugar. We have a beautiful stand of sugar maples in the rear of the farm. Tapping and boiling time for maple sugar is mid-February through March when the ground is still too cold to plant, and spring births haven't begun. We have time on our hands. There's a big sugar operation on the other side of the Connecticut River. What if I went over there and had a look at what it might take to do the same here?"

Mr. Wells' lips tightened. Oblivious, Aaron pushed on.

"The trip wouldn't take me away from the farm for but a morning or an afternoon to go talk to the folks."

Mr. Wells visibly curled his lip.

"I know the *folks*, Aaron. Man named Williams. He came sniffing around here a few years ago wanting to buy our back acres. With four sons, I'm not interested in selling any land."

"I'm not thinking we should sell any land, Father, or rent it out either. I'm thinking we could tap our own trees. It takes a lot of sap to boil to get syrup, but once you have the fires going under the kettles, it's not hard work. I'm told Mil Williams has more orders for syrup than he can fill. He has to buy syrup from other farmers to meet the requests. The father of my friend Hank Arnold is planning to buy some land with maples on it north of here and go into the sugar business. I thought I could—"

William made every signal he could think of to get his brother Aaron to stop talking about the subject that so irritated their father. He frowned. He pulled his forefinger across his throat. He laid his hand flat on the table in a time worn signal to drop the subject.

Aaron ploughed on. William raised his voice to talk over Aaron.

"Brother Aaron, I was away from the farm in Boston for a long time, and I have been terribly busy since my return. The farm records are not up to date. There's a lot I need to be brought up to speed about. I've lost count of the number of horses Pierre is working with and the stage of their training. Madeleine hardly recognizes my voice. Could we meet at the corral on Monday Morning at nine and go over a few things? I could get here earlier if you prefer."

Mr. Wells cut off William's effort at changing the subject. He confronted Aaron directly. "Haven't you got enough to do running the farm? You just stopped talking about joining the militia, and now, you have another plan. When I get back on the farm full time, we'll talk. Right now, just stick to your job and report everything to me."

Aaron looked over to William for support. William thought tapping the trees for sugar would be a good project for his brother—especially if their father allowed Aaron to handle the sugar-making on his own. William thought of talking to his father when he had a chance. But how could he ever persuade his impetuous brother to think before he sprang ideas at the dinner table? To do so immediately caused their father to dig into an opposing position. And then Aaron tied up the package of mistakes by mentioning that scoundrel Henry Arnold Sr!

Instead of arguing, William tried introducing an entirely different subject to change the direction of the conversation.

"The couple of weeks Father and I spent in Boston made me appreciate our life here in the mountains, but one aspect of the big city I thoroughly enjoyed—reading the Boston and New York newspapers every day. I hadn't realized how cut off from the news we are. Father, you enjoyed the news, too. You wanted me to read articles to you when you couldn't even raise your head from the pillow."

"Yes, I did. I hadn't even known about the Union successes in Tennessee under General Grant, nor that Grant was heading straight for Vicksburg, and General Banks had his eyes on Port Hudson. With the Union now occupying New Orleans, we could soon have the entire Mississippi River under our control. That's important. The Rebels would be done for," Father continued.

"I agree we need better communication. The eastern theater is where we have problems. The President has named a new Commander, General George B. McClelland. He is well credentialed. A lot is happening we need to know about. William, do you have any idea how we can get news out here in the west?"

Again, Aaron inserted himself into the conversation. "I have a thought on that subject, Father. Now that the railway comes to Greenfield, someone in Boston could put a bundle of newspapers aboard a railcar, and someone in Greenfield could make a bit of money by carting the papers down here from the Greenfield depot. Or perhaps Mr. Barnett at the Deerfield Community Center could send someone up there to pick up the papers. I'd even do it."

Mr. Wells slowly wagged his head from side to side. "No, Aaron. Is there no end to your bad ideas? No one who matters in Greenfield will win any friends supporting a plan to cut *The Greenfield Gazette* out of being the first to report the news in the west."

Aaron slapped his forehead. "Of course, Father. I should have thought of that."

Mr. Wells snapped back. "You not only should have thought of that, but it would also be an improvement if you thought at all."

At this point, Aaron stood up from the table, asked his mother to excuse him, and stormed out of the dining room. He went through the kitchen, out onto the back porch, and disappeared. He slammed every door on the route.

William's mother had tears in her eyes.

"We do have a problem getting information," Will said. "How can we be expected to have intelligent opinions about anything if we don't know what's going on? Perhaps I could bring the lack of current news to the attention of our representatives. They might have some ideas."

Diana Wells put down her fork. "Will, why on earth do we want to punish ourselves by trying to get information? War news is always dreadful. Blood and more blood. There isn't much going on right now, anyway. People tell me there will be major confrontations in the spring. But I can get along quite nicely not knowing anything. Can we think of something a bit more pleasant to talk about at this table to celebrate the return of Father to our Sunday dinner?"

William hadn't planned to bring up politics, but for once, even that topic seemed safer than either changes on the farm or the lack of progress of the war. He asked his father to tell Elizabeth about the visit he expected from the representatives. The topic put a sparkle in Elizabeth's emerald green eyes.

Mrs. Wells stood up to clear the table for dessert. "Elizabeth, could you help—"

William interrupted his mother. "I'll give you a hand, Mother." Elizabeth thanked her husband with a smile and a nod. Then, she listened intently to her father-in-law's conjecture about what the representatives might have on their minds that prompted them to want to meet.

When Diana Wells and William were back at the table, Mrs. Wells served Indian Pudding from a deep tureen. William had a grand time giving a detailed evaluation of the pudding the Durgin-Park Restaurant had delivered to their Boston hotel room.

"The consistency of the pudding was exactly the same as yours, Mother, but I think we've all forgotten the taste of the original dish. Not a bit sweet! You've improved the flavor tremendously. I thank you for giving Elizabeth your recipe. It's time to forget the Boston version! Do I detect maple sugar is your secret ingredient?"

William's eyes popped open when he heard the words *maple sugar*. He hoped the words didn't magically bring Aaron back into the room!

William's mother happily turned the conversation into a serious discussion of how many teaspoons of maple syrup should be added to the pudding bowl. The best recipe for Indian Pudding, or any recipe for that matter, was an even safer topic than politics.

~~~

The potholes on the road made homemade conversation impossible. After William put away the horse and wagon, he and Elizabeth sat on the back porch of the cottage enjoying a glass of blackberry wine.

"I probably should plan to stay at the farm Wednesday night after the meeting with the representatives, Elizabeth. You're welcome to come and stay as well." He smiled. "Of course, you and Mother will not be invited to meet with the men."

"I know, I know. We'll be expected to appear with dinner, say little more than how do you do, serve the men, and vanish. I decline your invitation, my love. I'll have school that day and the next. I admit I'll be anxious to hear what the representatives have in mind. I'll just have to wait until you come home for supper the following day to tell me the details."

"I promise to be home early."

Elizabeth continued, "I have a thought about the problem of delayed news, William. Do you want to hear it, or is it beyond what I'm supposed to be concerned about?"

"Go right ahead, please, Lizzy."

"I don't think the new telegraph line reaches the town of Greenfield, or anywhere in western Massachusetts for that matter. If the representatives could get the line to Greenfield, *The Gazette* would have news as quickly as anyone in the state. The paper would be greatly improved. Greenfield might even find it profitable to distribute *The Gazette* throughout Franklin and Hampton Counties."

"What a great idea, Lizzy. I'll see if Father might want to bring it up at the meeting." William stroked his chin. "Do you think Father should give the suggestion to all three of the representatives? If he does, and they are successful getting a telegraph connection out here, I bet the powers select Springfield, not Greenfield, to link to the telegraph first."

Elizabeth tipped her head to one side. "Springfield probably *should* get a telegraph first, Will. It's by far the largest town in this part of the state. I suppose they have a newspaper of sorts, although we don't see it. I think all three representatives should hear the idea at the same time. If this little group is going to amount to anything, they should be upfront with one other. But leave that decision to your father. He'll know what to do. He's the politician."

"I believe you are also, Love."

William and Elizabeth continued rocking as the sun slipped behind the mountains.

Elizabeth spoke again. "You know what I think about the meeting of the three western representatives at your father's house, William?"

"No. Tell me."

"I think they've found themselves a location for a mini caucus. The western caucus. The meeting may be the start of something important. The first time some eastern state politician asks to visit the meeting, you'll know they've arrived."

"Ha!" William struck his forehead with his open palm. "They could call themselves The Wells Club—the western Massachusetts version of The Bird Club. Father would love that!"

"I love it too," said Elizabeth. "You should be proud of your father, Will. A lone voice is less persuasive than one representing a larger group. There's a skill to determining a common opinion and promoting it without losing support of those whose opinion does not prevail."

"You're right. I've watched my father at meetings of the farm hands. Even if the hands arrive with a complaint, they usually leave smiling."

"How does he pull it off?" Elizabeth asked.

"I've been trying to figure out his technique. Looks to me as if he first decides—but doesn't say aloud—what he wants the group to do. He lets everyone talk. As they do so, from time to time, he sums up what's been said, managing to emphasize the positions that agree with his. Then he phrases a conclusion. He refines the wording until they reach close to unanimity. Sometimes, I'm not sure everybody realizes what he's done."

"That's amazing."

"Whether Father can do the same with experienced politicians has yet to be determined. It's a slow process. I don't think I'd ever have the patience to practice it. And, of course, the first requirement is to know what you want the group to decide. Often, I do not."

"Our friend Nat could probably do it. He doesn't talk much, but he has a way of giving simple explanations of complicated ideas," said Elizabeth.

"Aww. You're taken in by those wide blue eyes as clear as the summer sky! But so is everyone else. If he doesn't have to spend all his time with the militia in eastern Massachusetts, I'm going to get him involved in our meetings."

William became quiet. Darkness fell, and the fireflies appeared before he spoke again. "I think we're going to have to accept the probability that Aaron will not be happy spending his life working on the family farm. I've put my hopes for that with our little brothers. But before Aaron stormed away from the table, he did renew his promise to me that he will do the job now while we're in a bind. He's excellent with keeping records and doing the numbers, you know. Father may have to stop the heavy work, but he can get back to management if Aaron will just keep doing it until he is able. I'm certainly relieved Aaron stopped talking about joining the militia."

Elizabeth's expression clouded. "No, Willy. I hate to break to you. He hasn't given up thoughts of the militia. Occasionally, he takes your advice. He doesn't bring up the subject at the dinner table. It's still on his mind."

William paled. "Really? How do you know that? From Susanna?"

"I wish that were the case. Aaron doesn't show any interest in Susanna. I know about Aaron's continued desire to join the militia from my father. He told me Aaron and a couple of friends were overheard at the tavern in Greenfield saying they were just what was needed in the militia to give them the added push it's going to take to march on to Richmond. They also talked about going over the border to Hartford, where they could say they were 18 and enlist right now. One of the friends said the only reason he hasn't done so already is because he wants to serve the Commonwealth of Massachusetts."

"Oh, my goodness. Father would be wise to do whatever it takes to keep Aaron on the farm. The militia does not need impulsive hotheads. Being a hothead increases the danger, especially for the hothead himself. From what Nathaniel tells me, the first lesson a soldier must learn is blind obedience to the orders of a superior, whether you think the order is wise or not. Can you see Aaron accepting that?"

"No, I cannot. I think you're saying that if Aaron doesn't understand what is necessary for a soldier, he's increasing the danger for himself and his companions in arms?"

"Yes. I am."

"Will, I think you should try to make your mother understand that. She is very protective of Aaron, but I don't think she would support something that would increase his risk. Your father, on the other hand, has a different motivation for sheltering Aaron. Father thinks he is easily led astray. Your father's motivation for intervening is to try to keep him out of the company of scoundrels."

"My love, I don't know if anyone can do that. I will try to keep my eyes open, but Aaron pretty much moves around on his own."

CHAPTER FIVE

Pierre opened the windows to air out the parlor. With tidbits from the kitchen, he coaxed the dogs, who had appropriated every soft surface as their own, to relocate to the stable. When the doors closed them in, they whined like three-year-old children. Black Prince, the big sweetheart who looked so ferocious but wasn't, dropped his nose to the ground. He could not believe his best friend Pierre intended for him to sleep on straw in a horse's stall. He had become accustomed to a softer bed.

Pierre set to work on the parlor removing evidence of the canine occupancy as best he could. He took the loose cushions outside and beat them within an inch of their lives. He bent like an Arab facing Mecca to scrub the floor. The job complete, he stood in the center of the room, raised his chin, and sniffed the air to test his success. The best grade he could give himself was a half-smile and a sigh. John Wells watched it all, smiling and shaking his head.

"I appreciate your effort, Pierre, but you know our guests will not notice if the room smells like dogs. In truth, they'll probably miss the smell of animals."

"You may be right. I guess I'm cleaning to please Madame Wells. She's doing all she can for your guests."

"I know she is, and I know why. She hopes they'll give me a project to keep me content in her prison. That won't happen, but the guests will be happy indeed if she remembers to bring out the spirits. Remind her for me."

Pierre reported to Mrs. Wells in the kitchen, where she supervised the preparation of a sumptuous meal.

"Thank you, Pierre. As usual, Mr. Wells is right on all counts, but I have my standards."

Indeed, the guests were happy, including Representative Thomas Cole of Pittsfield. Representative Davis had sent a messenger to find Representative Cole, who accepted the invitation. The first sips of whiskey set in motion a flurry of ideas for projects to benefit the western part of the state and to provide a way to promote the opinions of their constituents. By the time they came to the dining room for supper, William had been assigned to take notes. He put a star next to a few projects for his father's special attention.

Representative Davis told the others he had made a visit to Massachusetts General Hospital. The director deflected his interest in pursuing a branch hospital in the west, but the idea of a Rest and Recovery Facility piqued his interest. The other two representatives welcomed the idea. Representatives North of Springfield quickly volunteered to spearhead the effort. The other two bowed to the inevitable. Springfield, the largest town in the Connecticut River Valley, had the best chance to be selected; let Springfield lead the effort to make it happen. Father and son Wells agreed.

One concrete project having been assigned, the group engaged in a free-flowing exchange about the problems the Union faced and how the rural areas could play a bigger role in finding solutions. They agreed they would have more influence at the state level if they could speak for a larger number than the five present. They appointed Representative Davis, the senior member of the group, to recruit for their meetings. William passed on the sobriquet he and Elizabeth had given them: The Wells Club. The representatives loved it, John Wells most of all.

Word of their meeting traveled among the politically aware across the western part of the state. "Our friends and neighbors are signing up to belong to the caucus as quickly as snowflakes melt on a horse's tongue." Mr. Wells reported that several eastern Massachusetts politicians asked for an invitation to appear at the next meeting of the group.

"You'll know you've truly arrived when Frank Bird or Senator Sumner asks to appear," William said. The others raised their glasses to that prospect and had a good laugh.

"The sentence should begin; *we'll* know *we've* truly arrived. *We,* not *you*," said Representative Davis. "You're a member of the club. We need to be more than a bunch of old codgers."

"What if I invite Nathaniel Bradford to join us?" William asked.

A chorus of agreement. "Great idea if the militia is not in training.

Fine young man."

"And his father also if you can handle another man with a few years. I'm sure he's lonely since he lost his wife. His oldest daughter, Susanne, will be helping him with the baby girl. Perhaps you remember Pierre teaching Susanne and Aaron Acadian dances at the reception at the Putnam house after our wedding."

They set their third monthly meeting for November, to be held at the Deerfield Inn.

The Army of the Potomac under General McClelland suffered another defeat in late October at Balls Bluff, 30 miles north of Washington. That battle proved to be the last significant encounter before winter weather set in.

~~~

Western Massachusetts had not yet had a major snowstorm, but by November, all plans were subject to change if one should occur. Meeting in the town of Deerfield, on the well-traveled route between Greenfield to the North and Springfield in the south, following the west bank of the Connecticut River, passing through Northampton and all the little settlements in between, optimized the chances the members of the Wells Club would have a clear road to travel.

The November meeting would probably be the last before the spring. Now too chilly on the back porch of the cottage, on the eve of the meeting, William and Elizabeth sat on a settee in the parlor before a crackling fire. Elizabeth commented on their good luck the clear weather held.

"All signs indicate you'll have a successful meeting, Will. No snow so far, and the Inn is just a short walk from here. Your father will spend the night with us, and you'll take him home the following day. As a bonus, your mother is delighted she won't have to prepare and serve dinner to your group, now up to a dozen."

"I applaud your optimism, my love, but we need more than favorable weather to deal successfully with the controversial issues on our plates. The minutes of the Republican conventions tell me our representatives don't all have the same opinions."

"Have you figured out if your father has ideas for some positions your group might agree to endorse?"

"Only for one of our issues. He thinks we'll have no trouble coming to a collective opinion about the necessity for more decisive military action by the Army of the Potomac. President Lincoln is too reluctant to interfere in strategy. He cannot be so passive. He's the commander-in-chief, for God's sake! Please excuse my language, but he frustrates me beyond belief. General McClelland lacks the will to use his skills. The President needs to confront General McClelland, get him to be more aggressive, or replace him. My prediction is we'll spend considerable time talking about how our Governor can persuade the President to make McClelland strike early and often. Maybe no President previously told generals what to do, but this President has already taken bold steps no one thought he could. It's time for another."

"What Massachusetts wants to have done is only the opinion of one state in the Union. The President must serve every state. Right?" Elizabeth asked.

William smiled. "Technically, that's true. But President Lincoln listens to Massachusetts. He knows we can be relied on to answer a call to duty. We always have, and we always will. Our Sixth Regiment shed the first blood of this conflict while marching through Delaware to give relief to the threatened Capitol. One columnist quoted a statement President Lincoln is said to have made while visiting the wounded after that confrontation. *The North? I don't believe there is any North. Where are the promised troops from New York, Rhode Island, and Pennsylvania? A myth. Massachusetts men are the only reality.*"

William did not notice Elizabeth's tight lips.

"Our group will agree to urge the Governor to push the President. Unfortunately, I don't see answers on any of our other issues."

"For example?" Elizabeth asked.

"Everyone agrees that our forces are depleted. No argument there. But no one has an acceptable plan to raise more troops."

William stood up and began to pace the room.

"The President could continue with his program of appeals to patriotism and financial bounties for enlistment, but he's been doing that for some time without producing the number of volunteers needed. He has very few options. Maybe he will have to go public with something unpopular."

"Like what? You told me there would be no draft," said Elizabeth.

"There will be no draft in the Commonwealth of Massachusetts, stated William. When duty calls, the men of Massachusetts answer. I can't say the same for the rest of the Union. But no one likes the draft."

William went to the window and stopped. He had a faraway look as he spoke to the dark glass.

"Representative Davis has it on good authority that Secretary of State Seward devised a scheme for the President to save face: have the Union governors ask him to issue a call for each county to produce forces. Then, the President would be responding to a patriotic appeal. He would say the governors requested more troops be sent from their states."

William continued staring at the dark glass, although there was no way he could see through to even the branch of a tree on the other side. "There's the master politician at work. Take the pressure off your boss, the President, and give it to the states."

"I'm confused, William. Are you saying he *will* call for a draft?"

"Relax, my dear. A draft will not happen in Franklin County. You can count on that."

Elizabeth closed her eyes and let out a sigh. William turned from the window and resumed pacing the room.

"Another controversial option is arming negroes, he said. People in western Massachusetts have come late to that idea because we have so few negroes no one thinks they could help much. I could count on one hand the number of black faces I've seen here in the west—free blacks, of course, probably born and brought up here, living in this nation longer than the Irish. There are more free blacks in the eastern part of Massachusetts."

William continued his pacing and musing.

"Opinions on arming negroes are all over the place. Governor Andrew is on record as being in favor of forming an armed colored militia, as is Representative Cole. But the minutes of the last Republican convention indicate that George Davis is not. And he's the one we appointed to bring reports of our decisions to the Governor!"

"No one talks to me about negro soldiers," said Elizabeth.

"People just don't talk about that subject to the ladies, my dear. Our neighbor Oliver hailed me, when I was riding to the farm last week to tell me he was dead set against putting rifles in black hands here or anywhere. *How about you, William?* He asked me. *If you were charging into battle, would you trust your life to some nigger? Or worse, a bunch of niggers?*"

"Is that what he asked you?"

"His exact words."

Elizabeth blinked hard. "How did you answer?"

"I told him I would count on the man's commander to evaluate the abilities of his troops and not send anyone who wasn't trained and ready into battle. That's the truth."

"Do you know if the negroes are willing to be in the regular forces?" Elizabeth asked.

"Not from personal experience. Most people, who claim to know, say negroes want to be soldiers who fight—not just laborers, which is what the majority has in mind for them."

"Are you telling me they want to go to war when they don't have to? Why?"

William's eyes popped open at her question.

"To demonstrate they are fully citizens and worthy of respect as such. They are thinking of their position after the war. They want to earn full citizenship."

Elizabeth started at the sharpness of her husband's answer. For a moment, she didn't speak.

"And you, William? What do you favor?"

"When I hear about the sacrifices our troops are making for what will benefit the slaves, I think our free blacks could do more for their race. But not at the risk of having the border states break away. That might happen if we put rifles in black hands. Do we give them equipment to fight to preserve the Union and thereby cause the Union to break apart?"

"We are told the enslaved do valuable work. The Rebels have the advantage of the enslaved to support their forces."

"Yes, Elizabeth. And I understand some of our troops resent that. Our rank and file must do all the support work for our side. But arming negroes is more controversial. At least we're no longer obligated to send escaped slaves back. They were being forced to turn right around and help the men who fight us. Encouraging slaves to escape and come north before we're ready to fit them into northern life creates another set of issues."

"Anyway," William continued, "there really aren't enough free blacks to solve our manpower problem." If the President should free the slaves, which Frederick Douglass is urging him to do, we'd have men but a whole new set of problems to solve. I still hold out hope the South will see our resolve, have second thoughts, and give up."

"Hope, but not conviction, it seems to me," Elizabeth mumbled

William stood up again and went to the dark window. He continued to stare where he could see nothing.

His back to his wife, his mind fixed on his own thoughts, William may not have noticed Elizabeth twisted a handkerchief in her hands, a universal indication of deep concern.

~~~

Although there were no major hostilities in the winter of 1861 to 1862, a procession of disasters gripped the northern states and produced one of the darkest periods in the history of the Union. Three weeks after the November meeting of the Wells Club in Deerfield, which lasted into the second day and reached no consensus on the issue of raising more forces with a call, a draft, arming blacks, or any other method, a harsh blizzard swept across Massachusetts, Vermont, and New Hampshire and north to the border with Canada. Another winter storm followed, and then another, without mercy. When schools tried to reopen after the Christmas holidays, they had to close again. The five-week winter break turned into almost three months.

In the Capitol, too far south to experience the full brunt of winter, fevers crept on a deadly course. President Lincoln's plan to take action on the issue of his overly cautious commander had to be delayed when General McClelland took to his bed with typhoid fever. The most devastating blow came to the first family of the Union when the beloved boys in the White House fell ill. Willie, the older boy, sickened, then Tad as well. Tad fought through the disease, but Willie remained in misery.

With no war news to report, the newspaper columnists scrambled to create content. They rehashed the failures of the Union commanders: McClelland, most of all. President Lincoln received the second of their vitriol. They praised General Grant's military successes in the West but managed to slip in references to his inability to stay sober. They had a field day with the extravagances of the President's wife and gossiped about arguments between members of the Cabinet and among their wives. Criticism of the government increased the temperature in the churches and everywhere people gathered.

Everyone was glad to see the year 1861 come to an end.

The New Year did not bring better times. Sickness continued. On February 20th, Willie Lincoln succumbed in an excruciating death. The President was devastated but brave. Mrs. Lincoln sank into a depression from which she could not recover.

The Union could count the naval Battle of the Ironclads as one military success. Facing the prospect of having the *Merrimac* fall into enemy hands, the Rebels scuttled the ship and allowed Union forces to open the entry point for McClelland to put into effect his plan for an amphibious landing between the York and James Rivers. He assembled

his troops for a drive to capture the Confederate Capitol of Richmond—
the Peninsula Campaign. After being stopped at Seven Pines, General
Lee drove McClelland from the peninsula when he was only four miles
from Richmond. The Rebels pursued, and before long, hostilities again
moved close to Washington.

During the Peninsula Campaign, ambulances carrying casualties from
all the field hospitals in the south—and field hospitals can be makeshift
buildings or even shade trees anywhere there are troops—pulled into the
Capitol and poured out the wounded. When no more beds were available
in Washington, casualties traveled deeper into the north by railcar,
thousands a day. Empty sleeves and crutches became a common sight in
towns of all sizes, including in western Massachusetts.

CHAPTER SIX

The return of responsibilities that came with the spring thaw lifted the mood on the farms. William worked longer days handling the birth of animals, but new life raises the spirits. Elizabeth felt the need to catch her students up with all the school days lost to the winter weather. They were so glad to see their friends again that they happily applied themselves to their lessons. She rewarded them with extra recess.

Winning the war assumed its rightful place as a priority for the nation. John Wells resumed monthly meetings of the Wells Club. The pace of enlistments did not replace the casualties; the need to raise more forces dwarfed all other issues. He and William believed President Lincoln dreaded making an unpopular call but would have to do so soon.

In April, just before school let out for the summer, William forgot to put the need for more forces on the Wells Club agenda. How could the major issue before them slip his mind? Easy. He remained fixed on the news Elizabeth had given him the evening before; she suspected they would be welcoming a new life by the end of the year—their secret until they could be certain.

With hope, Elizabeth declined her usual summer assignment teaching adults and dealt with morning nausea. William handled excuses for two Sunday family dinners. "Elizabeth seems to have a cold that just won't go away," he told his parents and hers. By the third Sunday, the couple decided to share the good news. Over the moon with happiness and expectation, the prospect of a grandchild banished the gloom in both families.

As if it had been his idea all along, John Wells bragged to his friends about the success of his initial season tapping the maple trees for sugar sap, giving no credit to his second son for the original idea or his management of the operation. Two kettles stayed bubbling. Mil Williams said he wanted to buy every drop,

"Let it go, Aaron," William told his grumbling brother. "You got what you wanted, right? Father has agreed the farm will buy another kettle and back all your plans to expand."

Elizabeth's nausea passed. The ground thawed. Spring burst out throughout western Massachusetts. One last snowfall dusted the forsythia blooms, but by ten o'clock in the morning, she couldn't stand up to the force of the yearly return of warm sunshine. Pollen fell on the paths around the Wells and Putnam farmhouses. Crocuses and snowdrops poked up green shoots as the ground thawed. Three weeks later, home gardens began to yield the first flowers of the season. The gentle slopes of the foothills turned a glorious new green.

On a day Elizabeth and William would not soon forget, William did not see his wife waiting on the porch when Madeleine turned into the corral at the end of the day. Concern pricked. William jumped down from the saddle and threw the reins over a post. Calling his wife's name, he took the steps up to the porch two at a time. No answer. When he entered the back door, he heard a whimper. "I'm here in the kitchen."

Elizabeth lay on the floor in a pool of blood. The sight of her husband turned loose her tears. He dropped down into the wetness and held her in his arms. She choked out, "the baby ...

"I see. I see. How about you?"

She nodded. "I'm still shook up, but I feel okay. It's been at least an hour. I'm just too weak to clean up."

"Of course you are, my Lizzy."

Familiar with everything about birthing, William swung into action. He bathed his wife, found her clean clothes, and settled her on the bed. He lay down beside her.

"We won't know if the baby was a boy or a girl," Elizabeth mumbled through tears.

"Hush," he said. "There's a good side. We know we can conceive. There will be another, and many more, both boys and girls." After a while, he spoke again. "As soon as you have your strength back, we'll take a few days and go to the Inn in the Mountains where we were almost a year ago."

"That would be wonderful." She buried her face in his neck. A few minutes later, she raised her head and tried a weak smile. "I think your mother will be happy to know you will not miss a meal tonight, my love. I have last night's Beef Stew *à la Diana* warming over the coals."

"Seriously?"

"Your mother told me never to let noon pass without knowing what dinner I will put on the table."

William gave her a playful tap on her shoulder. "You're a tease, you know. You inherited that streak from your father. Maybe teasing comes with red hair. I'll have to watch out for the trait in the next generation." He kissed her on the forehead. "I'll wash up from my day in the stable, then see what I can do about serving dinner."

~~~

For both sets of parents, the loss of the baby triggered a return of last winter's depression. They had limited optimism for a change of fortune any time soon. Returning to the cottage in Deerfield after a week-long visit to the Putnam farm, Elizabeth tossed her carpetbag from the wagon and released her irritation.

"Do you think it would do any good for me to tell my family we do not share their doom and gloom? The list of grumbles today was longer than ever. Even from my father, for goodness' sake. He usually can't stay down very long before something comes along to make a joke about."

"My dear," William responded, "I believe you and I are on a different page from both our families. Our good feelings are *not* apparent to them. They are way too deep into *woe-is-me* to notice." He pantomimed a stab to his chest and a swoon.

Elizabeth chuckled. "Can you recall the many ways they turned on the gloom? Trying to be pleasant, you said you were grateful the winter confinement provided an opportunity for your mother to teach Abigail to do such beautiful needlework. Abby snapped back. *Soon, the dogs are going to have roses embroidered on the cushions in their kennels.*"

"I'll raise you one," William responded, catching his wife's mood. "How about when, just to say something pleasant at *my* family's dinner table, you described how beautiful you thought the sight of lines drawn in the new fallen snow by the shadows of the trunks and branches of the bare sugar maples? In response, my little brother whined: *snow is not beautiful to me when it buries all the good stuff to do outside. Underneath there's a layer of ice guaranteeing you'll smack your rear end if you try.*"

Elizabeth could barely get her next words out of her mouth for her giggles. "Your little brother thinks any day lost when he cannot fish. Seriously, Will, only one other person in our families is smiling: Aaron.

How did you win your father over to letting him make sugar?"

"I had time to sit with Father for a long conversation. I convinced him Aaron needed a project he could call his own. Come February, Aaron will be tapping the maples."

"I do want to ask you if driving spikes into the trunks of our beautiful sugar maples harms them. They're my favorite trees. I love to hear the big leaves rustling over shaded walks in the hot summer and see a full palette of orange hues blazing across the lovely hills in the fall. Now I've seen them wearing fresh snow."

"Tapping for sugar sap doesn't hurt the trees, Lizzie, if you don't put in too many taps and pull them out shortly after the end of March. The trees have time to repair themselves during the growing season. Aaron went to Mil Williams' farm to study their operation, so I know he will do it right."

"Your mother thinks Aaron's always dreamed of making sugar. When he was no more than ten years old, he went back to the grove with a spike, a spoon, and a pot he pinched from the kitchen. She caught him with his tongue out trying to lick something sweet! But your mother is also determined to be miserable right now. She'll be grateful to you when she realizes what you've done for Aaron. Speaking of your mother, during these long visits I think I made progress getting to know her better."

"And vice versa! You broke the dam, my love. I would go by the kitchen and see a big smile on her face and you two chattering away over her cooking pots. How did you do it?"

"I had time to use the tried-and-true method of making a friend; let the person do you a favor. What does your mother know more about than anyone else? Getting a good meal on the table. I asked her to teach me how to do the same."

William gave his wife a hug. "You know I love you very much, my Lizzie."

She responded to his shoulder. "That's a good thing because your mother thinks I don't give you enough to eat! All joking aside, my Willy, I love you more now than before the snow came! The very best part of this hard winter is that we've spent more time together than at any time since we married. We've used daytime and bedtime to learn how to really love each other."

~~~

"The Wells Club had a special guest tonight, Lizzy," William said to his wife a few weeks later. "An assistant to Secretary of State William Seward."

"From the Capitol?"

"Yes. From Washington."

"Wow! I'd say you are indeed the Western Caucus now."

William's brows lowered. "I'm not sure we want to be."

"You're wary? Why?"

"The Secretary of State and Representative Davis apparently go way back together. Thaddeus said we had to call this special meeting to accommodate him. The Secretary and his son are traveling all over the North this summer. But here's what I don't understand. They aren't coming to western Massachusetts! He's sending his assistant! I thought because of Seward's connection to Thaddeus, we might get some advance information, like when an offensive will begin. We can't put an end to this war unless we make a move."

"What did Seward's assistant have to say to you?"

"If the man had something important to say, I missed it. And so did my father. The assistant was nice enough, actually a charmer. One of those people who pay attention to your name, repeat it in the conversation, and then repeat it again when they say goodbye. He made a short patriotic speech about how we need to increase our forces so we can get this war over with. Nothing specific about how we would be doing so except to say Secretary of War Seward is offering a new enticement bounty of $25."

"From what you tell me, $25 will not do the job."

"No. Funny thing, our guest seemed to be more interested in the Wells Club than here to tell us what the Union plans to do. He wants us to send a delegation to Boston to visit the Governor. Then he changed the subject and asked me how long I'd been presiding over our meetings."

Elizabeth's eyes opened wide. "I didn't know you presided, Will. When did that begin?"

"In April. It's just easier for me to make the arrangements when we meet in town. I talked to my father for a few moments after the meeting tonight and he was also puzzled about why the man came. Nathaniel thought he might be testing the waters for abolition."

Three weeks later, Mr. Barnett at the Deerfield Community Center delivered a copy of *The Greenfield Gazette* to the cottage. He was sure

William would want to see the lead story. He did, indeed.

"I'll read the first few paragraphs to you Elizabeth," William said as they sat down for dinner. "*On August 4 the War Department in the Capitol issued an order for a draft of 300,000 men to serve for a period of nine months.*" Elizabeth caught her breath and put down her fork. William continued. "*Because of an uproar from the people and the governors, the Secretary of War changed the order to a call for 300,000 volunteers. The quota asked of the State of Massachusetts is nineteen thousand and ninety. A number will be requested of each county. The men of the Massachusetts Militia will be absorbed into the new nine-month force. A team of recruiters will be dispatched to assist in the work of signing up the remaining volunteers.*"

William's eyes skipped farther down the article. "Franklin and Hampton counties are assigned a number sufficient to man a regiment, to be designated the Fifty-second Regiment, Massachusetts Volunteers."

After a few minutes of silence, Elizabeth's voice cracked as she asked, "How many men in a regiment, William?"

"Usually over a thousand."

"Oh, my good God? From one of the most rural areas of the state? When we've already met our recruitment quota for the three-year enlistments? Who will find that many volunteers?"

"I think the reason for the visit from the assistant to the Secretary of State is now clear. I suspect the Wells Club is going to be asked to spearhead the recruitment effort in this area. We will have to find them."

"My God!"

~~~

John Wells didn't even know the order had been issued.

"That proves it," he said when William found him on the farm the following morning and showed him *The Greenfield Gazette*. "I'm not going to rest until we get the telegraph to reach us here in the west. We need a little warning when we have something like this coming at us."

Representative Davis appeared at the farm in the early afternoon. Before the sun went down, he and John Wells decided to travel to Boston to see the Governor. No, they didn't think it necessary for William to go with them, but Representative Davis exacted a promise. "Secretary Seward's assistant was impressed with you, William. He specifically asked us to be sure you were on board for the recruitment effort. He thinks young people are critical for success."

"If my father has a job to do, I'll help him. That's the way it is with this family. And, of course, we'll have Nathaniel from the militia."

As soon as he heard about the trip to Boston, Aaron wanted to go. His father shot back. "Stick to your job on the farm, Aaron."

Elizabeth had nothing to say. As William predicted, the Wells Club received the assignment to organize recruitment meetings in Franklin and Hampton Counties.

~~~

When John Wells brought the news home that the Wells Club would oversee recruitment, his wife Diana was beside herself. Her face froze.

"No, John. You cannot take that on. You know what they are going to want from you. Your two grown sons!"

"Now, now, Diana. We're not talking about a draft. They are seeking volunteers."

"Which you have to find."

Diana could barely breathe but was determined to get her point out. She spoke so softly John could barely hear her. "Do you remember what they told us last winter? We were only raising troops to deter the South. We know what happened. In no time, the casualties were streaming home from the Peninsula. Now we're hearing that if we have enough well-trained troops, we can wipe out the South in a short time. One thing I know is that as soon as any real war begins, anything can happen."

She began to sob.

"There, there, Diana. Aaron is not yet eighteen, so he needs my permission to enlist. I have already told him I will not give it. Aaron will not be able to go."

"And William?"

"He is a grown man who will make his own decisions. But, newly married to a wife he adores… I can't imagine he'll be rushing to volunteer."

Slowly, Diana Wells composed herself. She had to have the courage to say to her husband what she wanted to say.

"John. I hear some of the bigger farms are requiring their top hands to enlist. We could send Pierre. You know he'd do anything you asked of him."

Shock! John looked as if he'd taken a bullet to the chest.

"Diana! I cannot believe I heard what you just said."

"I said we could send Pierre from this family. Many of the larger farms are telling their hands they need to prepare to serve the Union if the need comes."

"Diana. I am speechless. Pierre is not a "hand." I don't want you to suggest that ever again."

"Of course, I know he is not a hand. He's family. But if someone has to go…"

Diana thought she knew every mood of her husband, but she had never seen what she looked at right now. He was stiff, white, frozen, furious. He held his breath for a frightening period.

She thought of calling for help.

When he breathed again, he put out one word at a time.

"Saving the Union is not Pierre's fight. This is the cause of the men whose roots are in Massachusetts soil. If he wanted to go, He might be able to do so. But… I am going to stop speaking now because I might say something I cannot take back. Perhaps I already have."

Over the next three weeks, the Wells Club convened six times. Each day, William, his father, Representative Davis, and Pierre traveled throughout the two counties contacting the powers in each town and the unincorporated settlements. William had supper at the Inn and came home to a silent wife. At night, she held him tight. When Elizabeth inquired how the recruitment proceeded, William told her they were doing better than he could have imagined possible. Far from being discouraged by the dreadful casualties streaming in from the Peninsula Campaign, every town and village wanted to host a recruitment meeting.

Soon, Elizabeth and William had a welcome visitor: Nathaniel Bradford. He joined them many times over the next two weeks.

All over the North, the pattern repeated. Just as the Order of June 26 for 300,000 three-year recruits had been successfully met, it appeared the Order of August 4 for nine-month recruits would be met as well. The rallying cry became: *We are coming Father Abraham, three hundred thousand more.*

"You know what my schedule will be over the next month, Lizzie. I'll be at the recruitment meetings and may or may not be home for supper. Perhaps you'd like to spend some time with your family."

"No, William, I want to be right here in the cottage whenever you are able to come home."

"I guessed you might respond that way, my love. I have a proposal. I'd like to have Black Prince stay here at the cottage with you for a while. I know you're fond of him, as we all are. He's company, and he'll let you know if some animal comes prowling around."

"Oh, I couldn't take him away from the farm. He loves being with the animals. Your father and Pierre are both devoted to him."

"Not as much as they are to you, my love. I can have someone from the farm come and close in the left part of the yard, so all you'll need to do to let him out is to open the back door."

"Will he be happy here?"

"With you to love him? Of course, he'll be happy."

The following evening, Pierre pulled up to the cottage with a passenger in the cart. That night, and every night thereafter, whether William was home or not, Prince—that's what Elizabeth called her new guardian—slept on a mat on the floor at her side of the bed.

~~~

The recruitment campaign began the first week of July and took place four nights a week until mid-August. The State supplied a military band. The ladies of each town sent plates of treats. Not a few apple tarts, cherry dumplings, and blueberry scones went home wrapped in a handkerchief and tucked into a pocket. Eloquent speakers made stirring appeals to patriotic pride. One of the most effective speakers was Nathaniel Bradford. He conveyed what he labeled *messages from President Lincoln and the Governor*. He promised recruits the rewards of a grateful nation and, should they fail to return, faithful care of their dependents. Flowers and praise showered those who signed on. When someone did so, the recruiter called out to those remaining, *"Now, who will take the next bouquet?"*

Aaron appeared at one of the very first recruitment meetings. He told his father he planned to enlist. His father exploded.

"No, Aaron. You are not eighteen years of age, and I will not sign permission."

"Everybody thinks I'm eighteen. I'm tall and strong."

"Do you realize what awaits the rank and file in the forces? It's brutal. Talk to any of the men with empty sleeves and pant legs you see coming to our new rehab hospital. They are rank and file, every one of them. There's no commission for you. Now William—"

Aaron cut him off. "Dammit! Why, always William? So, William gets a commission?"

"Nobody has said so. Nor has he told me he plans to enlist. I do know the War Department prefers men with experience in the militia. He will not have that, but the recruits want to be led by men they know from their own towns. Nathaniel has both qualities; he will be included in our number, of course, and will most probably receive a commission."

Aaron interrupted his father. "If you had let me join the militia…"

"You'd still need my permission, and I will not give it. The recruiting team talked about some of the skills they would be looking for in officers: maturity, experience with horses, and demonstrated leadership. My God, Aaron, you'll have the same in a few years."

On meeting nights, William came home late and exhausted—to a silent wife. She held him tight. One night, he told her that he planned to enlist. "I know," she responded and held him tighter.

On September 13, 1862, the Fifty-second Regiment, Massachusetts Volunteers, under the command of Colonel Halbert S. Greenleaf, assembled for training in Greenfield at what would be named Camp Miller. Company D included 1st Lieutenant Nathaniel Bradford, folded in from the militia, and 2nd Lieutenant William Wells. The Chaplain for the entire regiment would be Rev. John. F. Moors, Pastor of the Congregationalist Church of Greenfield. A year and a half previously, when Nathaniel Bradford had been Best Man at the marriage of William and Elizabeth, Chaplain Moors had assisted in performing the ceremony.

Elizabeth felt queasy on the morning she kissed her husband goodbye for him to go for basic training in Greenfield. An upset stomach was not worthy of notice and could be easily a product of the emotion of the day. When her nausea persisted, Elizabeth began to suspect she carried a new life within her.

Should she tell William? She owed him honesty, but not at the risk of causing him to scuttle his dream. If the pregnancy went well, she would have seven months left to go on her nine-months commitment by the time the regiment left for theirs. She told herself William would probably be home long before that.

And she might well lose this baby as she had the last one. She let the days slip by in indecision.

PART II: TO WAR–BATON ROUGE AND THE FEINT TO FORT HUDSON

CHAPTER SEVEN

The beat of the military band that roused the crowd at the final ceremony for the Fifty-second Regiment throbbed in Second Lieutenant William Wells' head and propelled his steps as he and 1st Lieutenant Nathaniel Bradford led the march of D Company from the parade ground of Camp Miller to the railway station at Greenfield. Railcars festooned with eight-foot banners of red, white, and blue awaited them. Nathaniel counted off fifty of the one hundred men of the company and ordered them to board the first railcars, keeping tight military formation as they did so.

William commanded the second half of the company. He did not believe military discipline necessary. "Follow up, men," he ordered. The men scrambled up the steps of the next few cars. They threw their knapsacks onto the overhead racks and settled themselves into the hard seats, all the while chattering like schoolboys on a vacation trip not an army off to war. Standing on the platform watching the second half of the company board the train, Nathaniel raised his eyebrows but did not speak. A patient smile turned up the corners of his mouth.

Two hours later, the Greenfield railcars reached Back Bay Station in Boston. The cars of Nathaniel's men docked first. A handful of people lolling around the breezeway in front of the Station surged forward, touting their wares. The windows and doors of Nathaniel's cars did not budge. Accompanied by a conductor, Nathaniel entered each car and issued orders.

"Men: We will disembark here and assume military formation. I will lead the march to E Track, where we will board the cars that will take us to Grand Central Station in New York City. When you reach the cars on E Track, fill the seats in the cars to which your Corporal directs you.

Make no contact with any civilians. That is an order!"

When Nathaniel's men had left for E track, a different scene unfolded around the cars of William's men. The windows lifted. The crowd swarmed toward them buzzing like wasps disturbed from their hive. The Massachusetts farm boys in William's care took the honey they were offered. The pressing crowd of vendors, amplified by street people, came to hawk their wares. "Delicious candy, just 5 cents." "Cold drinks 10 cents." "Sandwiches very cheap." Beggars asking for spare change sidled into the open breezeway and headed for the cars as well. Women appeared from nowhere, smiling with invitations. They tilted their heads, lounged against the pillars, and teased out whistles from the men in the cars.

William smacked his forehead with his fist and leaped down to the platform. Hastening to reassert control over his men, he bellowed orders toward the open windows of the railcars.

"Men of Company D. Take your seats immediately. Lower your windows and fasten the latches. Remain seated in silence. You will have no contact with any civilians. That is an order."

William visited each car carrying his men and repeated his orders until he had the scene under quiet control.

He issued another order. "Company, soon the railcar will be secured. The conductor will open the door at the far end and set a footstool below the stairs. Corporals descend first. The remainder of the men will step down and assemble behind their corporals in military order. I remind you; no one will interact with any civilians."

A headache found berth above William's left eye. Damn! How would he ever lead his men in battle if he struggled to get them onto and off a passenger train? By keeping discipline, that's how. He found Nathaniel.

"Lifetime friend, and appropriately, my superior, I think I just learned a lesson. When the privates clamored to be led by men from their hometowns they already knew, the Army insisted on giving command priority to those with militia experience. I should have known why. I had not remembered the lesson Pierre and I learned long ago in the corral. You put a loose rein on an unbroken horse at your peril."

Nathaniel laughed. "I told the recruiting officer my good friend William Wells had no command experience but was a quick learner. Ten minutes! That's how long you needed to master your first lesson."

A gentle rain fell during most of the rail trip from Boston to New York and was still falling when they left Grand Central Station and began a long march south on muddy Broadway to New York City Hall. The men immediately learned the value of the most versatile piece of equipment in their knapsacks: the rubber blanket.

Despite the weather and the imposition of the short leash, nothing dampened the spirit the men brought to their mission. When crowds gathered, they raised the volume of their marching songs and performed a snappy demonstration of presenting arms. When they learned no one had prepared for their arrival at City Hall, and they were to catch what sleep they could on the cold stone floor, William heard a mumbled imitation of the stock question asked by the recruiters at the summer meetings throughout Franklin and Hampton Counties after they presented flowers to the most recent volunteer. The recruiters would turn to the remaining men and ask, "And now, who takes the next bouquet?"

William had used the words himself.

Somehow, the men slept.

In the morning, Nathaniel and William assembled their men and boarded ferries to leave lower Manhattan and cross the East River to Brooklyn. More adversity followed: promised tents had not been delivered. William and Nathaniel overheard the recruitment call again with a change in emphasis, a sharper edge, but always a smile. "My good men, who takes the *next* bouquet?"

The men laid out their rubber blankets and settled on the wet ground. Their continued good spirits left not a crack through which William could allow himself to feel wet, cold, or put upon.

Proper shelter, along with sunshine and home-cooked, late Thanksgiving Dinner served by the local citizens, arrived at the camp in Brooklyn the following day.

~~~

After four days in Brooklyn, D Company marched to the Navy Yard, where a sleek steamer named the *Illinois* waited for their arrival. Following the direction of the ship's mates, William and Nathaniel led their men up the gangplank and onto the ship in descending order of rank. The ship's mates directed them to the quarters assigned. When all save the lowliest privates had been accommodated, the mate directed Nathaniel and William to lead them to the lowest deck.

William blanched at the sight of the area designated for these poor lads and at what passed for their beds.

Tiers of stacked boards lay ten abreast in the semi-darkness with a narrow aisle at the midpoint where only one man could pass. Racks at each end of the boards accommodated their packs. The ship's mate instructed the men to lie on the boards, side by side, heads pointing to the bow. There were no more than twenty inches above the nose of each man to the bottom surface of the board above. The men barely had room to turn over.

"For the safety of all," the mate continued, "you must remain in your space, rising only for necessaries, day and night."

Would the men take this instruction without complaint? None that any could be heard.

When the privates had all settled in, if that is what you would call it, the mate led William and Nathaniel back to the ladder. He directed them to climb up two decks and turn to the port side to find their assigned quarters. Relief washed over them when they were shown the cabin they were to share with three other officers. Each man had his own cot, his own shelf, and room to breathe. Nathaniel and William took the two cots on the port side, leaving three identical cots on the starboard. These were soon occupied by the Chaplain and two officers from Company C.

An hour later, the mate came through with tin plates of a stew, source animal unknown. William thought the food terrible until the mate passed again, this time carrying the fare for the privates below.

"Lieutenant, sir, don't you think potatoes should be cooked?" asked one private when William went below to check on his men. The private wiggled a hand into a tight pocket and extricated two solid objects the size of turkey eggs. He struck them together like symbols. Crack! "I'll save these rocks to carve into dice in case we have an opportunity to shoot some craps," he said.

"Give me one of those potatoes, Private," William said. "I'm going to discuss them with the cook."

An hour later, a ship's mate arrived with a tin plate of steaming potatoes for each row. Later that night Col. Greenleaf commended William and told him that act of consideration might return tenfold as help in a far more critical situation. He said he didn't have a lot he could offer the privates but thought he could make a bit more space for them by arranging to move a few of the men to an open corner on the deck above.

During the past five days, William and Nathaniel had spoken to each other only as needed in the line of their duties. They had been within a few feet of scores of human beings, far closer than they liked to be, yet both felt unmoored. Now each lay under warm, dry blankets a few feet from a good friend. Neither had energy for but a brief conversation.

"Are you as spent as I am?" Nathaniel asked.

"Leaving was hard. The two people who had the most difficulty saying farewell to us were your father and my wife. *Saying farewell* is not correct. Neither one spoke a word."

"My exact thought, William. I hadn't seen my father so bereft since the week my mother passed. Seeing him like that again about broke my heart. I'm grateful his sister is coming for the holidays. Susanna always cheers him up. She'll give him a hand with my two little sisters."

"Elizabeth was rigid as a stone," said William. "Over the last two months, we talked a lot about my serving. I know that was not her wish, but I thought she had adjusted to the idea. I guess the reality hit hard. She came to the final review with my parents. They tried to persuade her to go home with them, but she just shook her head no. She did promise to go to the farm for Thanksgiving." William stopped abruptly. "By God, Nathaniel, I can't believe Thanksgiving has already come and gone! Life is going on without us. We don't even know where we're going or what army we'll join. Col. Greenleaf says our orders are sealed. They will open the orders when we've been on the water twenty-four hours."

"I may still be out cold by then, William. Goodnight now. We'll talk more in the morning."

From the depths of sleep, they barely heard the chains grinding as the *Illinois* crew raised the anchor in the middle of the night. The *Illinois* set sail at dawn.

Nathaniel woke at first light. A dreadful odor permeated the cabin, and closed his throat. He raised his head and his voice.

"Good God, men! Get your asses up on deck for some fresh air. You're stinkin' up our bedroom!"

~~~

The two lieutenants from C Company were bent over a bucket in a corner of the stateroom, retching. The Chaplain stood by the open hatch, breathing deeply. The three of them mounted the ladder and disappeared through the open hole above.

"I feel okay, Nathaniel. How about you?" William asked after the three left.

"I feel okay, too. I thank the Lord. I had no idea how I'd fare on the water. The only boat I've ever been on is a rowboat to the far bank of the Connecticut River—which isn't even as wide as the East River where yesterday we crossed to Brooklyn."

"The same for me. Could we be so lucky?"

They were. Their cabinmates stayed gone all day but sent up a couple of privates to clean up the mess they'd left behind. The odor lingered.

~~~

As promised, twenty-four hours after sailing, the Captain of the *Illinois* summoned Col. Greenleaf of the Fifty-second Regiment, and the ranking officer of every unit represented aboard to the upper deck for the opening of the sealed orders. He read the orders aloud. Everyone learned his fate almost at the same time. They were all assigned to the Ninth Army Corps under the command of General Benjamin Butler, Department of the Gulf, and over the signature of General Butler, the *Illinois*, and several additional ships received orders to proceed down the Atlantic Coast and sail around the Florida Peninsula to Ship Island in the Gulf of Mexico, south of New Orleans. When three additional ships arrived, they were to replenish their provisions, sail upriver to the Port of Baton Rouge, and await further orders. Nathaniel and William raised their eyes heavenward and offered thanks to God they had not been sent to the ill-fated Army of the Potomac. At last report, General McClelland still floundered about in Virginia.

~~~

Most of the passengers on the *Illinois* acclimated to the rolling sea after a few days on the open sea. Seasickness eased—but only briefly. Six days out, the wind kicked up waves, rain fell in sheets, and the open ocean threw up a major storm, pitching the ship about for the following three days and nights. Only a small number of the passengers aboard stayed well, Nathaniel and William among them. The whole ship reeked. The worst odor seeped up through the hatchways from the lowest deck. Word spread that one unfortunate lad had died.

"Died? My God! You can die from being seasick?" William asked Nathaniel. "I thought you just wished you'd die."

"Doc Sawyer said the poor boy had no other maladies. He thinks when vomiting got the best of him down there in the dark, he couldn't get out of the racks fast enough. He probably choked to death." A *frisson* traveled down William's spine.

The men of the dead private's company tied weights to his ankles, sewed him into his blanket, and laid him on a board. Chaplain Moors said he would conduct a short burial ceremony on the aft deck at dawn the morning after the seas calmed. Men from the private's own company would slide him off the board into the sea.

Without a Rebel shot fired, the Fifty-second Regiment suffered their first casualty of the war. Chaplain Moors performed his first burial.

The Fifty-second Regiment traveled on the *Illinois* with the Eighteenth New York Battery, numbering about fifty men and a score of unconnected passengers hitching rides south. These passengers hoped the ship would sail past the Mississippi River delta and deliver them to Galveston or another port on the Texas coast. They had been given no guarantee. Rumor had it that General Nathaniel Banks and members of his staff were passengers on the *Illinois* as well, but they were never seen. No one had any idea where they were going or what they were going to do.

The wind abated after a few more days, and the temperature slowly warmed. On the ninth day out of New York, the *Illinois* reached Ship Island, the first of the Union ships to arrive at the point of *rendezvous*.

Alas, Ship Island was no tropical paradise but a desolate barrier island off the mouth of the Mississippi River, the only sign of habitation, a rambling, partially ruined fort flying the Union Jack. The mates dropped anchor and tied off the *Illinois* at a broad dock. Green-hued ghosts emerged from the lower deck to take the air. To their disappointment, Col. Greenleaf picked up the megaphone and delivered an order they did not want to hear. "We are now docked at Ship Island. No one may leave the ship. The Fifty-second Regiment is ordered to remain on board until further notice." The privates climbed slowly back down the ladder to return to their board beds in the hold. Nevertheless, when they were allowed on deck the following day, the absence of the rolling sea had brightened their faces and restored a bit of color.

"My guess is we're headed to attack Port Hudson. What do say you?" William asked Nathaniel.

"My thought as well. Col. Greenleaf is under the impression General Banks has come to replace General Butler as Commander of the Department of the Gulf. It is well known that General Banks has had Port Hudson in his sights for some time. Port Hudson and Vicksburg control the Mississippi River. General Grant has already been assigned to take Vicksburg. You know, William, we could be the ones to take Port

Hudson, cut the Confederacy in half, and end the war!"

They smacked each other on the back.

William had a question for his friend.

"Nathaniel, can I ask you to help me decide something?"

"Of course."

"Chaplain Moors says he hopes to send and receive mail when we arrive in Baton Rouge. I wrote a letter to Elizabeth last night. This morning, I read it again. I had second thoughts. I tore it up."

"Why did you do that?"

"I did entirely too good a job of describing the conditions for the privates on this ship. I turned my own stomach." Nathaniel laughed.

"My friend, why did you ever think you wanted to tell Elizabeth about that situation?"

"I wanted her to pass it on to my brother Aaron. You know, he's not yet 18 years old. He argued long and hard for Father to let him join the militia, and then, at the time of the call for volunteers, he pitched a fit when Father wouldn't sign for him to volunteer. The life and death of the privates in the eastern zone is dreadful. I'm sure that is the story everywhere. Aaron is determined to serve, but Father knows there is no chance Aaron to have a commission. Aaron might understand Father's reasoning if he heard what the trip here was like for the rank and file."

"Hold on to those second thoughts, my friend. Elizabeth doesn't need to know about life in the hold. She could probably handle it, but she might tell her sister Abigail!"

"I could write directly to Aaron, but he'll blab, and Elizabeth will tell me I'm not sharing everything the way I said I would."

Nathaniel thought about the situation for a few moments before speaking.

"William, Aaron is not a priority problem right now. As I remember, his eighteenth birthday is several months away. We may well be done with the whole business by then." Nathaniel ran a hand through his curls and thought for a minute more before continuing. "I won't say the Union wouldn't ever change the policy and start taking younger men without parental permission. We'll do almost anything we must to win this war. But for now, being underage requires a father's consent. The policy will only change if matters are dire. I expect we'll know beforehand if that's the case because we're going to be in the thick of it."

"You're convinced of that?"

"My best guess would be more accurate."

"Maybe by then Susanna will persuade Aaron to stay on the farm."

"You dream, William. I have not heard of any moves in her direction by your brother Aaron since they danced at your wedding. That doesn't count as a "move." No one could resist the music that night. As a rule, Aaron seems to pursue more dangerous women."

"What? Do you know something I should know, Nat?"

"Not really. Just my impression."

Aaron and *dangerous women*? One of my little brothers? William thought he should pay more attention.

~~~

Two more ships and an escort of seabirds arrived at Ship Island the following day. The Captain of the *Illinois* released the crew from confinement and restored their routine assignments. The officers did the same for the enlisted men under their command. A beautiful day. No one grumbled about tasks to be performed in the warm, fresh air. The rank and file spent the morning scouring every inch of the vessel, which diminished but could not eliminate the reek of sickness. Only a three-day nor'easter on the ocean could do that. After they scrubbed the upper deck within an inch of its life, they had priority leisure time up there for a few hours in the afternoon. Then, the poor lads went back to the hold.

Mid-afternoon, the Captain of the *Illinois* picked up the megaphone and gave an order for the assembled vessels to complete putting on supplies. He planned to lead the armada up the ship channel in the morning. The ships finished provisioning from the fort against a bloodred backdrop of the setting sun. Elegant herons, magnificent pelicans and two spectacular black frigatebirds, who had strayed a bit north, swept in and out of the picture.

The armada assembled in the morning to sail the serpentine path of the channel up to the City of New Orleans. Squawking seagulls rode the wakes behind the ships and dined on what the passengers and crew threw overboard. A beautiful trip under a sky the color of a dutchman's britches! At the water's edge, scampering shorebirds fished for tasty bites left behind by each retreating wave. Magnificent herons fished for minnows. Above them, pelicans soared over the masts of the ships and plunged fifty feet into the water, then emerged with cargo in the brilliant orange baskets hanging from their lower jaws. They haughtily tossed their heads inviting all spectators to give them a round of applause.

First vegetation, then signs of habitation, then modest farms emerged on the windswept shore. With irony honed by impatience, the men aboard the *Illinois* referred to them as *plantations*. Little negro boys appeared from nowhere, scurried among the stunted trees, and pulled fresh, sweet oranges right off the branches. The boys tossed the fruit to the ships without concern for what did not reach the target but landed in the water. The soldiers hollered back greetings and threw coins to the boys. The owners of the groves were nowhere to be seen.

"Do you suppose the boys have permission to do that?" William asked Nathaniel.

"Not a chance. Little black boys are the same as little white boys. Untended fruit is there for the taking and tastes the sweetest."

The *Illinois* slowed to make the turn to go north. The steeple of St. Louis Cathedral poked up over the levee. A small tender took off a few of the passengers, some disappointed they would not be delivered to Texas. No one from the Fifty-second Regiment disembarked. All they saw of New Orleans was the spire, a long dock, a collection of barges, and an exotic paddle wheel vessel blaring music in their direction.

"I'd love to see the city, Nat, if only for an hour. I thought they might let us go ashore now that Admiral Farragut took New Orleans for the Union. I'd stroll the streets and lift my cap to everyone I saw. I'd say *Bonjour, monsieur. Bonjour, madame.*"

"That would be the extent of my conversation, Will, but I wager you could do a lot better."

"Wouldn't Pierre be happy if I could give him a report on the patois they speak here? Maybe we'll get a chance to see the city after we've done what we have come to do, especially if we're the ones who end the war. I hope we will."

William continued straining his neck to see over the bank. Soon, the shore showed nothing but wooded wilderness.

William rewrote his letter to Elizabeth. This time, he described the rank and file on the trip down as "packed in like the lower layer in a cigar box." He said nothing about the effect of the sea on their digestion other than to report that, miraculously, he and Nathaniel had no problem with seasickness.

"How's this letter, Nathaniel? Is it gentle enough for sister Abigail to

read over Elizabeth's shoulder?"

Nathaniel laughed. "Good job!"

The day before Christmas Eve, almost two months after they left the Greenfield Railroad Station, the *Illinois* and now four companion ships, pulled up to the long dock of the City of Baton Rouge. They had been nineteen days on shipboard. The passengers on the *Illinois* cheered long and loud. Col. Greenleaf ordered the companies at ease on the deck. He took the First Lieutenants to accompany him on a brief inspection of the harbor area.

CHAPTER EIGHT

Hearts that soared with their first steps onto the dock plunged when a ten-minute walk revealed the deplorable condition of the city they had come to. An extended tour of the city deepened their dismay.

"This place is a ruin! What destruction is wrought by war!" Nathaniel exclaimed.

Trash and rubble strewed everywhere. Every structure showed serious damage. Shattered oaks and badly damaged houses lined the wide streets. Five months before, Union occupiers sacked the city as they fled after their first occupation. From their departing ships, they took final shots at the stately walls of the Capitol. The Rebels did the same when they left a month ago. The Rebels were now nowhere to be seen. Only a few dogs openly claimed the city as their home. Many other creatures were no doubt hiding within the rubble so as not to become the next meal for the skinny hounds. Hoofbeats and the rattle of wagon wheels echoed in the abandoned streets.

Slowly, another picture emerged. When the Union soldiers moved aside the rubble, wide streets showed the new arrivals graceful curves along the riverfront and deep, shady neighborhoods. Like an aging beauty whose regal carriage and fine bones reveal her past glory, Baton Rouge showed the vestiges befitting her former life. Stately mansions along the streets cried out for ladders, repair crews, buckets of paint, and workers willing to restore what once was elegance.

But the Northern troops had not arrived to undertake rebuilding the city. The entourage moved through as quickly as they were able to clear a path and reassembled on a wide, flat plain above and east of the former Capitol of Louisiana.

Col. Greenleaf summoned his lieutenants and instructed them on the general layout of the camp he had designed from information brought to him when they were all still shipboard on the *Illinois.* Following the plan, the lieutenants ordered their men to set up a tent city on the upper plain. They made no attempt to occupy more than a few of the more permanent buildings in the city below. Although they had been given no specific timetable, William and Nathaniel expected an order to march to Port Hudson at any moment. Would they be given a few days' notice, one day, or perhaps only a command to assemble? Should they try to ameliorate the location or expend minimum effort with the expectation they would soon be gone? They chose the latter.

They hoped to proceed to their mission quickly.

All arms had been secured aboard the *Illinois* on the trip down from the north. Now, the quartermaster distributed weapons and a caution. "Remember!" he said, "You are in the Rebels' backyard. Be vigilant." As if to emphasize his point, appropriate sound effects in the form of a volley of Rebel gunfire resounded from the upriver woods. Col. Greenleaf dispatched a watch party to investigate and subdue the enemy if necessary. It was not necessary. They found no one.

"Don't get tired of being cautious, men. One Rebel with a gun is all it takes to change your life."

Some exceptions to minimal effort were essential. They found and appropriated a sound building with a fine kitchen that became the mess. They erected a large tent to use as a hospital and moved in the patients who had become ill on shipboard. Seasickness was not the only malady the men brought with them from their trip on the *Illinois.* Dysentery, measles, and a variety of fevers, including typhus and malaria, hitched rides as well. Doc Sawyer and his assistants busied about tending their patients.

"Where could all those diseases have come from?" William asked him. "Everyone seemed healthy when they came onto the ship. We had no contact with anyone from the outside world after we sailed. Did the crew bring illnesses aboard when we stopped for fuel and other necessaries?"

Doc Sawyer had no answer. When William asked Nathaniel the same question, Nathaniel said he had his doubts the doctors knew what anybody had or how to treat what ills they did recognize. They'd scratch their chins and advise Col. Greenleaf to relocate the tents farther from the river, already the distance of what had been the entire city of Baton Rouge. "Do they think the Mississippi River pours out fevers with the morning fog?" William asked, disgusted.

After three days, Nathaniel realized that maintaining high readiness ate at everyone's nerves, especially when the balmy days they enjoyed on the sail up the Mississippi River turned sour. A breeze chilled the air, and a light rain fell.

Soon a cold front swept in with a winter storm. Their hastily constructed camp provided little protection from the harsher weather. Nathaniel wore a long face two days later, when he returned from a briefing of company commanders.

"Gentlemen, we can settle into our camp. An attack on Port Hudson has been indefinitely delayed."

A chorus of moans met the announcement.

The only additional information Nathaniel extracted from the briefing was that Rebels were threatening the Union outpost down the Mississippi River at Plaquemine. Command sent four companies of the Fifty-second Regiment to give them relief. Col. Greenleaf said Rebel General Franklin Gardner was well dug in at the Port Hudson fortifications, and the terrain was quite difficult. They were going to need to be at full strength for an assault, and therefore must wait for resolution of what was going on in Plaquemine and the return of their four companies before launching an attack. No one knew when that would be.

"And in the meanwhile?" the troops asked Nathaniel.

"The Colonel instructed us to have our sergeants undertake a continuous training program of at least three hours every morning and await further orders."

"But you heard nothing inconsistent with moving on to Port Hudson, did you?" William asked.

"No. That is the good news. I still believe Port Hudson is our goal. There will be delay."

Nathaniel continued his report on the briefing. "At this point, I'm embarrassed that I said something stupid. I hope my thoughtlessness will not reflect badly on you men. I suggested to Colonel Greenleaf that we take advantage of the delay to send out our scouts to get some idea of the terrain we'll have to deal with when we do make our move. The Colonel smiled at me like a father whose teenager has just realized old Dad knows a thing or two. He said they had already done so. Ouch!"

William laughed. "I'm glad to know you make a blunder, occasionally. I thought only I did that." Col. Greenleaf read them the detailed description of the forests and fissures that encircled the fortifications he had received from his scouts.

As instructed, every morning for three to four hours, rain or shine, the regiments marched and trained in the manual of arms and the protocols and procedures for different situations. By noon, they were hungry. They ate well, the meals much improved by the addition of local provisions and the confiscation and renovation of the kitchen building in town.

Intermittently, they received reports of Rebel activities in the vicinity, but none turned out to require more than a brief and uneventful check. The Rebels who had been occupying Baton Rouge had disappeared.

William had not been notified that anyone in his company was ill. When the Chaplain told him that he found the father of Elizabeth's student from South Deerfield, Pvt. Samuel Harris, in the hospital, William was dismayed. As a member of Company C, notes of his illness were not routinely sent to William, a Lieutenant of Company D.

William immediately went to the hospital tent. To his relief, Pvt. Harris was not feverish or congested. He did not look ill. He was pale and tired, but that could be expected. William asked the orderlies to move Pvt. Harris away from those who seemed sicker and asked Doc Sawyer to keep him abreast of the private's progress.

William pondered whether to inform Elizabeth. Elizabeth had told William that Sammy was quite upset when his father marched off to board the *Illinois*. She always released the boy from school as soon as his grandmother came for him. His mother stayed home to care for a younger child. Theirs was one family for whom she knew the signing bounty was the motivation for enlistment. William hoped Pvt. Harris would be well in a few days, and he wouldn't have to tell Elizabeth at all.

The illnesses brought up a topic William hated to think about. If someone died, should he be buried in the cemetery already developed below in the city of Baton Rouge? That was Rebel ground. Should he swallow his embarrassment over his prior blunder and ask Col. Greenleaf?

He did so. The Colonel said he dedicated an area on the upper plain overlooking the parade ground for that purpose as soon as he started laying out the camp. Preparing a cemetery is one of the priority tasks in establishing an encampment. William resolved to have someone else ask the next question.

~~~

William supposed that a Chaplain's main duty was to preach on

Sundays, but delivery of the mail was by far the most popular task Chaplain Moors performed. He took note of lads who received no mail. He would investigate to determine whether the problem was illiteracy on one end of the correspondence or the other. He added teaching and being a scribe to his growing list of tasks. He would need to find an assistant to help him with all the duties he took on.

Within a few days after their arrival in Baton Rouge. the Chaplain had Dolly roll the mail wagon into the camp. The Chaplain rang a bell to announce he had mail to deliver—the first since they sailed out of the New York harbor. William received a letter from Elizabeth in which she apologized for being speechless when she said goodbye. She assured him she was incredibly proud of his service, and he had her full support. He tried to believe her.

Christmas Eve and Christmas Day passed with only an exchange of greetings and a red ribbon on the table at mess to mark the occasion. The Chaplain held a service in the morning and spent the remainder of the day at the hospital tent.

William let his imagination take him to the Wells farm, where Elizabeth would join his family for Christmas and then spend the week with her family until after the New Year. Elizabeth also allowed her imagination to take her to Christmas next year. William would be at the table, of course. Would there also be a new little person at her side? Her morning sickness had passed; she felt wonderful.

Elizabeth tried to calculate the time when it would be safe to give William her news. Maybe Dr. Thomas would say she was past the danger of miscarriage by the end of January. In the meanwhile, she swaddled her thickening waist in her long winter scarf.

One mail day, Nathaniel watched William hold a letter from Elizabeth to his nose and take a deep breath. "I thought I might catch her lingering scent or at least the smell of the Green Mountains," he said. "No luck. Home is just too far away."

Nathaniel dropped his eyes to ask a question. "William, would you ask Elizabeth something for me?"

"Of course I will. What is it you want to know?"

"Would it be presumptuous of me to request permission to correspond with her sister Abigail?"

Elizabeth conveyed Abigail's assent by return post.

"Nat, I do believe she was waiting for that request."

Letters took about two weeks to arrive from Massachusetts, which seemed a long time to Chaplain Moors. William thought it was truly remarkable for letters to arrive at all!

Second to his work with the mail, the Chaplain endeared himself to the regiment by taking special interest in those in the hospital. He visited the patients almost every day. He consulted with the doctor about their care. He checked to be sure the instructions were faithfully followed. Occasionally, he took boys who needed close monitoring into his own accommodations and tended them himself. William was proud of his special relationship with the Chaplain and enjoyed helping him when he could. He tried but he could not soften the Chaplain's rigid prohibition against gambling. Late in the afternoon, someone passing by a tent might catch the rattle of dice and shouts of glee and gloom. The lieutenants turned a blind eye, but not the Chaplain. The evils of gambling were a regular topic of his Sunday sermons and just as regularly ignored.

In the afternoons, the officers exercised the horses the quartermaster supplied them, which gave William an opportunity to serve the Chaplain in a significant way. The horse provided for the Chaplain was totally unsuitable—a fiery-eyed stallion standing at least 16 hands high. The Chaplain couldn't control him. In the saddle, the Chaplain looked like a chubby toddler having a turn around the corral on his father's mount. He might slide over the rump and hit the dirt at any time, if the horse didn't throw him off the front end first. William wished he could share the ludicrous sight with Pierre.

William located a gentle but strong little mare named Dolly; Dolly and the Chaplain took to each other right away. William helped train Dolly for what they expected to be her assignment when they attacked Port Hudson—pulling a wagon and obeying instructions to wait patiently for commands. William gave the discarded stallion, whose name was Excalibur, a trial period as his own mount. After a half day working with Excalibur, William knew all the mount needed was a confident hand holding the reins—a judgment Pierre would have made after five minutes on his back.

William explained what the Chaplain thought was his miracle.

"Chaplain Moors, I know you're happy to have an appropriate mount and happy that I have one also, but believe me, miracles are your department, not mine. I have a lifetime of experience with horses and understand them very well. The overwhelming emotion of a horse is fear. A horse fears being startled, confused, or dealing with a rider who cannot be trusted. At first, even Dolly had no idea what you might do. Now, she trusts you. You have made her your friend, and she is sure you will treat her as such. I see you caressing her neck and sharing your thoughts."

Chaplain Moors kept abreast of goings on at home in Western Massachusetts. He wrote to his wife every day and received many letters from her in return. Come sundown, William and Nathaniel invited him to visit their tent to share news. The meetings attracted other officers also. When the tent became crowded, the Chaplain offered his quarters, now a comfortable house in the town. One drawback: no gambling is allowed over there. Many officers gave up the game in return for information, good company, and news they found nowhere else.

William visited the hospital after the first of the year. He was happy to find the father of Elizabeth's student, Sammy, still looking well, but his cot was again close to men with high fevers and rashes.

"I know you're the doctor, but it seems to me in his weakened condition, he's likely to contract something from your other patients more serious than what he already has. Could he be located farther away?" William asked.

Doc did agree to move him. Elizabeth wrote that his son Sammy was beginning to read now and had made new friends.

~~~

Adding to the depressingly long wait in Baton Rouge, William was picking up hints that, once again, all was not going smoothly on the family farm. Elizabeth wrote that his brother Aaron asked to be excused from the dinner table when the conversation turned to William and the war. Aaron should have been grateful. Thanks to the intervention of big brother, their father had done an about-face of making sugar. He now supported the sideline for Aaron. Mr. Wells laid in a supply of buckets and taps, located a second boiler, and added to the sugar shack to set up for producing molasses in the spring, just a few months away. Elizabeth wrote that Aaron would have been even harder to live with without his special project to work on.

Elizabeth didn't want to tell William anymore about Aaron's malaise. That was not news. Aaron giving his father anxiety was the rule, not the exception. But there was a new issue. The father of Aaron's friend Henry Arnold Sr., the man who owned the mill in Northfield, wanted Aaron to quit the family farm and come work for him. He had shipments of cotton coming in from Boston and a crew of green hands. He knew Aaron managed hands on the Wells farm and did it well. It just happened the offer came on the fourth day in a row Aaron's father had Aaron driving

pigs to the slaughterhouse, a job he detested. Good grief! William
exclaimed when he read the letter from Elizabeth. If Aaron thought the
job on the farm repetitive and beneath him, he sure wouldn't be happy as
a private in the Army!

William knew the father of Aaron's friend was involved in
questionable schemes and there was an older sister, a known beauty, who
worked at a pub in Boston. Rumor had it she lived there also. William
took time to write to Aaron to tell him all the reasons he should have
nothing to do with the family, especially the sister in Boston.

~~~

William and Nathaniel were accustomed to living too far west for
timely news, but now they yearned to hear about the progress of the war
elsewhere and the opinions of the people at home. Nathaniel had more
tolerance for the way the brass kept those of lesser rank in the dark, but
even he grew impatient. He wanted to know what the columnists had to
say. Any newspaper someone received traveled around the camp until
the pages crumbled and fell apart.

Nathaniel read that a columnist in the *New York Daily Tribune* said
since General Banks was doing nothing. His forces should be sent to help
the floundering Army of the Potamic in the east.

"My God, no," Nathaniel exclaimed. "Probably Horace Greeley
wrote that. He always has a bad word to say about General Banks."

William recalled what Elizabeth's mother asked at the dinner table
back home. *Why do you men try so hard to get news of the war? It's always bad.*

"I'd like to know the ultimate plan for the Department of the Gulf,"
said Nathaniel, "even if I don't like it. The South has seen our resolve,
but our dedication doesn't appear to have diminished their thirst for
rebellion. My faith in a speedy end to the insurrection is fading. And
apparently, that of the President is as well. He is also persuaded that the
South's support from the work of the slaves contributes significantly to
their strength. Removing that support might forestall the necessity of
other measures."

~~~

In the fall of 1862, President Lincoln floated his plan to remove from
the Confederate Army the aid and support they received from the
enslaved. On January 1, 1863, he formally issued The Emancipation
Proclamation. First, from that day forward, all persons held in bondage
in the states or parts of states, like Louisiana, still in rebellion against the
Union would be free. Second: negroes would be eligible for service in

every branch of the Union forces. Parts of Louisiana occupied by the Union were not included in its effect, but that was an unimportant detail to abolitionists who rejoiced and Lincoln's detractors who decried his action. The Sundowner Sessions with the Chaplain, as William had taken to calling them, buzzed with the topic.

"I'd love to know what changed Lincoln's mind," William said. "Last I heard the President thought slavery was in the Constitution and therefore legal by definition, at least in the ratifying states. He thought the problems presented by abolition were overwhelming. Freedom, and then what? President Lincoln didn't ordinarily go down a road unless he had an idea what the destination would be and what difficulties might be encountered on the way. William agreed with him on that policy. Did the President now have a plan for freed slaves they hadn't heard about?"

Chaplain Moors passed on what he'd heard from one of his fellow Chaplains.

"The President made his decision in favor of the Emancipation Proclamation based solely on his assessment of the military situation. He became convinced they had to end the dreadful war by draining the manpower and resources of the North. They were almost in a position to end the war except for the contribution to the Rebel cause made by the slaves—keeping the farms and plantations in operation and doing the fatigue work for the military so white men could fight—tipped the balance against them. He no longer feared the European nations would intervene to preserve the source of the raw material on which their economy depended; the war was increasingly seen by the people of Europe as one to preserve the institution of slavery and the Europeans themselves no longer approved.

As everyone predicted, the problems presented by the Proclamation bubbled to the surface. A few of the officers of the Fifty-second Regiment objected to any talk of negro officers. When they found no fertile ground for their opinions in the meetings of the Sundowner Sessions, they stopped attending.

"Just as well," William said. "I'm not going to oppose abolishing slavery, but I do hope President Lincoln has a plan to deal with the freed slaves and just hasn't yet told us what it will be. It cannot be to send them to some other country, which he once proposed. They are as much Americans as someone with white skin."

"Chaplain Moors, I think you'd be interested in what Elizabeth told me about a program at the men's club of a church at home she attended to serve refreshments. She heard the speaker, a female abolitionist from eastern Massachusetts, read accounts of slave life now appearing regularly in the Eastern press. Elizabeth was quite moved by the descriptions of what the slaves endure."

The Chaplain raised his eyebrows. "How was that received at the men's meeting?"

"There was much grumbling in the audience," William reported, "and some open criticism of the Pastor for having allowed the guest to attend. Too controversial for church. The owner of a mill in Northfield, perhaps the father of Aaron's friend, said the woman was just a trouble-making busy-body. He said he was totally in support of preserving our union, but we must have cotton for our mills. You can't grow cotton without labor. Only slaves will pick cotton."

"Too controversial for church? Is there a better place to take our differences than to church? What do you think?" the Chaplain asked William.

"I think the man just doesn't approve of women having opinions. Elizabeth tells me she knew enough not to say a word. No one could know her thoughts unless they could read her mind."

Nathaniel had also been doing some thinking on the subject. "Nothing is sadder than the slaves in rags who come to our camp asking for food. They flee plantations at night, even more since the President issued the Proclamation. I don't know what will become of them. No one is prepared to undertake their care. You know, there were those, including myself, who thought dealing with former slaves would just be a problem for the South. But we're fighting a war to preserve the Union. Any problem for part of the Union is a problem for everyone and for our President, who has the issue on his plate. We will need to support him. Perhaps he has plans we just do not yet know about."

At the end of January, during the morning training period, a hospital orderly gave William a message that stopped him in his tracks and sent a stab of fear into his gut. He said the two men who had taken sick on the Illinois had both taken turns for the worse. One of them was Sammy Harris. William raced to the hospital tent and found Doc Sawyer.

"I can't believe it! How could that be? I saw him yesterday. He was tired and pale, of course. He hadn't been out of bed for a month. But we had a long conversation. He was so proud of how his boy was coming along in school. Before Sammy became Elizabeth's student, he couldn't read a word. Pvt. Harris didn't look sicker to me."

"Don't panic, William. You tend to your business, and I'll tend to mine. His fever has gone up a bit, but he is far from critical. We'll keep a close watch."

William wondered if they ever did anything except "keep a close watch!" His experience with the state of medical care in the field was giving him some understanding of why casualty numbers ran so high. William returned to the parade ground, but anxiety over Sammy made him cross with his men. Those who went out on picket duty received instruction that plunder of livestock was strictly forbidden. The men disobeyed, more for the adventure of hunting than the need for food. When William chastised them, they claimed they saw a twinkle in the eye of the officer who transmitted the prohibition. William had to admit they could be speaking the truth. He had witnessed officers digging their forks into a succulent roast piglet or baby lamb they well knew hadn't been shipped upriver from New Orleans. William never saw their supply ships unloading fresh meat, and he certainly never heard the bleat of young lambs or piglets in the fenced-in area next to the mess. He put the issue out of his mind.

William and Nathaniel yearned even more to hear about the progress of the war in other parts of the South and to read the opinions of the people at home. Nathaniel had more tolerance for the way the brass kept those of lesser rank in the dark, but even he grew impatient. He wanted to know what the columnists had to say. Any newspaper someone received traveled around the camp until the pages crumbled and fell apart.

~~~

The real winter weather set in at the end of January, not as cold as what they left behind in New England but wetter. A depressing pattern repeated itself time and again. Darkening clouds gave but a few hours warning of trouble ahead. Terrifying lightning, swirling wind, and deluges of rain ushered in a twenty to thirty-degree drop in temperature. Over the next few days, the temperature slowly climbed twenty degrees until the men felt they were in Massachusetts in July. Then the air turned heavy with sticky dampness, the temperature plunged, and the cycle began again. One chapter of the pattern often got stuck and overstayed everyone's patience. And it seemed that it would always be one of the least pleasant chapters in the cycle, such as the precipitous drop in temperature or the lightning and swirling rain. The repetitions destroyed good humor because everyone knew once the cycle began, they would have to endure the remainder of the cycle before coming around again to one of the spells of pleasant weather.

"Can we get any warning when we're going to have these violent changes?" William asked the Colonel. All he would say is that weather in the semi-tropics is unpredictable.

~~~

Chaplain Moors often preached about maintaining cheerfulness— indeed, a challenge for the rank and file closed off from being with loved ones and not able to do what they came so far to do. His suggestion? Every night, think of three good things that happened that day for which you can thank the Lord.

William agreed that being gloomy did not help. Shut indoors last winter in Massachusetts, he and Elizabeth did well because they were still virtually honeymooners, and they had each other. So many of the poor lads, now confined in rainy winter weather in Baton Rouge, had no reservoir of experience to tap. They did not know what war would be like but had not expected to be miserably cold, wet, idle, and in the company of strangers for weeks on end.

At the end of January, the order came for all who had been physically cleared for battle to assemble on the parade field at eight a.m. the following day. What industry that afternoon and late into the night! Everyone was sure they were off to Port Hudson to do what they had come to do.

The men put their gear in order. Many dashed off letters home. Those seeking to be restored to duty reported to the regiment's doctors for reexamination to certify their ability to fight. Everyone anticipated a hero's return after they had captured Port Hudson. A few woke up in a nightmare of a battle resembling the bloody field at Bull Run described by reporters in such detail nine months before.

Not William. At dawn, the Chaplain had come to his tent to tell him that Samuel Harris had died. William dashed to the hospital tent. He received the only explanation the staff was able to give him. Sammy had suddenly taken a bad turn. His chest became congested, and he had trouble taking a deep breath. They tried hot compresses for over an hour but had no success. In two hours, he breathed his last. William had no alternative but to bear his grief. He had to be with his men as they prepared for battle.

~~~

An excited regiment assembled on the parade ground. Company A passed in review after presenting arms, with flags flying and band playing. They were followed by Companies B through K. Each flag dipped before General Banks, and he raised his cap in acknowledgment of the salute.

The regiment marched due east for approximately an hour, paused, and then heard the following order. "Company A: right, march." After Company A, companies B through K received and obeyed the same order.

March to the right? What was the General saying? They were marching south! Not north in the direction of Port Hudson but downriver.

The regiment marched south for several hours, halted, and were ordered to turn about face and march back from whence they came. When they again reached the Baton Rouge parade ground, they heard the next order. "Companies dismissed." They broke ranks within a few feet of where they had first assembled.

Incredibly, instead of disappointment or any other dispiriting emotion, the men held their chins high and their backs straight. The patriotic display and pounding music had raised their spirits!

Back at their tent, Nathaniel couldn't keep a straight face.

"Forget all my razzing of General Banks, Will. He is one smart commander. The men were low as worms, so he dished out the pageantry. The men fell right into it and emerged on a high."

But For William, nothing helped. He kept thinking of Sammy Harris. He visited with the Chaplain. The Chaplain knew that talking with those who suffered losses would be part of his job. In fact, he had read a lot on the subject. But he expected the grieving parties to be strangers. He began his grief counseling with someone with whom he had become very close. It was hard.

~~~

By February, Elizabeth knew she would soon have to tell the families her secret. Her winter scarf could no longer conceal her condition. But all did not go well. She saw signs of difficulty. She confided in Pierre.

"Pierre, I suspected I was pregnant the day we went to the final ceremony before William left. I didn't tell him. One day, I said I must; I owed him honesty. The next day, I said I mustn't. William would probably have decided to stay with me and miss something he really wanted to do. Perhaps for naught since I fear I am having difficulty again."

Pierre hopped right on the problem. He arranged for Dr. Thomas to come to Deerfield to see her.

"Into the bed with you, my dear," the doctor said. "Your well-being must be our first consideration. The difficulty will probably pass, but I'll keep a close eye as you watch for developments. Do you know someone who can stay with you? Perhaps Abigail?"

"No, no! Not Abby, Doctor. Pierre knows a young woman from the Acadian farm. She has come to William's family when needed. She is discrete. Would that be possible?"

The doctor agreed with Elizabeth that they could keep the pregnancy and the problem a secret for a few weeks. He approved the young woman staying with her "until the fever of a bad cold" broke—as they labeled their ploy.

At the end of a week, all signs of difficulty had passed. Elizabeth stayed in bed for another few days. Then she wrote to William and told him her news. She visited each family to tell them as well. She said nothing to any of them about the difficulties.

William stopped breathing when he was but a line or two into the letter from Elizabeth with news of her condition. *Dr. Thomas has just left the cottage. He confirmed what I knew to be true. My love, you are going to be a father!*

William headed for the nearest tree stump to sit down before reading further. The Chaplain came over to ask if there was something wrong.

"No, No. More than right. Elizabeth tells me she is pregnant. We are expecting a baby."

"Congratulations to you both! Does she know when the baby will arrive?"

"Late June, beginning of July is the doctor's best guess. Elizabeth says she felt unusual on the day we left but thought her emotions were responsible. Then she wanted to wait to ask Dr. Thomas to come until she'd passed the time when she had lost the baby before. She didn't want me to have anything to worry about! To think I'd been feeling sorry for us that so much time would pass before we could try for another child!"

"God was taking care of you all this time, William, and you didn't know it."

"Indeed. I am so thankful. Surely, this news counts for all three of my reasons for thanks today, Chaplain Moors. Dr. Thomas says Elizabeth and the baby are both doing fine. I've gotten control of myself now. Do you know where I can find Nathaniel?"

"He'll probably come to the mail wagon sometime soon. We have a couple letters for him—written in a woman's hand."

"Would you tell him I have news? He should come to the tent to find me. I'm going to dash off a letter to my parents to tell them to see that Elizabeth has everything she needs. She's sure to have told them the news already because she said she planned to do so on the following Sunday. What do you think of the coincidence that we both have nine-month assignments?"

"Coincidence, my friend, or God's plan?"

"Yes. God's plan."

"Now wipe away those worry lines between your eyes. You do realize women have been doing this since Eve was in the Garden of Eden. Elizabeth and the baby will be fine."

Not always fine in my family, William thought.

But at least something finally chased William's gloom—unless he stopped to think about the poor unfortunate Pvt. and his son Sammy.

CHAPTER NINE

n mid-March, the Fifty-second Regiment again received an order to assemble on the parade ground, battle-ready, at 8:00 a.m. the following day. This time, they were to be joined by the Ninety-first New York Regiment, Nims's Second Massachusetts Battery, the Twenty-fourth Connecticut Regiment, and several bands of cavalry, all of whom had moved to the vicinity of Port Hudson over the past two weeks. Now, that was promising. They would be a brigade of over 2,000 men. Surely, the long-delayed assault on the fortifications would begin at last!

Col. Greenleaf instructed the Fifty-second Regiment only to pack what they could carry in a knapsack. Only the high command would have horses for a march of just under twenty miles. Now experienced with changeable Louisiana winter weather, their rubber blankets found priority location in their packs.

The Chaplain, with Dolly and the wagon, would accompany the regiment. Rev. Moors offered to carry small treasures on his person. William gave him a bundle of letters from Elizabeth and a small likeness.

Picking up the regiments coming in from other locations and assembling them into a brigade took an undue length of time. The march north did not begin until 4:00 in the afternoon. After only four hours on the route, Col. Greenleaf halted the caravan. They pitched camp in a cornfield. The headlands remaining from the recent harvest provided firm, dry ground for their tents.

"I'm seeing the same fire the men had four months ago when we left Camp Miller," Nathaniel commented to William as they bedded down for the night. "I feared the long delay might snuff their spirit."

"No, indeed. I see plenty of spirit! Do you smell roast lamb? I know the distinctive aroma well. I believe they are foraging, cooking, and feasting behind our backs."

"Let them be," said Nathaniel. "It's better they be in a good mood than a bad one. I believe we're in for an assault on one of the most well-fortified strongholds of the Confederacy. We'll crack down when we have to."

William raised his eyebrows. "How about *just before we have to*? Remember the lesson I learned about discipline the day we took railcars to sail on the *Illinois?* I haven't forgotten."

"Agreed. Or, as you are fond of saying, *d'accord!*"

The next sunrise brought an order to "fall in." The weather was warm and by noon, had become hot and sticky. Early afternoon, Chaplain Moors took pity on a straggling lad sweating in his woolen blues. He offered to let the lad ride Dolly for a while. Alas, he didn't first ask permission from Dolly! The ordinarily gentle mare reared up, shuddered like a volcano, and slid the lad straight off her rump—the second try was the same reaction. Second try; same reaction. The company enjoyed the circus act, but the Chaplain did not. He tried in vain to get Dolly to accept an unfamiliar rider.

William to the rescue! He tightened the bit and had Dolly under control in three minutes! Dolly behaved from then on but at all times kept one big brown eye cut sideways toward William.

"Do you suppose word passed among the horses that the tall fella is the one we must obey?" asked the Chaplain.

They marched all day. When they reached a thick stand of trees south, and below the fortifications, a messenger from command delivered a special assignment for the Fifty-second Regiment. *Pass up the location for the base camp. Leave making camp to others; march forward to the fortifications on reconnaissance and await further orders.*

"*On reconnaissance*? What the hell does that mean?" William asked the messenger.

The messenger responded, "I asked Col. Greenleaf, and he told me to take it as "*advance and don't fire unless ordered to do so or unless fired upon.*" They advanced.

When the Fifty-second Regiment had the moveable canons of Port Hudson in view, a tremendous blast came up from the direction of the Mississippi River. The shriek of mortar shells hissed in the air and exploded, changing the calm evening sky to a quivering, fiery crimson. A ferocious battle on the river had begun. Following his orders, Nathaniel led the company to the most forward position, under the moveable canons and behind the rear of the fortifications, nearer to the enemy than any other regiment.

The participants in the battle raging between the Union fleet on the Mississippi River below and the Rebel cannons of the fortifications of Port Hudson appeared to take no notice of close to 1000 men of the Fifty-second Regiment at the back door of Port Hudson.

"Opportunity is knocking," Nathaniel said to his second Lieutenant with a smile on his face. "Everyone inside Port Hudson has eyes on Admiral Farragut out there in the river. We could probably come in the back and take the whole damn fortified area by ourselves."

"I'm on! Let's do it!"

"No, No. We'd be court-marshalled for not following orders. But I'll send a messenger to ask permission."

The messenger who returned from Col. Greenleaf ordered the Fifty-second Regiment to remain in place behind the fortifications for a half hour and then return to base camp.

William saw Nathaniel's lips draw into a tight line, but he complied.

Before the Fifty-second Regiment reached the base camp, Col. Greenleaf himself rode up. He ordered them to go no farther.

"I remand my order to you to return to base camp," Col. Greenleaf called out. "Instead, go four miles deeper into the woods, north of the trail. Make camp there and bed down for the night. You will return to base camp in the morning."

A night without rest. A ferocious exchange of firepower between the Union ships on the river and the batteries of the fortifications raged through the night and until 5:00 in the morning. The Fifty-second Regiment could see flashes lighting on each other's faces even in the wee hours. No one could sleep through it. At dawn, the red sky faded down to a rosy glow. Unfortunately, a rosy dawn portends a wet day ahead.

The Fifty-second Regiment gathered themselves and left the woods. They returned to base camp for a few hours of sleep in their tents.

~~~

At noon, General Banks called a meeting of the field command. Nathaniel learned that in the night, Admiral Farragut, with the *Hartford* and the *Albatross,* had slipped under the guns of Port Hudson and traveled up the Mississippi River toward Vicksburg. The remainder of the Union fleet had been torched by the Rebels. Every Union ship sank or, gravely damaged, floated helplessly down the river.

Nathaniel returned to base camp with the last words of General Banks burning in his ears. *I have ordered the equipment wagons to return to Baton Rouge. The object of the expedition has been accomplished; the Army of the Gulf will return as well. We march as soon as we are able to assemble.*

William controlled his reaction until he was alone with Nathaniel. Then he exploded.

"The object of the mission having been accomplished? How can he say that? The Union fleet is destroyed. The fortification is unharmed. We are pulling out. By any measure known to reasonable men, we have once again failed our mission!"

Nathaniel could do no more than repeat the announcement made by General Banks. Again and again.

The Fifty-second didn't receive orders to begin the march back to Baton Rouge until early afternoon. By then, an ominous eggplant color covered the lower half of the western sky.

After less than an hour on the route, a storm roared in as if shot from the cannons on the heights. High wind, then thunder and lightning, put on a display for twenty minutes. Rains joined in the display—the most violent downpour the Fifty-second Regiment had experienced since they had been in Louisiana—and they had seen a few storms. For the remainder of the day, curtains of rain swirled about them. The rubber blankets used as rain gear were impotent against the torrents. Most seriously, the packed dirt road that had been perfect for the march from Baton Rouge to Port Hudson began to dissolve. The road became a gutter full of slow-moving mud. Almost immediately, the equipment wagon became mired—irrelevant because there was no ground on which they could have pitched a tent. Dusk indicated the approach of darkness. Alternative footing became impossible to find.

The men stood between thick stands of trees and underbrush on either side of the sluice of mud and pondered their dilemma.

"By God, it's as if a Sky God broke a dam and freed every bit of snowmelt from the Green Mountains of Vermont," said Nathaniel.

The deluge kept up for an hour, let up for spells of no more than fifteen minutes, then started up again as hard as before. Brought to a standstill by the disappearance of the road beneath their boots and the total absence of any ground on which to take another step, William expelled a sarcastic laugh when Nathaniel ordered, "Company halt!" They had been involuntarily "halted" for quite some time.

Even though there were no good options, there was indeed a need for leadership. Nathaniel summoned the corporals of both parts of Company

D. "We need to make a plan for the night before it is completely dark. Will, what can you remember about the terrain on either side of what used to be the road?" Nathaniel asked. "Do you think the right side or left side of the road looked more promising for an alternate path foreword?"

"Neither one. As I remember, they both seemed about the same: not virgin forest but vigorous second growth and heavy impassable underbrush. The best we'll find in the way of material to help us get some sleep is probably a downed tree we can drag to a high spot to sit or lie down upon."

"Gather your corporals, Will. Have them see what they can find on the Mississippi River side. I'll keep my corporals on this side with the same mission. We had no idea we'd need training in the double buddy system, but once it's dark, we'll have to institute that system to keep track of everyone. It was providential; we had three hours of drill every morning when we first landed here. Now, we have to put the drills into practice."

A huge crack and crash sounded on the river side of what had been the road. The top seven feet of a tall tree snapped off and fell to the ground.

"I believe the rain God has just made you a present of a tree trunk for your side, Will. Probably a pine tree by the way it snapped clean, but I can't see details in the dark. I'll have my corporals see what they can find on my side, the one away from the river. Something, anything to keep our rear ends off the mud."

They were still making tentative forays within twenty feet of what had been the road when they heard a horse approaching. Col. Greenfield appeared. He greeted them.

"Gentlemen, everyone is trying to find the firmest ground on which to spend the night. I suggest you do the same."

"We are doing so, sir."

William requisitioned the fortuitously felled tree, and Nathaniel found a similar tree trunk on the other side of what had been the road—now a slow-moving sludge of muck moving toward Baton Rouge.

Sitting on a log, dozing off with chin on chest, was as close as anyone would come to "bedding down" this night.

The rain slackened around midnight. The moon attempted an appearance in the southern sky. The men used the brief respite to see if there was any way to improve their situation. There was not. The

Colonel rode up again.

"If the rain holds off and the moonlight continues, we could resume our march."

The moon quickly scuttled that plan by ducking under a layer of clouds. The rain increased.

The Colonel delivered a message. "General Banks made me an offer. The first two companies of the Fifty-second Regiment who take the offer may divert from the route to guard a posse escorting some cotton to New Orleans. "He can't tell you who'll get the money from the sale, but you're entitled to know there's a way out of this hell," he said.

Nathaniel declined the invitation for his part of the regiment; William agreed with the decision and did the same.

Sometime around three o'clock in the morning, best guess because, of course, there was not a moon or stars to give anyone a clue of the time, one of Nathaniel's corporals and his buddy from Nathaniel's men crossed what had been the road and found William with his buddy dozing on his felled tree.

"We have a crisis, sir," Nathaniel's Corporal shouted over the noise of the storm. "A man is unaccounted for."

"What? How long has he been missing?" Will asked.

"Perhaps 30 minutes, sir."

"Tell me who and what you've done to find him."

"His name is Pvt. Dart, sir. During a blinding squall, he and I were on opposite ends of the same fallen tree. About fifteen minutes later, when the rain let up a bit, Pvt. Dart wasn't there. I followed the procedure for a missing man—two buddies went out from each point on a clock face from where he was last seen. They called his name. There was no response. They returned. What do we do now, sir?"

"I'm coming back with you, Corporal. Let me get my buddy. Can you mark our route so we'll be able to find our way back? Red-Riding Hood's breadcrumbs won't work tonight."

"Yes, sir." He did so by digging in flagged stakes.

William, the Corporal, and their buddies found the spot where Pvt. Dart had last been seen. They repeated the clock search maneuver once, twice, and a third time. On the fourth, when William called the private's name, by chance, the noise of the storm let up. William thought he heard a whimper. He located Pvt. Dart at the bottom of a hollow in collected rainwater about four feet deep. With the Corporal holding his foot, William lowered himself into the hollow. He tied a rope around Pvt.

Dart and called on his buddy above to organize a lift crew to pull Pvt. Dart up. Dart didn't think he had any injuries except surface scratches, but he was completely tangled in a thicket of briars. He was soaking wet and chilled to the bone. William made the decision he and his buddy would stay with Pvt. Dart until dawn or until someone could bring the medical crew.

The Fifty-second Regiment did not go to bed anywhere that night. The rain fell without let-up. Rain fell again the following day, less violently but virtually nonstop. The command was in total sympathy with the men. The medical crew arrived and took charge of Pvt. Dart. Nothing could be done but endure the conditions. They resumed the march as best they could.

To take a step, the men had to drag their feet out of deep, sucking muck.

Someone who thought he found a log to sit on came to grief. He slipped off frontwards. He must have hit his head. William found his body damming a stream, but he was still alive, muddy water going around his feet, sliding under his neck, and filtering through his clothes and hair. "Damn lucky he didn't drown. Another exposure patient for the medical crew."

"Better he would have stayed home working in his father's pigpen," said William.

At one point, Nathaniel watched a private from Conway, north of Greenfield, take out a knife and slit the leather of his boots straight down the back of the heel. Nathaniel thought the private had gone mad from the desperation of his situation. The private smiled when Nathaniel questioned him.

"No, I'm not crazy, sir. I raise racehorses. I know a good mudder when I see one. A mudder doesn't carry around a heavy load. The farrier raises the back end of his horse's shoes. The mud goes in the opening in the front and then out underneath in the back."

"But you've ruined your boots, Private."

"I know. I checked with the Quartermaster before I took the first cut. He said the boots were near gone to start with. He has some better ones waiting for me."

Most of the men were not as careful about how they dealt with the damage to their boots or their feet. They just kept going, damage be damned. The sergeant-major cut a hole in the great toe of each boot to drain the water out and marched on, flinging squirts of mud and water from the toes as he went. Everyone had blisters, sores, and worse and came to the end of the forest with flapping soles and holes in their uppers. Some marched barefoot because shoes had blistered their feet so badly that their feet couldn't tolerate any cover.

And, of course, everyone was hungry and exhausted.

Nathaniel and William were proud of their company. Some other officers had to resort to lying: "Keep moving, men, keep moving; the Rebels are hard on us." Company D set their faces and pressed on, albeit slowly. William marched twice as many miles as the men of the company because he circled the regiment time and again, checking the very last men in the rear to be sure no one was left behind.

Exposure, exhaustion, and no sleep took a toll.

Why had they been sent on this mission? They still did not know. How could anyone say it was a success?

They were not as fond of General Banks as they once were.

Col. Greenleaf rode up to them when they limped into camp that afternoon. Some men went straight to the hospital tent, but the docs ran out of supplies to tape up their feet and boots.

"I'm proud to report that everyone is accounted for," said the Colonel. "We all returned to Baton Rouge."

"Even Pvt. Dart?" Nathanial asked.

"He came to camp. I confess it is an open question whether he and the poor soul who fell forward into the muddy sluice will recover from the effects of hours of exposure in cold water in time for us to move again. We'll not know for weeks."

~~~

The men showered and dressed in clean, dry uniforms. They ate a fine dinner prepared by their cook. With dessert came an announcement by Col. Greenleaf.

"The steamship. *Marie de la Mer* is sitting at the dock below us. Tomorrow morning, she will take the Fifty-second Regiment down the Mississippi River to the mouth of Bayou LaFourche."

The following morning, the regiment packed their still-damp clothes and excess gear into the army wagons and struck the tents. They gathered and set fire to the floorboards, the cookhouses, and all the debris of the camp—hopefully including the resident fleas. To the beat of the drums, they marched through the ruins of the city and boarded the *Marie de la Mer*. Two starving stray hounds tried to board with the Chaplain. Col. Greenleaf caught them in the act and tried to tempt them into a building, but they growled and snapped. He apologized to the Chaplain and shot the hounds in the head.

Company D had sailed from New York with one hundred healthy men. When they left Baton Rouge, Doc Sawyer pronounced sixty-five fit to travel. Another ship waited at the dock to take others to a hospital in New Orleans where they could receive proper care. William, Nathaniel, the Chaplain, and several others immediately found soft surfaces in a cabin on the *Marie de la Mer* and fell back to sleep. They had no memory of the trip down the Mississippi River to Donaldsonville.

Nathanial and William had no opportunity to speak at length about the entire experience of the feint to Port Hudson for several weeks.

PART III: THROUGH THE *GARDEN OF LOUISIANA—* THE BATTLE OF IRISH BEND

CHAPTER TEN

B lind hog found an acorn!" Chaplain Moors called to a few friends when they disembarked on the wharf at Donaldsonville, the town a few oxbows of the Mississippi River below Baton Rouge near where the Bayou LaFourche flows out of the river to wend its way southward toward the Gulf. Chaplain Moors pointed out the sign that read *Happy Days Tavern*. "See that sign over there? The captain of the *Marie de la Mer* pronounces the breakfast there a fine treat. He says he stops at the *Happy Days* every time he's anywhere in the vicinity. The cook is the tavern owner's wife. She serves a feast in the morning and, if she is in the mood, at other times. I invite you gentlemen to join me. With a twinkle in his eye, the captain of the *Marie de la Mer* suggested that if we enjoy the breakfast, we should ask the tavern owner to introduce us to his wife. He said we would have a surprise."

Indeed, it was a happy day for Nathaniel, William, and a dozen other lucky members of Company D, the Chaplain included in his invitation. They enjoyed the first meal without the lingering taste of tin since they left New York. They had real pottery plates, knives, and forks for their fried eggs, ham, and buttered corn biscuits. At the end of the meal, the tavern owner served something he had some imagination to call "coffee" with milk in it.

When they were sated and tipped back their chairs—true chairs and not barracks benches—the tavern keeper came to the table with a bottle of fine whiskey and a stack of shot glasses. He offered each man a chaser. Everyone indulged except Chaplain Moors. The Chaplain jovially refused their host's repeated urgings.

"You just want to see me take the first drink of my life and fall on the floor, my generous host. But I will take the suggestion of the captain of the *Marie de la Mer*. He said we could ask you to bring out your wife from the kitchen to introduce us and thank her personally for a breakfast better anywhere outside of New Orleans."

The Tavern owner disappeared behind and returned with a tall woman on his arm.

"Gloria, my dear, meet my friends from the north."

They were not just surprised by the tavern owner's wife. They were astounded. A striking, coal-black, bejeweled negress wearing a spotless billowing apron loped in as elegantly as a giraffe, bending one knee and then the other.

She was at least a foot taller than her husband. She piled up her hair to add an additional six inches to her height. She spoke with the patois and the lilt of the Caribbean Islands.

Chaplain Moors expressed the appreciation of the group and gave her a generous tip. Nat gave her a second tip just so he could see again the one tooth of gold shining in her mouth.

"Do you suppose the captain brought Gloria home for his friend, the tavern owner, as a souvenir of a trip from Jamaica?" Nat mumbled the question to Will after they had moved far from earshot. "I received a letter from a friend I knew in the Militia who told me that different parts of the South are very different. He said we'd be lucky to go to Louisiana. I thought we lost our chance to experience the interesting state's sights when we passed up New Orleans without stopping, but perhaps there will be some others to discover. I hope we get to see more than ruins our own army left. I'm not sure we'd ever meet a couple like the tavern owner and his wife any place else."

~~~

That night, the Fifty-second Regiment pitched camp in a field of fragrant clover. White-topped mini pompons waived slowly in a light breeze and wafted a soft scent into their tents. The men were thrilled to leave the fleas that bedeviled them in Baton Rouge but found dark, buzzing, and thirsty mosquitoes took their place.

"By Golly, they've got a lot of critters south of the Mason-Dixon line! Southerners must have tougher skin than Yankees to be able to live down here," said Nat.

The morning dawned to another jewel blue sky. The entire regiment of Fifty-second men enjoyed a big breakfast at the *Happy Days*—with the addition of a tall stack of pancakes and syrup dusted with powdered sugar.

The tavern owner watched them pushing around the syrup on their plates. He went to the back and came out with a plate of bacon, which they relished.

"I believe you don't like the taste of our cane syrup, my northern friends. Most people get used to it, but you may not stay around here long enough for that. To be honest, even a spoon of powdered sugar doesn't help the bite. Gloria and I prefer maple sugar from your part of the world."

After the usual chaser, Nat thanked the tavern owner and Gloria again.

Col. Greenleaf had a short meeting of the officers. He appointed Will to lead company D down the left bank of the Mississippi River to Bayou LaFourche. The tavern owner accompanied them. He explained the significance of the Bayou. Although only wider than the Connecticut River at home, the LaFourche had a big impact in bringing life-giving water from the river to the entire area and made apt the name *The Garden of Louisiana.*

"The march on the top of the levees to the west, your planned route, is particularly beautiful," the tavern owner said. "Everything is quieter now, but less than six months ago, you Yankees did a lot of damage over there. Most of whose homes and crops were damaged have gone away now, but you may encounter some who are resentful. I hope you have good information about what to avoid. Good luck. Return sometime if you're here again."

~~~

At the first sight of the wide path on the north levee, the men scampered up the slope. Astounded at the panoramic view, they stopped, turned, and gaped in every direction. They were stopped in their tracks by an order barked from the colonel.

"Men of the Fifty-second. Halt! This is an order!" The men froze.

Col. Greenleaf beamed when they did so. "Excellent, men! The view on this levee is the most pleasant in the entire adventure to the south. You are entitled to enjoy the walk after what was probably the most miserable trudge down from Port Hudson in the rain. But we still have to remember we are in a war. My congratulations that you did not forget so. You responded instantly to my order and thus passed the first test. Now we have another lesson to learn well, mark, and inwardly digest before we take the march."

"The views from the levees are indeed astounding, and we could enjoy them for a brief time before the sun has risen well. But there are hazards here of which we must be aware. The first hazard is alligators. Perhaps you have seen one or two Louisiana alligators already."

He heard mumbles from the men. When he again had their full attention, he continued. "Louisiana alligators are the ugliest animals you could ever see; their behavior is even worse. A serious danger. They look like prehistoric creatures who, by some happenstance, escaped an epic disaster of ancient days that wiped out all the other creatures who once roamed this area with the dinosaurs. As the survivors, they now rule the kingdom of the vast rivers and swamps."

"For most of the winter, the alligators hide in the mud. When spring comes and the sun warms, they rise from the muddy rivers and swamps to seek out high, warm perches on which to sun their bumpy backs in the warming rays. In the nesting season, which is now, they hold their two big grapefruit-sized pop-eyes wide open to guard their nests of sticks in which they have hidden their clutches of eggs. Watch every step, men, or you will encounter their enormous jaws, each with a row of pointed teeth. If you misstep, you will quickly become a side dish for the alligator's breakfast."

He had their full attention.

"The second hazard of the glorious walk up here is a human threat: young hunters. We have cleaned out all the organized Rebel forces in this area and vetted most adults remaining you might encounter like the amiable owner of the *Happy Days*. You are safe from organized or disorganized adults who wish you harm. But Rebel lads in these parts are crack shots. They have been hunting squirrels, ducks, wild hogs, deer, turkeys, and even bears—everything with feathers or fur—since they've been old enough to hold a rifle. They have no access to big city excitement growing up out here, but they have plenty of adventures in the outdoors. They live for the secret, sole hunt. Every one of these boys would relish to pick off a trophy from a dead Yankee to decorate the walls of his hunting cabin."

"Men of the Fifty-second, we may enjoy walking early while there is dew on the grasses, but the moment we feel rays of the morning sun or spy human activity, we must be alert for gators taking the sun and young boys out for sport. See them, and we make haste down the levees to the lower roads immediately."

~~~

The cautions dissipated the excitement that had puffed out the excited chests during the first run up the banks of the levee in the morning. Now, they walked without a word. Thirty minutes on the walk, a sharp-eyed Corporal noticed a shudder in the left side of a bundle of unkempt brush some fifteen yards before them on their intended path. He sent the alarm. The men were already starting down the lower road when the other side of the brush pile rose and began to lurch along the empty levee. The brush fell aside, and a monster waddled out on his stumpy legs. The men tore the last twenty feet down the levee within twenty seconds. They continued their walk on the lower road where the tops of their heads were on a level with the surface of the water flowing between the two levees carrying the water of the Mississippi to the *Garden of Louisiana*.

~~~

On the lower road along the Bayou LaFourche, the day continued clear and warm. Soft breezes suffused the air with the fragrance of orange blossoms. The foliage in every direction glowed with the yellow-green of new growth.

Bird song accompanied their walk. Not a few men made responses to the mating calls of scarlet cardinals, tiny wrens, and mockingbirds, which prompted other men to rag them by saying they were so desperate for female companionship they were announcing their availability for mating to anything female, even creatures with bird legs!

The little farms they first passed had only slipped a little. A few days with hand tools and a weekend could bring them back. The men could not believe they were in the same "enemy" country their armies had left devastation up the Teche country, north of Baton Rouge, or such damage to the untended fields of sugarcane and cotton north of St Martins. Neat beds of garden flowers decorated even the most modest homes and more elaborate beds around the larger homes. Colorful flowers found sufficient nutrition to survive even in the ditches. Asters and zinnias found water holes to feed their roots. It was as if the owners left in a hurry and planned to return soon. Although in need of attention for perfection, a "garden" was still an apt description of where they passed.

Then, the homes became finer. They saw groves of fragrant blooming orange trees between them—stately magnolias with open-petaled white flowers and green waxy leaves scattered in green swards. Elegant blooming Bradford Pears marched to the front doors of some homes.

Rambling roses twined between the spokes of fences, wisteria vines fell in cascades and set out suckers to anchor delicate purple flowers over any branches that became bare over the winter.

The fields between the larger home tracts indicated the tragedy that had taken place to the sugar crop. The fields had been abandoned before cane knives cut the year's harvest for hauling to the mill and planting the next crop. The sugar canes lay uncut, fallen over in the fields, starting to rot. The farm boys from New England knew what effort and time would be necessary to return the fields to productive land. For them, uncared farms were painful.

The mills stood empty, beginning to tumble, and broken carts to rust piled in heaps. The weeds shot up a foot tall. They were many seasons away from returning to condition for sugar production.

Then, abruptly, everything changed from bad to worse. Devastation. For more than a mile fine homes and white pillared plantations stood abandoned and ravaged. There was no sign of any effort to raise even sustenance crops. The appearance of white people became scarce and then nonexistent. A few negroes ran from behind the ruins to tell the men riding by, "They gone, Missus and Massa been gone." And then the worst damage: fire. For several miles, every house was nothing but a pile of cold embers. The officers mounted and walked their horses as in a funeral cortege. They saw no human, animal or turned earth to support a crop: just rubble.

Further on, a few negroes dressed in rags ran from behind the houses, calling, "They gone. All gone." Wooded tracts between the larger homes slipped even further toward a natural state of weeds and thicket. Acres of uncut sugarcane lay tangled and rotting in the fields behind the tracts as far as they could see.

A few hundred feet beyond lay piles of black rubble as if prepared for an opportunity to return. They rode past a few dozen homes devastated but not burned. Division D dismounted. They found a road and walked looking for signs of renaissance.

And they found some such signs. They saw tiny green buds on brown vines, probably purple flowered wisteria vines hanging on the trees, and walked to the edge of home tracts. They saw branches of roses snaking through fences and spotted green leaves of bulbs breaking the dirt in abandoned garden beds. Green leaves wound up the trunks of oaks and magnolias to find their old haunts.

In the rubble, they saw wisteria vines putting out feelers to anchor suckers on broken oak and magnolia trees, and confederate jasmine slipped through the branches of stately oaks and blooming magnolias. They thought these must have been fine-looking farms before suffering the ravages of war.

A troop of Negro children came from behind one cluster of unpainted quarters behind the ruins, calling out praises to the Lord and the Yankees that had come to save them.

Still, there was not a white man or woman to be seen.

"Do you see any food crops to keep them fed? Maybe rows of vegetables coming up around the quarters?" William asked. "I don't see any crops for people to feed themselves, their animals, or to sell to buy what is needed to sustain life in the countryside. You call it the *Garden of Louisiana,* but it needs serious attention soon, or it will return to a jungle."

The Fifty-second Regiment remounted, passed through the destruction, and found the path to Brashear City again.

~~~

Col. Greenleaf gathered all the leadership of the Fifty-second Regiment and announced a change of plans for the route to Brashear City. They had all seen enough of the ravages their own troops had made to the "Garden." He ordered everyone to remount, pass through the destruction, and seek the lower route toward Brashear City. They found the route without difficulty and could have continued from LaFourche to Brashear City. However, Col. Greenleaf realized many of the men needed to rest, their feet still sore from the ordeal of the trip down from Fort Hudson. He decided to make camp and wait for the railway expected to come from New Orleans on its way to Berwick Bay. The regiment bedded down for the night.

The decision turned out to be an unfortunate one. The expected train did not arrive. The following day, they rested but had to complete the hike on one of the hottest days.

William searched his pack for the two letters he had written to Elizabeth days ago. He could not find them. He put off the chores and wrote a report to Elizabeth about the journey from Baton Rouge to Brashear City. Unfortunately, he ended his letter telling her they would probably soon run into General Taylor. Thoughtless! That sentence might make Elizabeth think they were heading to an armed encounter. She would be anxious until she heard that her husband and the father of the baby she expected was again somewhere relatively safe and not about to face a confrontation with the Rebel army. He was too tired to get up to correct his mistake. He turned the letter over to the private collecting the mail for the Chaplain.

CHAPTER ELEVEN

Nathaniel, William, and everyone else in the Fifty-second Regiment expected to rest and recover for a few days before they entered hostilities. General Banks had other ideas. As soon as the General received word of their arrival in Brashear City, he ordered General Cuvier Grover to take the Fifty-second Regiment and the regiments from Connecticut and Maine aboard the gunboat *St. Mary's* the next morning. They were to join in an assault on Rebel General Richard Taylor wherever they could find him. Nathaniel chafed at how little the Fifty-second Regiment understood about the strategy of the Rebels' forces, let alone that of their own. William reminded Nathaniel he was the one who said they had no right to know anything. It was sufficient for them to follow whatever orders came from their superiors. Nathaniel sought out Col. Greenleaf for further information.

Nathaniel learned that Rebel General Richard Taylor did not wait idly by as the Fifty-second Regiment enjoyed the glory of spring in the *Garden of Louisiana*. While they marched down from Baton Rouge, Rebel forces had been engaging other units of the Union Army in the lower Bayou Teche and with the Union Navy gunboats. Rebel artillery greatly damaged the fleet of Union gunboats on Grand Lake. They had mixed success at Butte–á–la Rose and on the Atchafalaya River, capturing a prize Union gunboat, the *Cotton,* which now flew a Rebel flag. When the Fifty-second Regiment arrived at Brashear City, General Banks had Rebel General Richard Taylor challenged on land at Bisland southwest of the outlet of the Bayou Teche. Nathaniel learned that the next assignment for his Regiment would take them to assist in that challenge.

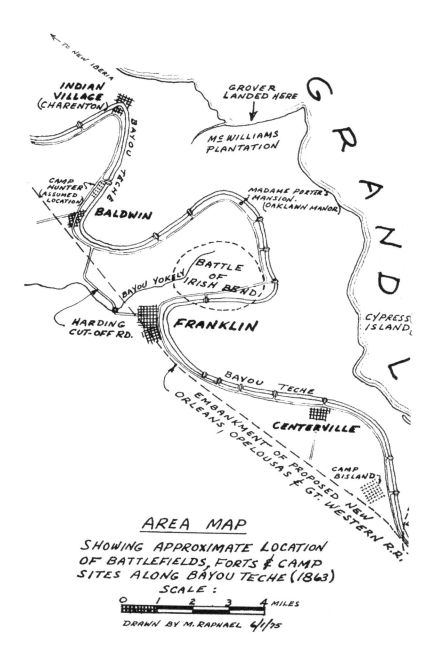

TO NEW IBERIA

GRAND L

INDIAN VILLAGE (CHARENTON)

GROVER LANDED HERE

McWILLIAMS PLANTATION

BAYOU TECHE

CAMP HUNTER (ASSUMED LOCATION)

BALDWIN

MADAME PORTER'S MANSION. (OAKLAWN MANOR)

BATTLE OF IRISH BEND

BAYOU YOKELY

CYPRESS ISLAND

HARDING CUT-OFF RD.

FRANKLIN

BAYOU TECHE

EMBANKMENT OF PROPOSED NEW ORLEANS, OPELOUSAS & GT. WESTERN R.R.

CENTERVILLE

CAMP BISLAND

AREA MAP

SHOWING APPROXIMATE LOCATION OF BATTLEFIELDS, FORTS & CAMP SITES ALONG BAYOU TECHE (1863)

SCALE:

0 1 2 3 4 MILES

DRAWN BY M. RAPHAEL 6/1/75

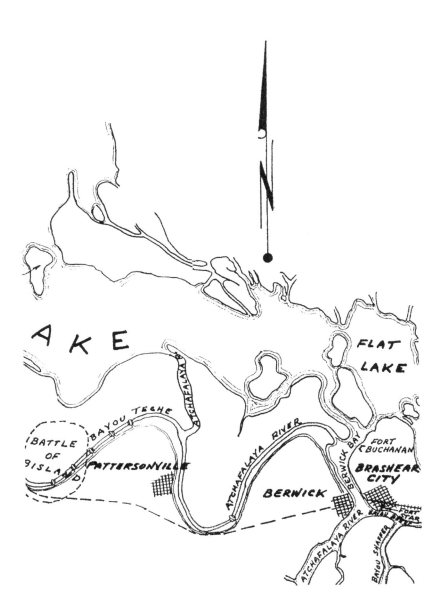

The Fifty-second Regiment packed aboard the *St. Mary's* almost as tight as they had been on the steamer *Illinois* from New York to New Orleans. This time, they did not complain about the conditions. They were not concerned; they expected a one-day trip on the water traveling west across Grand Lake to the Bayou Teche.

At first, fog and mechanical trouble sent the *St. Mary's* back to port at Brashear City. Launched again the following morning, they were delayed by time-consuming maneuvers necessary to avoid Rebel gunboats threatening from Butte-á-la-Rose. Then, for half a day, they were dead in the water as scouts searched for an undefended landing spot on the west bank of Grand Lake. The afternoon of April 13, on shore at last, William, Nathaniel, and their company stretched their arms above their heads and kneaded out the indentations made by the gear on which they had been trying to find comfort for two days and nights.

The regiment reassembled. Support forces brought up the batteries and horses. Nathaniel and William mounted and marched the company across the Bayou Teche bridge near what was labeled on their maps as Mme. Porter's mansion. They made camp inside an oxbow of the Bayou Teche, checked out their men, and turned in for the night.

"Not as bad as the conditions the enlisted men endured—on the *Illinois,* on boards stacked five high in the hold or with bedmates," William said. "I prefer sleeping on the hard deck of the *St. Mary's* with my pack as my pillow to sharing a bed with others."

"As you would say, *d'accord.*"

The regiment rose at first light and organized by companies. General Grover ordered a march to the left, the south arm of the oxbow, and then headed due west toward the sound of battle. When they had been on the route for about twenty minutes, a splatter of bullets fell into the woods some twenty feet to their right. "Ready or not, my good pal Nat, I believe we are now going to do what we came to do. May God and good fortune be with us!"

Unknown to General Grover, during the night, a message sent to him by General Banks from his location at Bisland instructed General Grover to change the route previously ordered. Communications were always unreliable. This lost communication was perhaps tragic. For reasons never made clear, the message did not reach General Grover. Under the revised plan, had the message reached him, General Grover would have taken a right turn toward the upper or northern arm of the oxbow. Some believe if he had done so, later in the day, the Fifty-second Regiment would have been in place to intercept and destroy the cream of the Rebel forces fleeing Bisland in the lower Teche and thereby change the course of the war. Such are the mischances of war.

General Grover led the Fifty-second Regiment toward the rising din of the Battle of Bisland. Nathaniel followed him with the first half of D company, William, and the second half trailed.

After about a half mile, Nathaniel abruptly ordered a HALT. William came from the rear for an explanation. William blanched when he saw the reason for the stoppage in their advance. A blanket of seething flies dined on a bloody, five-foot high pile of human legs, arms, and hands at the side of the path. As William's eyes fell on the grisly scene, a severed leg, still wearing a boot, hurtled through the front opening of a nearby sugarhouse on the right of the path and landed splat on the pile of body parts. The arrival of the booted leg turned up the velocity in a swarm of buzzing on the stinking banquet. On his right, William could see surgeons bent over tables inside their makeshift hospital in the sugarhouse. Blood dripped from under the sugarhouse to a gully leading to the bayou. After a few deep breaths to settle their stomachs, Nathaniel and William resumed the march.

William felt a sharp sting on his upper thigh. Excalibur stumbled as William's weight shifted. William gripped Excalibur's flanks with his knees and thighs, steadied, and then urged his mount forward. Excalibur's hooves found solid footing. William leaned forward, uttered soothing words, and stroked the stallion's neck.

A few minutes later, Nathaniel moved the company to the left side of the path to make way for several wounded men walking with assistance from the battlefield toward the sugarhouse "hospital." Men bearing stretchers carried others who were too badly mangled to walk. Their moans competed with the sound of the buzzing flies. A few minutes passed before the Fifty-second Regiment could resume the march toward the sounds of battle.

Nathaniel did not realize his second in command had been hit. William said nothing about his injury. There was no field hospital for Second Lt. William Wells as long as he could hold his seat in the saddle! And William did not realize that Excalibur took a splatter of gunshot on his flank.

Company D soon came upon the area where other Union troops had already formed a line of battle and were poised to engage a band of Rebel troops approaching straight toward them from the direction of Bisland.

Additional men in grey emerged from a swampy area to the right in the center of the oxbow where unknown to the Union, they had lain in wait since the previous day.

Instantly responding to Nathaniel's command, William dismounted and moved his men into the Union battle line. The men climbed over the carnage of the slain Union and Rebel men who had engaged before them. They took battle positions beside the Connecticut regiment. General Grover issued an order to fire. The Union bullets found their targets. The Rebel line twelve yards ahead dropped half its number.

First kill. Company D, Fifty-second Regiment, Massachusetts Volunteers lost their virginity. Several lost their footing as well and slid into the gore of death. William felt a rush of energy fuel a fire in his chest to kill those who had killed his own.

The half of the Rebel line still standing took position to load and fire again. William noticed one of his men, Pvt. Mathew Harbor, stagger and quickly step to the left to leave the fray. Harbor bent double at the edge of the engagement and collapsed to the ground into a pile of his own vomit.

Without hesitation, William took the private's position in the Union line. He crouched and, responding to Nathaniel's order, fired again—just as a Rebel yell came screaming over the field. "Withdraw! Withdraw!"

The grey line did so in confusion. General Grover's Union brigade fired at their backs and took pursuit.

~~~

At the intersection with the road that ran north along the right bank of the Bayou Teche, the Union forces ran smack into their own men chasing General Richard Taylor and General Alfred Mouton's troops fleeing the battle at Bisland. Now, the Union had the Rebels on the run from the sites of both battles at the lower end of the Bayou Teche, Bisland, and Irish Bend.

For William, the details from that moment swam in a blur of the pain shooting up and down from his wounded thigh. Later, he remembered General Grover directing the medics and a burial detail back to the battlefield. Six negroes appeared from nowhere and proceeded to dig a mass grave. He remembered the Chaplain following the detail, probably to say a few words over the bodies.

He remembered the smell of gunpowder, seeing General Mouton join General Taylor in flight, and First Lt. Nathaniel Bradford, his buddy Nat, galloping past Union officers who outranked him to the head of the Union forces in pursuit. The remainder of the Union men followed behind Nat. The Rebels occasionally paused to turn and fire upon their pursuers and were met with Union fire in return.

The Rebels had a head start. Nathaniel and the Union officers could not catch them. They stopped occasionally, and William remembered a tense discussion among the officers concerning General Grover's decision that morning to take the southern arm of the oxbow toward the sound of battle rather than the northern arm. The armchair strategists were certain receipt of the lost communique sent to General Stover would have placed the Union force in the path of the fleeing rebels and enabled the Union troops to wipe out the forces of Generals Taylor and Mouton, causing the South to withdraw all their plans to secede from the Union, end the war, and alter the course of history! All that?

~~~

For three days and nights, from Irish Bend up the Bayou Teche to the Vermilion River, First Lieutenant Nathaniel Bradford led the main body of Union forces in a forced march in pursuit of the Rebels. On the first day, they covered twenty-five miles before making camp, and on the second and third days, twenty miles. The sun burned brutally hot. To the west, stretched an endless prairie dotted with herds of cattle grazing on tall grass—a bucolic sight. On their right, they passed magnificent bayou-side plantation homes. Beyond the Bayou Teche, deep woods lead to the Atchafalaya River.

Slaves ran from the plantation homes to follow the Union march. The slaves wreaked havoc—plundering and setting fires. Nathaniel and other company commanders gave orders against such conduct. Still, they did not delay the pursuit of Generals Taylor and Mouton and the Rebel troops to enforce the orders against either the slaves or some of their own men who joined them. The wanton damage was horrendous. Through his fog of pain, Second Lieutenant William Wells remembered three fleeing slaves carrying a massive walnut dining table from a mansion. They dropped it. The table broke apart. The slaves left the pieces where they fell, went back, and carried out a dozen matching chairs and a wide sideboard instead.

When the pursuing Union troops arrived in New Iberia, General Godfrey Weitzel and Companies A, E, F, and G of the Fifty-second Regiment peeled off to remain and secure the town. They set up camp on a clearing in the prairie west of the Bayou Teche curve from St. Martinsville. Nathaniel, the Chaplain, and the main body of the Fifty-second Regiment moved on north toward Vermilionville. William, weak from pain and loss of blood, could not go with them. Doc Sawyer made the decision to leave William in New Iberia with the four security companies for treatment of his wound. The main body moved north. When most of the regiment reached Vermilionville, they discovered the Rebels had crossed the Vermillion River and set the bridge on fire. As a result, they made camp and awaited the arrival of engineers who could rebuild the bridge.

PART IV: GATHERING CONTRABAND, HUMANS AND GOODS

CHAPTER TWELVE

William woke in unfamiliar surroundings. Shadowy scenes floated in and out of his consciousness. He knew for sure he was no longer on Excalibur's back: the only fact he could hold onto. He lay on smooth sheets stretched tight on a cot in a large indoor space.

He raised his head and looked around. There were a dozen other cots in his view, several occupied by sleeping men. He looked straight up to a high ceiling. Where could he be? Long benches with high backs pressed against the far wall. Was he in a church?

A painful twinge down one leg halted William's attempt to sit up. He reached down and felt a bandage on his right thigh. Then he remembered; he had been wounded. Was he in a hospital?

William hailed the first person he saw pass by his cot: an attractive young woman with a large red cross stitched on the swell of the bodice of her stiff white uniform. A little pleated cap perched on her head above a loose circle of soft dark hair at the back of her neck.

"Where am I, ma'am? Please, can you tell me?"

"You are in a hospital in New Iberia, Lieutenant. The hospital is temporarily located in the Episcopal Church."

William asked a second question. "And where is my horse, Excalibur?"

"Ah! So that's his name." Her face opened in a lovely smile. "A big fella! Knowing his name might have helped us last night. He was not happy to have us take you off his back. I suppose Excalibur is stabled with the other Union horses at the Yankee camp west of the town unless they've banished him for bad behavior."

"Bad behavior?" William frowned. "He is not known for bad

behavior."

"Getting you off his back was not easy, Lieutenant."

"I understand. Excalibur is very loyal to me. I can imagine you had a tussle."

"Loyalty like the men say they've never seen the like. They tried to clean up his wounds, but as soon as they touched him, he went wild! He acted as if he'd never had as much as a rope on his neck."

A striven look landed on William 's face. "He is wounded?"

"Very Slightly. He took a splatter of glazing bullets, even less than you did, but they wanted to clean him up. They decided it wasn't worth getting a hoof in the face."

"I'm sorry he misbehaved. Was anyone hurt?" William asked.

"No harm done. Cush-cush and coffee for breakfast will be here in a little while, Lieutenant. Cush-cush," She answered before William had a chance to verbalize a question to match his expression, "is like a porridge. Is there anything else I can get for you in the meanwhile?"

William asked if she had paper, a pen, and a bottle of ink so he could write to his wife. "I would appreciate that very much. She'll worry if she hears I'm in a hospital. We're expecting a baby. And a glass of water would be very nice if you please. I'm quite thirsty."

The nurse complied. William set the ink on a table by the cot and tried, as best he could, to lean over and scratch words on the paper. He debated with himself whether to expend the energy to explain to Elizabeth that writing from an almost prone position and not injuries caused the ink splotches and dreadful handwriting of his letter. He thought he must explain, or Elizabeth would not believe he had not been seriously hurt.

An hour or so later, William sensed the presence of another person standing by his bed. He looked up to see a man in a white coat and, above the collar, a smiling face beneath a full mustache and bright blue eyes. The man inside the coat carried a black medical bag in his left hand.

"Good morning, Lieutenant. My name is Dr. Alfred Duperier."

"Good morning, Dr. Duperier. I hope I pronounced your name correctly. Lt. William Wells, Fifty-second Regiment, Massachusetts Volunteers here, sir."

"The nurse cleaned and dressed your wound last night when they brought you in, Lieutenant. General Weitzel asked me to look at your wound if that's agreeable. He'd like an opinion about when it will be safe for you to join your unit and move on."

William raised his full eyebrows, and four deep lines appeared across his forehead. "Do you know that I am a Union soldier?"

"Of course I do. And a tall one. Your feet are hanging off the end of our cot. And I'm a Rebel. But first, I am a doctor. So, you are from Massachusetts?"

"Yes, doctor. Northwestern Massachusetts. Near the Berkshires."

"Ah, the mountains. I regret we have no mountains in Louisiana. But we have some very nice forests."

After a pause, the doctor asked William if he would let the doctor look at the wound.

"Of course. Proceed, sir."

Dr. Duperier opened his medical bag. He had a fine supply of needs. He removed the dressing on William's thigh and picked carefully at the wound. "The nurse did a fine job, Lieutenant. The bullet that did the damage is no longer there, and I see no remaining threads of your uniform or anything else that should not be present." He rebandaged the thigh. "I expect you will heal well." He glanced at the remains of Elizabeth's tintype on the crate beside the cot. "Unfortunately, the likeness of that lovely lady will not."

"My wife, doctor. I should have given the likeness to the Chaplain to hold for me. He's done that before. This time, I didn't have the opportunity. We left in a scramble."

"That was your good fortune. The presence of the tintype in your pocket probably deflected the course of the bullet, and your wound is less severe because of it. I expect you'll be ready to move on in a few days. Meanwhile, I recommend you alternate walking and resting for the remainder of your time in New Iberia."

William told the doctor he had not seen the town, but the church was lovely and seemed to have a fine location at a curve of the stream below.

"The stream is the Bayou Teche. May I take you to the front door to give you a better view—and catch the warm spring breeze?"

Dr. Duperier helped William to his feet. The doctor stumbled as William's greater height and his instability challenged the doctor's balance. Together, they walked slowly down the center aisle of the church. The two men looked out across the bayou to a large brick house on the opposite bank.

"That's a beautiful house over there," William said.

"My boyhood home, Lieutenant. I was born there in 1826. The house is still in the family. Slaves built it with bricks made from a clay pit behind the house, the same brick used to build this church."

They looked down to the Bayou Teche coming from their left and flowing slowly between the church and the Duperier house. Specks of color poked through fans of tropical plants that edged the muddy water below. In addition, wildflowers and foot-high knobby pillars of hard bare root rose on the shoreline at the base of tall, feathery-needled cypress trees. The doctor told William they called the protruding roots cypress *knees.*

"Lovely sight, but very different from our clear mountain streams gurgling over rocks in Massachusetts," William said.

Dr. Duperier chuckled. "Different indeed. Rocks are rare in these parts. I don't know if you'll get down to the bayou, but if you do, keep an eye out for the noses of small creatures. You won't be familiar with them; they're not all friendly."

The two men walked up and down the aisle of the church several times. The doctor said he'd be back in the morning to see William again. Not so! Mid-afternoon, he returned. He said there had been a change of plans. He expected William to be moved to a tent in the area where General Weitzel's men made camp. The Union needed the church to house prisoners. They walked some more and had a long conversation about their families, horses, and the crops they raised. Neither said a word about the war.

"Dr. Duperier, you speak slowly but don't have the heavy southern accent we all make fun of at home."

"No, I don't. Louisianans don't drawl like people in most of the South. Maybe it's the influence of the French. If you know the rest of the South, you will find in many ways we are different."

When the doctor had gone, William fantasized about one day returning with Elizabeth for a visit to New Iberia.

~~~

William finished his letter to Elizabeth. He gave it to the nurse for delivery to the Union camp. He missed Chaplain Moors. He hoped Elizabeth knew he was safe and only slightly wounded and that the companies to which he now found himself attached had a system to send and receive mail. His eyelids lowered, and his chin dropped onto his plate before he finished his dinner.

Nightmares again interrupted William's sleep. He saw bleeding bodies in ripped uniforms of grey and blue spread before him. He heard his own orders to his troops to mount the bloody piles, close a tight line, and fire at men in grey a few yards ahead. He watched men fall. He heard again his order to his men to act with deadly purpose and felt the rush of heat fueling his order to pursue the Rebels, firing at will toward any who seemed within range. He woke in a sweat.

He picked up the glass of water on the crate by his bed and drained it.

Questions swirled in. Do very smart men go to the military academy to study how best to conduct a battle and come up with the barbarity of a plan to have hundreds of men armed with lethal weapons face off yards from one another and fire until everyone on one side or both falls dead in a bloody heap? Does this strategy of warfare survive because the thrill of the kill fuels an excitement that enables ordinarily humane people to become killers?

William wished he could talk with Nathaniel. Nat might endorse the current military practices, or he might want to go to the military academy to ponder other possibilities now that the available weaponry performed more accurately at a greater distance than during the conflicts with French and Indian enemies. Would Nat be the one to come up with better strategies to wage a war?

These thoughts made William wonder if Abigail knew of Nat's ambition to have a military career. She must have figured that was a possibility. No doubt she'd heard about his childhood fascination with war stories and toy soldiers. Nat joined the militia immediately after Fort Sumpter, not waiting until the call for troops. In any case, it was not for William or Elizabeth to tell her.

William felt certain he and Nat would agree—on one aspect of the first battle experience of Company D. Their mission had been to train their men to respond quickly to commands and maintain courage under fire. Mission accomplished—for all except poor Pvt. Harbor. They had prepared their men for dealing with the freeze of fear: the common response to a first battle experience. They were unprepared for plain old-fashioned nausea. William forced his mind to move on. He hoped Col. Greenleaf did not punish the lad too severely.

Two days later, after more long walks and conversations with the Rebel Dr. Duperier, Captain Storrs of the Forty-first Massachusetts Regiment brought William his orders. The main body of D company was still pinned down at the Vermillion River. William was to join the four other companies of the Fifty-second Regiment, which had been left in New Iberia, and support the mission of Col. Thomas E. Chickering, who was attached to their command. They would cross the Bayou Teche and travel north through St. Martinsville and beyond. Their mission would be to gather from the plantations contraband sugar, cotton, and any other provisions useful to the Rebel war effort, take the plunder safely to Port Barre on the Atchafalaya River, and ship it south for Union use. In addition, they were to gather negroes, also considered contraband, who were fleeing from slavery and recruit those suitable for service in the Union Army. They would attempt to reunite with the main body of the Fifty-second Regiment when they could safely do so.

William had a different order of priorities. Whatever the assignment, he wanted to reunite with Nathaniel and the remainder of his regiment. For him, gathering contraband ranked a distant second in importance.

~~~

With nothing but his knapsack, the damaged uniform he had been wearing for days, and his mount Excalibur, William could be ready to leave New Iberia with little notice. At eight o'clock on the morning of the third day, after he woke up after the march up from Irish Bend, he reported to Col. Chickering and the Forty-first Massachusetts Regiment at the Union encampment. Dr. Duperier had cleared him for service the day before.

A smart-looking brigade. Col. Chickering must have been well trained in his prior service with the New England Guards. He rode a splendid roan horse at the head of the officers. Others in blue, including General Godfrey Weitzel himself who was technically in command, flanked him. They carried the Stars and Stripes and their regimental colors.

Additional officers rode behind. They held the reins of their mounts in their left hands; their right arms pressed rifles across their chests. The Union soldiers did not anticipate hostilities but were armed and ready for any angry plantation owner or Rebel sniper they might encounter. Behind them came the rank and file.

William slipped into the formation at the rear of the officers. He made sure to leave his bandaged thigh visible through the tear in his uniform to explain his failure to meet their sartorial standard.

A ferry awaited them. Once across the Bayou Teche for the first of several times on this route, General Weitzel divided the brigade. He ordered William to accompany Col. Chickering and his group. They turned right, then left to follow the left or east bank of the Bayou Teche up and around the Fausse Pointe oxbow. The remainder of the force turned left as soon as they crossed the bayou and took a more direct route to St. Martinsville. They would cross the bayou again before it turned to Fausse Pointe. Both groups pursued the same mission: gathering contraband goods and fleeing slaves.

Col. Chickering's group made slow progress. They stopped frequently to admit behind them oxen and mule-driven carts and wagons piled high with furniture, boxes, and crates, all containing confiscations. Negro men, women, and children streamed out of the plantations shouting alleluias and praising the Lord! Barely clothed children climbed up and perched on top of the cargo. None of the negroes who joined them wore shoes, and their feet were grey with grime.

"My God! Those boys look like laughing monkeys riding on the backs of animals at the county fair," exclaimed one of the officers with William.

A half dozen mounted Union officers tended the growing caravan of wagons like herding dogs guiding a flock of sheep. The sound of hoofbeats, the clatter of the loaded wagons, and the cheers of the riders as they greeted the newcomers grew louder as the numbers increased.

~~~

The caravan stopped for a longer time than usual at the easternmost limit of the Fausse Pointe oxbow of the Bayou. William heard voices rise in a heated exchange behind him. One person spoke in French; the other in the clipped English of eastern Massachusetts. William rode next to Col. Chickering and asked if he might ride back to see if he could help sort out the difficulty.

"I speak some French, sir," William told him.

"Good God, yes! Go back there!"

A cluster of loaded wagons had drawn up next to the caravan. An older negro with a tight cap of grizzled hair held the rope harness of an old mule. He stood waiting at the animal's head. A Union officer screamed instructions to him in English; the mule driver looked as dazed as his mule. The volume kept rising.

Why is it that when one encounters a language he doesn't understand? Does he think higher volume will improve comprehension?

A younger negro came up and took a position before the first French speaker. They exchanged a few rapid phrases incomprehensible to William. He couldn't tell if they spoke English or French. Then the younger negro addressed the Union officer more slowly in French and English.

"*Français, monsieur! Il parle seulement français. Pas d'anglais. Il ne comprend pas anglais."*

William urged Excalibur forward and supplemented the younger negro's explanation in English. In a few moments, the Union officer nodded his head. He now understood that the runaways understood only French, Acadian French, slightly different but close to the *patois* William and his ranch manager Pierre spoke with each other in the corral back home in Massachusetts. William demonstrated to the older negro how to work his wagon into the line and to those already in line how to make room for new arrivals.

The incident resolved, William continued to ride next to the caravan, helping runaways find places for their carts and wagons as the caravan made its way slowly in the direction of St. Martinsville.

The plantations the runaways fled from were more modest than those the Fifty-second Regiment passed on the road up the Bayou Teche from Irish Bend to New Iberia. Chickering's men did some foraging in St. Martin Parish. Still, they brought mainly farm produce rather than hogsheads of sugar or fancy furnishings they had confiscated on the ride up to New Iberia from Irish Bend. William, who was wounded, had not been conscious of the extent of the wanton destruction of the fleeing slaves and the Union soldiers who enabled them to carry out the pursuit from Irish Bend, but now he heard. Col. Chickering made it clear to his band that he did not want to see a repetition of that disgraceful conduct.

Now William understood why Dr. Duperier, who had graciously treated him in New Iberia, was strangely silent when William told him that one day he would like to come back and visit the Teche country with his wife. William supposed it would be many years before the people of St. Mary Parish would want to see a Union soldier again.

The fleeing men and women looked the same as those William had seen before. The women wore simple, well-worn cottonade shifts and tied their hair in bright red scarves. The men wore threadbare cottonade work pants and shirts. No one had shoes.

With one stunning exception, a husky young man came running from a large farmhouse wearing a fine silk suit, tall, polished leather boots, and an elegant sun hat! The caravan crowd cheered his arrival. He took a deep bow and doffed his hat. The one who had originally tried to explain the language problem to the Union officer returned his greeting.

"Mon Dieu, mon ami Alphonse. Vous êtes endimanché."

"Oui, mon ami Louis. Je suis endimanché pour la liberté!"

The new arrival, Alphonse, must have clothed himself from his master's closet for his freedom. Understandable, William thought. He'd probably been working in the cane fields since he was a boy without seeing a penny in wages.

Col. Chickering's officer in charge of the caravan returned to his position with the other officers, delighted to leave William to deal with those who couldn't speak his tongue.

Just before the Fausse Pointe Road curved around to join the route straight north to St. Martinsville, the train of wagons caught up with the other portion of General Weitzel's brigade. The General had added a dozen loaded carts into the caravan behind him. The families sitting on the carts in Col. Chickering's caravan jumped down and called greetings to those in the other. The helpful, somewhat bilingual one whom Alphonse had called Louis warned everyone to curb his demonstration or the mules' hooves would run over him. Louis said to William in what passed for English that he thought the big sugarcane plantation called Belmont was going to have trouble bringing in a crop this year.

He also suggested to the Union officer leading the other part of the brigade that he put the new mules and wagons onto the rear of his caravan rather than attempt to insert them into the middle. "Mules go easy where they don't feel hemmed in," he said. "And they do better when they think they have been part of the plan." William endorsed the idea because simple signals could more easily direct the arrivals to the tail of the caravan, but the Union officer shook his head. He would have none of the advice of a black and enslaved man.

In addition to a facility with language, William concluded that Louis knew mules. And he had unusual self-confidence. Most of the enslaved kept their eyes cast downward when talking to white men. Louis looked white officers square in the eye. Having no experience, William was wary. Self-confidence might mean the one called Louis would help their efforts, or it might portend trouble ahead. He knew he had a lot to learn about the enslaved, but at least he could talk to Louis, and Louis could talk some with him.

What a terrifying experience it must have been for those leaving the world they knew and couldn't even communicate with those leading them to a world they did not understand.

The caravan halted late in the afternoon. Word came back that they were to camp for the night. William left monitoring the caravan and rode forward to where the officers supervised slaves, pitching tents for the

Union soldiers only.

Later in the evening, Col. Chickering asked William to take a ride back to the caravan. Several runaways were objecting to keeping their wagons in line, and they were not happy no one gave them any food. They never had much, but they were used to getting something, and no food had not been provided. "Just tell them they must stay put. Tomorrow, they can forage. We all have to forage, even the soldiers," the Colonel said.

William delivered the message to each wagon. Some six wagons back he ran into Louis, who introduced him to his father, JeanLouis, and his mother, Marie Adele. Their friend Alphonse sat with them in their wagon. Alphonse was no longer *endimanché pour la liberté,* to use his words. He now wore plantation clothes like the others. They all had tin plates of food. William greeted them and said he was glad they found something to eat.

"*Regardez la fumée?*" Louis said, pointed to rising smoke in the distance. "*Des Acadiens là-bas. Le père, la mère et cinc enfants habitent l'étable.*"

The family was bitter, Louis said. They told Louis they never owned slaves, but a week ago, some Yankee soldiers came, stripped them clean of all their stored food, and torched their house. Louis thought they shared their duck dinner with his family because they were glad to hear French spoken. The Acadians wished them good luck, he said.

William asked Louis' mother, Marie Adele, if she found food for her mule. She said she learned a lesson. When she despaired, she looked at the cart ahead of theirs and saw a wagon packed with crying children. They had much bigger problems than she did. Yet when she introduced herself, the mother smiled a welcome and directed one of the older children to give her a bowl of mule feed. Marie Adele resolved not to panic but to have faith that things would work out and return the favor to anyone who needed help.

Louis and Alphonse planned to get up early the next morning and go foraging for food for themselves and their mule.

William had not received any mail since his company left Brashear City. He wrote another long letter to Elizabeth, describing their day with Col. Chickering's caravan and meeting the French-speaking slaves. He delivered the letter to the officer serving as postmaster for the four companies of the Fifty-second Regiment marching with Col. Chickering. The officer said he thought he would be able to post the letter but doubted he'd receive any mail addressed to William.

William resolved one way or another to figure out how he could soon reunite with his own company.

CHAPTER THIRTEEN

The sun hung high in the sky when they reached the town of St. Martinsville. To the right, the Bayou Teche flowed slowly past. Buildings and magnificent live oak trees lined both sides of the main street. Across the Bayou, they could see fields of unharvested sugarcane and a few buildings. Incredibly, there was not a soul to be seen in the town. Shops were shuttered. Lace curtains fluttered in the windows of the houses.

William, riding next to the caravan, asked Louis if he'd ever been to the town before. Louis said he came once with the overseer of the Broussard plantation to get a plow repaired at the foundry.

"Were there people in town?" William asked.

"Oh, yes! Crowds of people. The shops were bustling. The main street through the town was so packed with people and carriages we couldn't walk a straight line from one end to the other." William asked him where he thought everyone had gone. "They're not gone. They're probably hiding from the Union devils but watching from behind the curtains. *Regardez-bien. Il y a des yeux en dentelle, peut-être?"*

Ha! Eyes in the lace. That one has a sense of humor! William thought.

They passed a simple church. St. Martin de Tours, *L'Eglise des Acadiens.* Louis said the overseer told him the master brought his slaves there as babies and had them baptized. Of course, Louis didn't remember the trip. Louis didn't cross himself the way Pierre did when he passed a Catholic Church at home.

The caravan now stretched twice as long as it had when they left New Iberia. They kept the plodding pace through the town and out the other side. They still saw no one until they pulled up next to a fallow field where a half dozen Union soldiers scrambled to stand at attention as they approached, rifles at the ready. The soldiers took guard position before a dozen large wagons loaded with barrels and crates.

A Union officer riding by on the other side of the caravan signaled William that he needed help. He said he'd picked out some husky young negroes to move the wagons but couldn't get them to pay him any mind. He asked William to translate. He led William to Louis' wagon.

"Boys! Yes. You and you, also! Come here," the officer of Col. Chickering's brigade said, pointing at Louis and Alphonse and another. William raised one eyebrow as he translated: "*Garçons! Oui, vous et vous aussi! Venez ici.*"

Louis and Alphonse had their eyes on the loaded wagons on the right side of the road and hadn't noticed the Yankee soldier on the left side ordering "boys" to come. Or perhaps he did notice! To give his next command, the soldier gestured vigorously, circled his biceps, and made a fist. William told Louis he believed the soldier wanted some strong mule tenders to help move the wagons.

The deep wrinkles in Louis' mother's face turned a shade darker watching the exchange. She mumbled something about how they weren't free yet. Now, they took orders from the soldiers. Louis' father touched her arm and told her they couldn't expect the soldiers to take them to freedom if they didn't do their part. They could run off by themselves and be "free," all right, but if they did, who'd tell them where to go to stay clear of the Rebels? They'd surely run into a slave-catcher. When a slave-catcher saw they had no shoes, they'd be back on the plantation a few hours later with an appointment to get twenty lashes for their attempt to run.

"What about not having any shoes?" William asked. "How can you do hard work in all kinds of conditions without shoes on your feet?"

"We have shoes, but the overseer takes them away and locks them up at night. He knows we can't get too far away without 'em. Bare feet are a tip-off to the slave-catcher. We had to leave without 'em when we fled. Can you tell me, Lieutenant, do we get shoes in freedom?"

William thought the runaway slaves didn't understand how freedom would work. But then, come to think of it, neither did he! Nor anyone, he feared. What were they going to do with these people? Had no one started to make plans?"

Louis and Alphonse now had daily work. Over the next two hours, William caught an occasional glimpse of them working the mules at the head of the caravan. The mules moved large wagons from the fields to the parade of carts and worked them into line right behind the soldiers. William asked one of the soldiers what was in the wagons. He said hogsheads of sugar, barrels of syrup, bales of cotton, and bushels of farm produce like sacks of corn and other vegetables. "I hope some packages of meat," he said.

"We'll get to enjoy some of the food," the officer said, "but I wonder who'll pocket the money from selling the cotton and sugar. There's plenty of money being made on the side around here."

That night, the caravan camped on a prairie next to a bayou much smaller than the Bayou Teche. As they ate their plates of food in the mess, William and Nathaniel watched flocks of enormous white birds with red curved-down beaks sail in from the east. They banked, turned, then landed in the tops of tupelo and cypress trees that marched along on the bayou bank, chattering so loud the men could hear them a hundred feet away. They folded their black-edged wings and burrowed into the greenery where they had built their nests. They circled like cats and settled down to roost for the night.

After supper with the officers, William rode back to check on the caravan. He found several families praying and singing a mournful song together. Elongated vowel sounds rendered the words incomprehensible, but the sliding low notes pulled him into their spell. There were some wonderful voices in the company.

About six wagons back, he found Louis and his family sitting around an open fire, stirring a large pot of something that smelled a heck of a lot better than the mystery dish the officers had been served up front. William asked how the day's work had gone. Louis said it was OK. Alphonse said when they were finished getting the wagons in line, the big boss took their names. Alphonse guessed that was a good thing. He said he sure hoped so. They had no choice! Maybe they'd see some pay. William watched Alphonse's face open in a big grin. "That's freedom, right? You get paid for your work?"

"I think so, but admit I don't know when that happens," said William.

Louis had a request. "Do you think we could get shoes when we have to walk around in mule shit all day?"

"Are you working tomorrow?" William asked.

"Yes, sir."

William looked down at Louis and Alphonse's feet, trying to guess the size. The soles seemed to flatten out more than his own. Maybe it just seemed so, being many shades lighter in color than the rest of their feet. Their heels and soles, that is.

"I'm going to ask our quartermaster to be at Col. Chickering's camp tomorrow morning when the men start work. He'll have some shoes that might fit you, and if he doesn't, he'll go find some. I hope you don't mind if the shoes came off a dead Rebel."

The men broke out their widest smiles. "They'll guard the shoes with their lives 'cause that's what they're worth," said Louis. "They'll sleep with them under their blankets!"

Later, William worried that he may have made it possible for those two to run away. No, he thought. Louis probably wouldn't run away without his parents. And Alphonse seemed to consider Louis his leader.

Alphonse proved a boon for everyone's spirits. That started when he sported the *Sunday freedom clothes*. William took a chance to tease him a bit. He was rewarded by seeing Alphonse's dark, closed face open in a toothy grin. Basically cheerful, Alphonse could not help but smile when someone smiled at him.

William asked JeanLouis what he was stirring in the pot. *"Des poulets, de là-bas. Et des herbes du jardin."* He pointed to a column of smoke rising behind a line of trees. He said Alphonse got lucky. They talked about food for a while, getting better and better at understanding each other's words. William told him he'd never known chicken to smell so good. JeanLouis beamed at the compliment.

"I was cook for the whole plantation, white folks and slaves. JeanLouis raised his head and tilted it to one side. *"Est-ce que vous avez de riz, peut-être?"*

With difficulty, William squeezed the smile from his face. *"Oui, mon ami."* He turned Excalibur's head and took an easy canter along the side of the caravan to the mess up front. He returned in twenty minutes with a tin bowl full of steaming, puffed-up grains of rice.

"So, it's true what they say," one of William's tentmates commented later when William told him the story. "Darkies got to have rice for their chicken and gravy!"

William told the officer in charge of the mess that he had found someone whose skills they might put to good use. He used to be the plantation cook. What he stirred in his cookpot sure smelled good.

~~~

The sky looked dark when the officers returned to their tents for the night. "Weather coming," Louis had told them an hour ago when he saw the big birds come streaming into the nests. How would the people in the caravan make out without shelter for themselves or their open carts?

Howling wind and pelting rain woke William during the night. He groped for the edge of his rough blanket and pulled it up under his chin. Trying not to think about the caravan, he didn't open his eyes. He dozed on and off. Scenes of the battle of Irish Bend replayed in his head. When he no longer heard the plopping of raindrops on the canvas of his tent, he got up and stepped outside.

Wisps of clouds scudded northward across the surface of a glorious full moon. He watched until both the clouds and the moon dissolved in the morning light.

A long line of women carrying baskets of wet clothes and blankets streamed from the caravan to the Bayou. The caravan must have received a soaking. Soldiers jingled coins in their pockets and circled the women, looking for someone willing to earn a few coins doing the men's laundry.

William walked to the mess for breakfast. To his left, he heard the big white birds dig out of their nests and greet the morning with clacks of their wings and chattering beaks. They rose, circled, rose, and circled again, then took off in the direction from which they had come last night. "Good hunting!" William said to no one in particular. A few nests kept small, fuzzy white occupants. Newly hatched nestlings, perhaps? As he passed small trees and shrubs at the edges of the tracts of land, William's eyes picked up the sight of iridescent blue birds, no more than five inches from beak to end of tail, flitting around in the branches. Their feathers flashed in the angled rays of the rising sun. Scattered in the flock were a dozen birds identical in size and shape but not solid blue. They sported patches of every color of the rainbow. He had never seen so many birds of similar variety swarming in one place. He knew people at home who kept lists of the different birds they saw. If they came here and counted the numbers of birds and not varieties, they could start a new pastime.

Larger birds flitted above him in the taller trees, and smaller bright yellow, black, and red ones flashed by. He began to recognize a few of the summer birds common in Massachusetts: orioles, robins, finches, rose breasted grosbeaks, and cardinals. The very same birds, perhaps? Did they fly through Louisiana and then all the way to Massachusetts? How did they find their way in bad weather, such as came through last night?

William swallowed his breakfast cakes and coffee. He jumped on

Excalibur and rode through the camp to find the caravan family he had befriended to ask if they had ever seen a bird display such as he had witnessed this morning. He found the older couple, JeanLouis and Marie Adele, but not the young men, Louis and Alphonse.

As of this morning, the daily routine of the family had changed. The men had jobs. Louis and his friend Alphonse reported to Col. Chickering's tent quite early. They were to be given a work assignment. Later in the morning, JeanLouis planned to report to the mess. He would work as a cook.

William asked JeanLouis about *les belles oiseaux*. Yes, he knew about them, he said. C'est *la chute des oiseaux de printemps*. Every year at this time, hundreds of birds come with early fronts.

"And the big white birds?" William asked. "Where are they going?"

"For a day in the big swamp to feed on what the spring floods bring in."

Without Louis to rephrase William's efforts at speaking French, they stumbled through the conversation. The older couple kept their eyes on the ground, spoke softly, and mumbled. Were they just timid? Or were they afraid there might be something wrong about them having a conversation with a white officer?

William returned to the officers' area of the camp and reported to Col. Chickering. He came only for information about the plan for the day; he had no part in decision-making concerning the gathering of contraband. He served at the pleasure of Col. Chickering as he waited for the opportunity to be reunited with Nathaniel and his own company. He had been told that would occur when they left the dust of St. Martinsville behind. Perhaps today would be the day.

William received disappointing news. A scout for Col. Chickering reported that Union forces in pursuit of the Rebel generals were still trapped on the south side of the Vermilion River waiting for engineers to complete a replacement span. He did not know how long the construction would take.

William watched the birds most of the morning. In the afternoon, he checked on and exercised his horse Excalibur and wrote again to Elizabeth and his parents to tell them about the bird shower. Which kicked in worry about what his brother might be up to—a long day.

Late afternoon Col. Chickering called William to the headquarters tent. His scout had pulled off a miracle. He had spoken with someone in the main body of the Fifty-second Regiment. He would not say where or how he did so. The scout expected to make contact again soon. He offered to deliver any messages William might wish to send.

"I will give you a message for my superior officer, 1st Lieutenant Nathaniel Bradford. I hope to see him soon. Our Chaplain tends to the post. Please try to find Chaplain John Moors. He might have letters for me. I haven't heard from anyone at home since before Irish Bend. And I will give you letters for him to send to my wife and my parents. They may not know where or how I am."

"I will do my best to find them."

"Will I be able to rejoin my company once they cross the river?" William asked.

The scout shook his head. "General Taylor and General Mouton have moved on and are now almost to Opelousas. The area they traveled through is heavily wooded and now thick with Rebel sharpshooters. Attempting a reunion there would be dangerous. With the caravan and the heavy wagons, we are far from a nimble force able to sneak up undetected!"

"Indeed! *Trop de tracca*, as my ranch manager would say in polite company." William did not translate the expression to give it the meaning the New England Acadians usually did.

Col. Chickering agreed with his scout. "I'm sorry to disappoint you, Lt. Wells, but I believe you will be with us until we get to where we gather all our contraband goods and runaway slaves for shipment south. That will probably be Port Barre."

William thought but did not say aloud that he and Excalibur alone might have better luck slipping through the few miles of woods to intercept their unit once the main part of the Fifty-second Regiment crossed the Vermilion River.

Buoyed by the prospects for a scheme to meet up with Nathaniel and the rest of D company, the next morning, William kept his good humor, helping Col. Chickering organize the contraband goods they had scraped up in the area north of St. Martinsville. After lunch, he made rounds of the caravan. Most of the men were away working. Women make a home for their families wherever they find themselves to be. They were busy with a great variety of chores around their wagons. Marie Adele now had in her care three children of the woman ahead of her in the caravan who had provided mule feed to the family on their first night on the road. She introduced the woman, named Colette, to William.

Marie Adele organized the children into promoting her side business.

Sowing read the banner the children fashioned from a discarded piece of a shirt she asked the quartermaster to give her. William asked Marie Adele if she wanted him to spread the word of her services to officers struggling to repair their clothes after the hard march up from Irish Bend. *"Oui, oui, lieutenant. Et merçi."*

For the first time, Marie Adele lifted her chin and looked William in the eye when she spoke. And she gave him an identity since the word Lieutenant was the same in French and English. William pointed to himself and added a note to the advertisement on her wagon. *Translator Available.* A translator would be necessary if her customers needed anything more complicated than sewing on a button or *sowing* as she wrote.

Marie Adele had a favor to ask him. It took some time for William to figure out what she wanted. Did the soldiers have a doctor who could look at the back of her friend, a woman who had fled from a plantation on Fausse Pointe? The woman had been lashed, and the stripes weren't healing as quickly as Marie Adele thought they should. Marie Adele said they had tried their usual measures but were lacking many of the needed herbs for the poultices. Her back still bled.

William explained that their medical team was with the main body of the regiment. He had a wound and was treated by a Rebel doctor. He told her they hoped to reunite the regiment in a few days; he thought the Union doctor would do him a favor and see her friend.

William asked what the woman had done to get the lashing. Marie Adele told him she was a runaway. The first time she ran, the slave-catcher spotted her and sent her back when he saw she had no shoes. The overseer on her plantation assigned her to work out in the fields. The second time she ran, the overseer gave her the lash.

In the evening, William made another round of checking on the caravan. Louis invited him to dismount and join them. He offered a post for him to tie up Excalibur and a log for William to sit on. The hospitality surprised William, as did the absence of a pot simmering over the fire. He expected JeanLouis would fix a sumptuous dinner for them now that they were in an area of abundant farms to *"visit."*

Louis explained. *"Ce n'est pas nécessaire. Notre cuisinier a réçu lagniappe pour tout la famille."*

This family had eaten the same dinner as William and the other officers.

William heard the French-speaking negroes in Louisiana using the

same expressions Pierre did at home. Probably neither knew how to spell
the words. Acadian French seemed to be an oral language in Louisiana
as well as in New England. In William's next letter to Elizabeth, he
would ask her to thank Pierre for sharing his language. Pierre was
probably unable to write letters to the Acadians here, but if he found
himself in Louisiana, he could communicate face-to-face fairly well.

Louis and Alphonse worked with the Union's mules, preparing the
contraband goods for the trip to the gathering place at Port Barre. They
said the job had a downside: listening to a serious effort by Col.
Chickering's second in command to recruit them into the Union Army.
JeanLouis asked William if it was true the Union Army recruited men
who looked like him.

The recruiter told him yes, but Louis had his doubts. William had his
doubts, also. He thought they only wanted negro men for *le travail
salissant,* dirty work the white soldiers didn't want to do, not to be real
soldiers. William admitted he had yet to see a negro with a rifle.

"But I believe that's coming soon, my friends. When we were in
Baton Rouge a few months ago, we were visited by a company of negro
troops; they had a negro commanding officer."

JeanLouis said he wasn't anxious to fight. He was too old for that. But
he did want to be treated decently and to be paid. Maybe he could cook
for the Union.

Alphonse also had an interest in joining the Union army; to fight or
not didn't matter to him. He expected he'd be working for somebody no
matter what. If army pay were decent and guaranteed to be paid as the
recruiter promised, he'd be taking a big step up from the plantation.

Marie Adele frowned through all that conversation. Louis saw her
concern and put his arm around her shoulders. He again made his
promise to her. He would never, ever join the Union Army. Having been
taken away from his mother as a small child and sent to be raised by a
relative of the man who enslaved her, he vowed to watch over her as
long as she lived. And he would never willingly put himself in a position
where someone could have that kind of power over his life. JeanLouis
looked as if he might cry. He said that if he knew his wife was safe and
taken care of, he could be happy cooking for the Union Army. As the
wife of a soldier, Marie Adele was promised an allotment to live on and
a pension when her soldier died, whether that happened during service or
after.

Louis was the one the recruiters really hoped to attract. William understood why. Louis would be an asset. No one knew what the world of freedom would be like, but Louis, more than others who ran away from the plantations, seemed to think things through. He was young, strong, and spoke some English.

William recalled the discussions they had at the Wells Club last year when they considered recruiting negroes to help the shortage of manpower to conduct the war. The President was not then in favor. Like his views on abolition, his opinion seemed to have changed. He was more and more convinced that the need to end the bloody war outweighed all difficulties with which they might have to deal afterwards.

William knew the moment he would see Elizabeth again would be many times more wonderful than his reunion with his regiment, but until then, anticipating the meeting with Nathaniel and the rest of his company thrilled beyond measure. The main body of the Fifty-second Regiment crossed the rebuilt Vermilion River Bridge and quick-marched almost to Opelousas before word reached Col. Chickering that a *rendezvous* with the rest of the regiment would be feasible. Col. Chickering reacted quickly. Within twelve hours, his Forty-first Massachusetts Regiment and the four companies of the Fifty-second Regiment he commanded—plus William—broke camp and marched north. They outflanked the sharpshooter-filled woods and closed a triangle formed by their camp north of St. Martinsville, the Bayou Teche at a point north of the Vermilion River Bridge, and the road to Port Barre.

Col. Chickering took charge of the reunited Fifty-second Regiment as well as his own Forty-first Massachusetts. He assembled the men by companies. He addressed the men and issued orders. William was correct about their next assignment: a continuation of the great gathering and packing for shipment of the produce of middle Louisiana considered critical support for the war effort of the Confederacy. As they had on the march through upper St. Martin Parish, they were to welcome those fleeing the plantations and recruit the men suitable for the Union Army. Col. Chickering left out the details. What were they supposed to tell the former slaves when they asked questions about being Union soldiers? How the former slaves would serve the Union Army was a matter of debate among the generals and the politicians all the way up to President Lincoln himself. Would they bear arms? Would they be limited to labor at what was known as fatigue duty? Would they be commanded by officers of color?"

"Do you know what to tell them when they want to know details?" William asked Nat.

"I asked Col. Chickering that very question. He suggested I say the details will be worked out when they see the official recruiters at Brashear City."

When the formal meeting was dismissed by the Colonel Chickering, Nathaniel gave William a big bear hug in greeting, then stopped him from talking.

"The hardest part of the march up the Teche for me was leaving you behind in New Iberia, but enough about me. Chaplain Moors has four letters for you from Elizabeth. I suggest you read them in order but of course that's up to you. When you are ready, find me in my tent. I'll be waiting, and we can tell each other what we've been doing."

William followed Nathaniel's suggestion.

In her first letter, without trying to alarm her husband, Elizabeth went through her efforts to get information after the battle of Irish Bend. Elizabeth wrote that she learned there were casualties. Still, all the families of the soldiers who were injured had been officially informed, and the most seriously injured were sent to New Orleans. Since she hadn't been informed, she could assume he had not been injured. But where was he?

The newspapers reported the main Union force moved on to Vermilionville. Still, the information she gathered from the families of others in William's company told her he was not among those there. Likewise, she learned that some companies were left in New Iberia to secure the town, but D company was not one of those companies either. So, she turned the world upside down. Now into her ninth month of pregnancy, she had Pierre take her all over western Massachusetts, chasing people who might obtain information about her husband. Representative Davis was the one who solved the mystery. He found out William was in a makeshift hospital in New Iberia with just a flesh wound.

Elizabeth tried to put everything in the best possible light, but her panic came through loud and clear. *Oh, my darling, you must have been frantic,* William thought as he read her letter. *I am so sorry to cause you such anxiety.*

By the fourth letter, that topic paled in importance. Elizabeth had something else to be concerned about. His brother Aaron. She followed the suggestion and let Nat convey 'the latest.'

Elizabeth wrote I'm going to let Nat tell you all we know about Aaron's situation because, by the time you read my letter, he will have more information than I have now. We all realized Aaron's eighteenth birthday was coming up, so we were nervous about what he might do. It appears he didn't wait for his birthday.

~~~

"So, did Elizabeth tell you anything about your brother Aaron's latest adventure, William?" Nat asked Will.

"No, she didn't. She said she would leave that to you. All Elizabeth told me about was that the sugar making was successful; in fact, she said father bragged to everyone he knew what a great job he—my father—had done. Not a word that the idea was originally Aaron's, and Aaron organized the project."

"Your father just will not learn how to handle Aaron, but I'm getting to think no one could. The chip on his shoulder is a bigger log than any sawmill could handle! Here goes, my good friend. Elizabeth wanted me to be the one to give you the details."

Nat took a deep breath. "One morning, your father opened the *Greenfield Gazette* and read an article about a fire in Boston. A club owned by Henry Arnold burned to the ground. There was one fatality, and several people remained missing. The fire department and the police were engaged in investigations."

Will drew in a quick breath. Nat continued.

"Later in the day, your father received a message from the Boston police. They *needed* to locate Aaron; he might have been inside the building that burned, and they needed to speak with him." Another quick breath. "Your father went to work. He found Aaron and his friend Henry Arnold, Jr. in Springfield with the family of another friend. Aaron told him they had indeed been inside and ran out when the fire began."

"Oh, my God, Nat! Henry Arnold again!"

"Yes. Two days later, your father had more information. Other occupants who ran out, leaving behind their tall-heeled shoes in the process, included a half dozen ladies of the evening in pink silk negligées and number of prominent Boston gentlemen, including a partially dressed senator and a well-known businessman without his trousers." Will gasped. Nat continued. "One body was recovered from the fire, which triggered an even more thorough study of the evidence. The investigation revealed that several known occupants were still missing.

Families had been notified and their whereabouts were being sought by the investigators."

"My family must have been in shock, Nat, especially my mother!"

"Yes, your father took it pretty well. After thinking Aaron might have been burned alive, life looked pretty good. And your father doesn't see any criminal charges coming out of this for Aaron; it can't be a crime to get out of a burning building. Aaron turned himself in—after Father twisted his arm. The family name has not been in the Boston paper nor, miracle of miracles, in the *Greenfield Gazette*. But then the word of the fire spread. Before long, everybody knew Aaron was there and what he was there for. Very embarrassing."

"And Mother?"

"That is the problem. Not taking it well, as you can imagine. Elizabeth wonders if her mother-in-law will ever get over it."

"Father was a genius to be able to keep the name out of the paper, but you know official statements are never lost. They're all in a file somewhere."

"What does Aaron have to say for himself?" Will asked Nat.

"He tried to say he and Henry Jr. stopped in for a beer after playing cards down the street, but because there was a fatality and missing persons, detailed statements had to be taken from everyone. The police placed every occupant where he or she was in the building. There's no doubt where Aaron was and what he was doing when a man was careless with a cigar and set a mattress on fire."

"So, it's all true?" Will asked.

"I'm afraid so, Will. They have to do a thorough job to determine whether the missing person is another victim or went home to bed. One good result: Henry Arnold will have a lot to answer for."

"I'm thankful for that. I guess that isn't being very Christian, but..."

"It's hard to be a Christian and love every fellow man when one causes such pain."

"I hurt for what my family has to endure, especially my wife and the new member we haven't even met yet. And you know what burns me up? I don't know if you know how it goes in our family, but after we all go crazy with concern about some escapade of Aaron's and how Mother will get over it, Mother is always the first to forgive him! She may already have. He's my brother, but I don't know that this time I'll forgive him, ever."

Another bear hug was exchanged between Nat and William, and they sat quietly for a few moments.

"On another subject," William continued. "I'm relieved to see you looking so well, Nat. "I heard there were skirmishes on the pursuit up the Teche from Irish Bend. I've learned the word "skirmish" covers a wide variety of events—an exchange of a few shots or a full-scale battle. All I see is that you've lost weight, but we all have. Tell me about it."

"The mounted officers didn't fare too badly on the march, but the infantrymen were force-marched past exhaustion. I had full responsibility for keeping our company disciplined and on the march. You were close to worthless with pain. Most officers were not able to prevent their troops from plunder and destruction. Other than foraging for food, which was necessary, our company was well-behaved. I can't say the same for some of the others. Or the runaways. We left many plantations as smoking ruins. I just don't understand wanton destruction."

"Nor do I," said William. "I was just fine. You and the company suffered in the pursuit. Elizabeth had major anxiety. In contrast, I had a pleasant visit with a kind Rebel doctor in a lovely town. Imagine! But Nathaniel," William continued, "your real accomplishment was leading the pursuit from Irish Bend when many who out-ranked you were indecisive. The word is out you'll be commended."

"I'm embarrassed about that. General Banks issued a triumphant report of our so-called success at Irish Bend. The truth of the matter is we failed. Generals Taylor and Mouton are still out there; we aren't going after them. We allowed, and in many cases, promoted, dreadful destruction through the plantation country."

A smile opened William's face, prompting Nathaniel to comment that he was sure glad to see a smile. He asked what was so funny.

"Elizabeth told me about a column in the *New York Daily Tribune* commenting on General Bank's ability to rewrite history to wrap a disaster in the clothing of success. Remember the words of Horace Greeley? *General Banks moves in mysterious ways his blunders to perform?*"

"I remember. Elizabeth also wrote that the know-it-all columnists who are usually so critical of General Banks have a positive view of his decision to pull us away from Port Hudson early last spring. They say we might have succeeded in entering the fortifications while Admiral Farragut had the attention of the Rebels diverted, but we'd never have been able to hold our position. We'd have been annihilated. They think it will take a massive force to pry General Gardner out of Port Hudson for good."

"Sometimes, we don't know what's good and what isn't, but I don't see any silver lining to Aaron's escapade."

The next morning, William complained to Nat. "Now General Banks is assembling troops to assault Port Hudson, and we don't seem to be going there. We'll be packing plunder and expect no open conflict. Stripping the countryside of anything the Rebels need furthers the war effort, but it is not an inspiring duty. I do not feel we have covered ourselves with glory. Elizabeth is the only one I know who is happy about our next assignment."

The day before Col. Chickering was scheduled to lead his Forty-first Regiment and Col. Greenleaf's Fifty-second on the route to Port Barre, William received a letter from Elizabeth with more news about Aaron. He and his buddies had gone down to Springfield to talk to some Union men who were putting together investors to rent plantations in the south—the locals called them carpet baggers because they brought their possessions in carpet bags.

"Damn it, Nat, he never stops!" Will said. "My mother is still inconsolable. Every time she passes Aaron's maple trees, her tears begin again. She hasn't yet passed to the second stage—the forgiveness."

William was a man under orders and could do nothing to help his family.

~~~

Trailed by the caravans of contraband goods and persons already gathered, the united Fifty-second Regiment began the march due east toward Barre's Landing on Bayou Courtableu, above the headwaters of the Bayou Teche. They were to assemble there with other Union troops who had the same assignment and together pack the contraband goods onto steamers. Some boats would go down Bayou Teche to Brashear City, and others would travel down Bayou Courtableu through a network of bayous to the Atchafalaya River and on to New Orleans.

~~~

The forces Col. Chickering commanded were the first to arrive. Col. Chickering's second in command directed them to make camp on a level prairie on the right bank of the bayou. The officers staked out what they considered the prime location. They directed the wagons and tents of the contraband caravan to locate farther back.

Not a good plan! The tents of the officers were on the traffic path to everyone's destination for bathing and washing clothes—a busy path indeed after weeks on the march. Col. Chickering came by to inspect the encampment. With a few harsh words for his second in command, he ordered a rearrangement according to a plat he had prepared.

Nathaniel expressed praise for the colonel. "I have no idea how Col. Chickering would perform in battle, but I'm impressed with his handling of this complicated operation. He always has a plan."

A half dozen additional regiments and their caravans arrived over the next twenty-four hours. The Fifty-second Regiment placed them as illustrated in Col. Chickering's plan. Then, two more regiments arrived. Eventually, they had a five-acre tent city with a network of wide paths, an orderly arrangement of tents for the soldiers, and a great conglomeration of carts and wagons for the contraband persons. There were more black faces than William had ever seen in his life.

Having been told they would be in this location for a while, the more ambitious of the contrabands, including the family William had befriended, launched into enterprise.

Louis' mother, Marie, set out her sign for sewing and mending: *Racommodage/Sewing*. She asked William to draw a picture of a thimble and a threaded needle. This time, she used the proper French word and spelled the English one correctly. Everyone's facility with the languages had improved.

A woman in a colorful, flowing dress advertised herself as a *Traiteur*. Marie's friend Colette took a group of little ones into her care for a few hours each day so other mothers could do their chores or conduct their chosen enterprises. Doc Sawyer checked Marie Adele's friend with the bleeding stripes of the lash on her back and approved the treatment Marie Adele administered.

Col. Chickering assigned several members of the Fifty-second Regiment to important duties at the encampment. He placed an officer William knew well in charge of sending out wagons to scour the area for additional contraband goods to supplement those brought in the wagon trains. Another officer set up a crew on an adjoining tract where he sorted and packaged the goods for shipment. Col. Chickering placed William in charge of the Landing itself—unloading the wagons and packing the goods onto the steamers. He gave Nathaniel the assignment of security for the entire encampment. Nathaniel tried to recruit Louis for the security team. No luck. Those managing the mules had already lined him up to be in charge of transporting contraband to the Landing for shipment. On that duty, Louis and William saw each other every day.

"You're looking at that steamer for a long time this morning, Louis," William said to him one day. "I hope you aren't thinking of taking a trip."

Louis smiled and confessed the thought crossed his mind to stow away and go on to New Orleans in a bale of cotton.

"But don't worry. I'm not going to run. I'm committed to seeing my parents to safety."

"I'm glad to hear that. You've taught me something. I'll be putting a security detail on the Landing. Maybe also on the steamers themselves."

"Have you seen the terrain on the route? I think you or the slave catchers can catch up pretty quick with anyone who tries to escape on the boats."

"My friend, what would you do if you got to New Orleans?"

"I hear half the black men in the city are free. They came here free from the islands and work in the trades. I did carpentry on the plantation. I think I could make my way. My father may join the army to cook. If he does, the recruiter says my mother would get an allotment. Then I'll have to see she has a safe place to live."

"But you aren't interested in the Army?"

"No, sir. I know they'd just put me back on some sugar farm with a carpetbagger because they'd find out I pretty much ran one before. They're looking for ex-slaves who would manage farms to get them going again. Freed slaves with experience would help." William said nothing about his brother Aaron.

The camp fell into a pattern of working days and relaxing nights.

CHAPTER FOURTEEN

William brought Nathaniel to meet his friends in the caravan. Nathaniel could converse easily only with Louis; he needed help to speak with Alphonse and the older couple.

"I'm kicking myself for not taking advantage of our French speakers the way you did, William."

"Louis had to be patient with me in the beginning. I asked him to say everything a few times. *"Encore, mon ami, s'il vous plait."* There are differences between the language here and at home. You'll get better. And they get better at understanding English."

"How did Pierre's family and the little band of Acadians in our part of Massachusetts ever get there from Quebec, Will? Most of the Acadian speakers in New England are in Maine, right over the border with Quebec."

"Pierre told me his family story once, but I've forgotten most of it. They were expelled from Quebec by the British but somehow a dozen families got separated. They were chased by some Indians and came down the Connecticut River. We were looking for settlers then, and Acadians are hard-working farmers. Only thing they missed was their church. They found one just over the border in New Hampshire. Then they built their own chapel, and the priest from New Hampshire came down often. When we get home, I'll have Pierre tell us the story again. Maybe he will recall some more details."

Nathaniel talked to them about their daily life on the plantations, the routine of growing sugarcane, what other crops they raised, and if there was any opportunity for education. Now that he had some exposure to the "contrabands," he could see Louis was unusual. For many, the future was a challenge for the North as well as the South.

"Do you know anyone with the last name Belanger?" Nathaniel asked Louis. "That's the family name of William's ranch manager, the one who taught him French."

The older couple and Alphonse looked blank. Louis smiled. He told Nathaniel a white man might have a second name, but the enslaved had but one. He heard the recruiters were giving out a second. "I don't know where I'll get another one."

He said every white man around his plantation seemed to have the name Broussard. "That's the one second name I don't want, by the way."

"Have you ever heard there are some Acadians in Western Massachusetts where we come from?" Nathaniel asked.

"The Lieutenant told me that, but I didn't know."

Nathaniel and William got the picture. The enslaved heard little about the world beyond the boundaries of their own plantations, and what they did hear, they had no frame of reference to understand.

"Does it strike you as ironic," Nathaniel asked William one night," that the only people we speak with who were born in the South are the negroes who were formerly enslaved? They're the ones who know the answers to our questions about this land the army sent us to, like the weather and all the hazards. They can make better guesses than the men who are supposed to be keeping us informed."

Being stuck at Barre's Landing still irritated William. He was adequately fed, not under threat, and assigned work not unpleasant to do. The only enemies he fought were the fleas and lice. He had the company of Nathaniel and occasionally that of the Chaplain—good friends. For these blessings, he should have been grateful, and he put them on his list of three good things every night. However, the original nine-month enlistment had but about a month to go. He'd heard nothing of any plan to be relieved. More importantly, the end of Elizabeth's confinement drew close. He resented being apart from her at the time of the birth of their child for the inglorious duty of packing plunder! She wrote with humor about her condition, but he could imagine how uncomfortable she must be.

I am grateful our letters travel back and forth speedily now. I know where you are and that you are well. But, my love, without you, I am only half myself. No!! No!! That is not true. I am now twice myself and getting larger every day!

Elizabeth knew William probably would not be home in time for the birth, but he should be soon after. Both impatient families kept asking her the name she had chosen for the child. She told them she would wait to name the child until William returned. Dr. Thomas said she could do that.

She did have some thoughts. If the baby were a girl, she liked the name Margaret. She responded cautiously to William's suggestion of Nathaniel as the name for a boy. One day, Nathaniel might want the name for a son of his own.

~~~

Three weeks after the Fifty-second Regiment arrived in Barre's Landing for the operation to assemble and ship the produce of middle Louisiana to the southern ports, Col. Chickering pronounced the gathering assignment complete. He ordered the regiments to pack up and move the contraband persons, goods, and themselves south to the Union facility at Brashear City. The Chaplain would not accompany the caravan on the trip. He had scheduled a respite visit to New Orleans. He would join them at their next assignment.

Before leaving, the Chaplain delivered to William a letter from Elizabeth. She wrote that Dr. Thomas had left the house after examining her. He pronounced her quite well and on track for safe delivery in a few weeks. The midwife had been informed, and Abigail was on her way to stay with her sister. Pierre insisted on picking Abigail up and delivering her to Elizabeth. He planned to bring his fiancée with him for them to meet her. They might be interested in having her come to help out after the baby was born.

Fiancée? That was interesting news.

Elizabeth wrote that Representative Davis arranged for Col. Greenleaf to be informed when the birth occurred. She didn't know how on earth he could do that but was grateful.

Elizabeth knew William probably would not be home in time for the birth of their child, but he should be soon after.

Elizabeth passed on to William the rumors she had heard about the Department of the Gulf. Columnists sitting in their offices in Boston claimed to know more about the plans than those serving under General Banks in the field! They believed General Ulysses S. Grant in the west wanted General Banks to join him for an attack on Vicksburg: Grant to come from the north and Banks from the east or south. They said the reverse was also true. General Banks wanted General Grant to help him take Port Hudson. The squabbling Generals held their ground and sent emissaries to compete for the president's ear. Like so many important events of the war, the lack of resolution delayed planning for the outcome. President Lincoln was still reluctant to tell his generals what to do.

Each general went forward with his preferred plan. The generals in General Grant's Army gathered their forces to assist him at Vicksburg. The generals in the Department of the Gulf amassed men and materials around Port Hudson. Probably neither had adequate resources for a speedy resolution.

William grumbled even more that the Fifty-second Regiment was not present in either where it really mattered.

One night, Nathaniel had a story to tell the other officers at dinner.

"Night before last, one of my men gave me a gift of a fine, fat tom turkey, so-said, he had just *found*. I accepted the gift, but at the time, I couldn't leave my post to take Tom to the animal pen at the mess. If I tied him up outside my tent, I knew someone would have lifted him before morning. All I could think to do was to take him inside my tent with me. In the morning, I delivered Tom to William's friend JeanLouis, the cook. I asked him to deal with my bedfellow in a particularly kind manner before he became a stew."

Nathaniel slapped his forehead. "Come to think of it, maybe we just ate Tom for dinner."

~~~

Col. Chickering's own regiment, the Forty-first Massachusetts, led the parade out of Barre's Landing. Two-mule Army wagons laden with ammunition and military supplies followed behind the Forty-first. A half dozen other regiments—including the Fifty-second Massachusetts—came next, some men left in marching order and some dispersed throughout the remainder of the caravan. From all reports, at least 6000 negroes and their belongings in carts and wagons followed behind the troops.

William and Nathaniel made good use of their friendship with French-speakers Louis and Alphonse as they lined up the caravan that had been assembled by the Fifty-second Regiment. Col. Chickering noticed the ease with which they did so and gave the Fifty-second a prime location as the first of the contraband caravans, directly behind the military supplies. Nathaniel and William kept the incredible assemblage moving under discipline—Nathaniel leading and William patrolling the sidelines. At one point, Nathaniel galloped back to share an observation with William.

"The last such parade of animals and people had ever before gathered in history may have been when Noah led the animals onto the Ark," said Nathaniel.

Behind the human contraband came droves of horses, mules, and cattle—beeves as they called them—taken from the enemy. More humans and animals fled the plantations with the *encouragement* of Union troops. They carted goods from the plantations as they fled, singing and shouting hallelujahs for freedom. Col. Chickering chose the route they took. For two days, they followed the left bank of the Bayou Teche, avoiding the Rebel troops thick in the woods around Vermilionville. On the third night, the entire caravan crossed the Bayou Teche above New Iberia. They made a wide arc around the town and bivouacked south of New Iberia at Nelson's Canal.

William felt a pang of disappointment not to stop and see again the people and town that had treated him kindly. He wanted to show Nathaniel the lovely church where he'd spent a couple of nights. But skipping New Iberia was a fortunate circumstance. William shuddered to imagine the upheaval the commotion of the caravan would have produced if they had taken the hordes of animals and laden wagons straight down Main Street!

From Nelson's Canal, the caravan followed the west bank of the Bayou Teche southward, down the same route from which Nat had chased Generals Taylor and Mouton up from the battle of Irish Bend. The Union did not secure all the routes, but fortunately, they encountered no Rebels. However, as they approached the land of the Chitimacha Indians, Louis suggested the Yankees be wary of the Redmen. The tribes thought the Northerners were looking for land. Indians, by experience, knew their tribal lands were vulnerable.

A rumor flowed through the caravan that a Rebel band was approaching from Texas to ambush the train. Col. Chickering dealt with that threat by canceling camping in Patersonville. Instead of being sitting ducks, they marched through the night and arrived at Brashear City before nightfall the following day. The forced march was all in a day's work for the mounted troops and even for those in the caravan who could ride on their carts and wagons. Not so pleasant for the foot-sore rank and file.

They moved into buildings in the large facility and enjoyed a dinner prepared by staff cooks. The camp was well equipped to deal with the contraband goods and the people brought in the caravan, or so it seemed at the time. Free of the responsibility for care of the freedmen, the Fifty-second hoped for a few days of rest.

Not to be. After one shortened night of sleep, the order came to the Fifty-second to be packed, battle-ready, and assembled for departure in the morning. Steamers awaited to take them upstream. William and Nathaniel had no opportunity to learn the fate of the enslaved family they had befriended. As usual, they were not officially informed of their destination, but this time they could make a good guess. There was only one reason to take steamers "up the Mississippi River:" to go to Port Hudson. They knew from the rumors of the past three weeks that General Banks was scraping together every regiment and company in the Army of the Gulf. They were on their way to action.

Nathaniel reviewed the company. He reported to Col. Chickering they were ready. The other companies did so as well, as did all the other company commanders. Col. Chickering returned the command of the Fifty-second Regiment to Col. Greenleaf. They boarded the steamers and departed for Port Hudson.

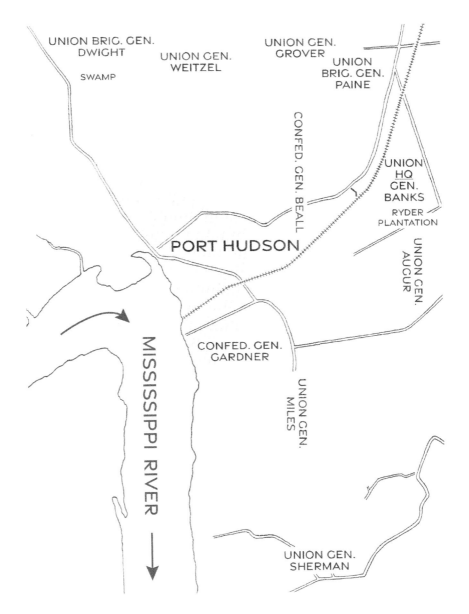

UNION BRIG. GEN.
DWIGHT

UNION GEN.
WEITZEL

UNION GEN.
GROVER

UNION
BRIG. GEN.
PAINE

SWAMP

CONFED. GEN. BEALL

UNION
HQ
GEN.
BANKS

RYDER
PLANTATION

PORT HUDSON

UNION GEN.
AUGUR

MISSISSIPPI RIVER →

CONFED. GEN.
GARDNER

UNION GEN.
MILES

UNION GEN.
SHERMAN

THE SIEGE OF PORT HUDSON

 HIGH GROUND

PART V: THE SIEGE OF PORT HUDSON—THE TRIP HOME

CHAPTER FIFTEEN

The steamers set the Fifty-second Regiment ashore at Springfield Landing, a wharf facility on the left bank of the Mississippi River five miles below the batteries of the fortifications of Port Hudson. The men were numb from the emotional seesaw of the past six months. Time and time again, they had expected to proceed to the capture of the Rebel garrison of Port Hudson and thereby play a decisive role in saving the Union. Instead, they were told there was another change of plans. One more delay plunged them into another disappointment. Now, the men stepped slower and stood less erect than when they sailed out of Baton Rouge in the early spring.

As the sun needs no command to rise or set, they fell into the routine of assembling by company to receive their orders. They lined up behind their corporals and stood at ease until the horses for the officers came off the ship.

Col. Greenleaf mounted his horse. Standing tall in his stirrups, he pulled up all the authority and enthusiasm he could. He thundered up and back each side of the regiment, then assumed a place at the head. He raised the colors and addressed the men.

"Gentlemen of the Fifty-second Regiment, Massachusetts Volunteers. We assemble here to join General Nathaniel Banks and the Army of the Gulf as they proceed to the capture of the fortification of Port Hudson. Union forces are just now settling back into their camps after their last assault. We are assigned to the direct command of General Godfrey Weitzel. We will now march by company around the arc of all the Union forces camped before the fortifications until we reach the encampment of General Weitzel on the northern arm of the arc. We will make camp as General Weitzel directs. As we proceed on our march, we will make reconnaissance of the Union presence and, at the same time, announce our readiness to serve. The batteries and support wagons of each of our companies roll behind them. Company commanders, in order, announce your readiness to serve."

"Company D stands ready to serve, sir," Nathaniel responded after Company C's report.

"Proceed with your company," First Lieutenant Bradford responded to Col. Greenleaf.

Riding next to Nathaniel, William mumbled. "Ready to serve, all right. We've been ready to serve for six months. March here, march there. So far, mostly what we've done is gather contraband and march some more. Even now, we're two days late to this party taking place at Port Hudson."

"Get a grip, William. Port Hudson has been our destination since the day we landed in Louisiana. We are here at last, and we have a clear assignment."

Advance scouts had warned Col. Greenleaf of extensive changes made to the terrain since the Fifty-second Regiment marched on Port Hudson from Baton Rouge in the spring. In the briefing for company commanders, Col. Greenleaf warned them the scouts advised that Confederate General Franklin Gardner had "hardened the defensive perimeter." Hardened, indeed. The Fifty-second remembered an easy march on a trail through a natural forest of oak and cypress toward the fortifications. Now, in midsummer, they looked out over deep ravines cutting a haphazard honeycomb into an apron of wasteland between themselves and the Port Hudson bluff overlooking the river. The men recognized nothing of their surroundings.

All the trees had been hacked off a few feet from the ground as if a mythical giant strode through the area wielding a hatchet. The severed trunks had been fashioned into abatis: defensive constructions designed to impale any human, horse, or wheeled device that might attempt to pass over or through the depressions on a path to reach the bluff. Devastation!

"My God!" William exclaimed. "We easily marched all the way up to the batteries last March. How did we do it? We couldn't march there now. What a dreadful violation of a beautiful forest!"

"Agreed. I'm puzzling over our challenge. In the spring, we also came from the south but easily found a well-defined path through the forest. I don't see any paths at all through this field of hazards. Hold the company at ease, William. I'm going to see if my mount will take me in there to have a better look around."

Nathaniel rode up to the edge of the wasteland. At the sight before him, his mount Thunder jerked his nose in the air, snorted, froze, and locked his knees. Commands delivered by the reins, Nathaniel's heels, and his encouraging words failed to persuade Thunder to take one more step. Nathaniel respected his mount's assessment of the risk involved. He turned the horse's head back to the waiting company of men and touched his horse's flank with his heels.

"Too dangerous," Nathaniel told William. "Thunder is as surefooted as a mountain goat. He took one step and knew he could break a leg if he put a hoof into an irregular hole. The new ravines look mostly natural, like the terrain that supposedly remained after the ice age and the subsequent floods changed the course of the Mississippi River. I recall seeing some indentations like them under the forest. But now the area has been salted with traps. Nothing on wheels can get through. If we attempt an attack on foot, the only armament we would have to support us would be what we could carry. No doubt the Rebels have sharpshooters in the fortification and on the high spots around targeted on the most promising pathways. An approach may be more promising from the north side of the arc. Let us proceed."

Nathaniel led Company D away from the river through an area untouched by the desecrating Rebel hatchet. William brought up the rear. When the fortifications were no longer in view, Nathaniel turned the regiment left, giving the encampments of General Thomas Sherman and General Christopher Auger a wide berth. William galloped up to ride by Nathaniel's side. He swept his arm toward a large plantation house, white columns and all, standing in a clearing behind a well-tended garden a few hundred yards to their right.

"That's the finest dwelling anywhere around here," he said. "The sign says *Ryder Plantation*. What do you bet Ryder's house is now the headquarters of General Banks?"

"No odds could tempt me. The General always finds the softest place to land."

Continuing around the arc of encampments, the regiment reached a thickly wooded area that had not been butchered by the hatchet of the mythical giant. Nathaniel ordered another left turn and led the regiment on the northern arm of the arc back toward the Mississippi River. They passed to the rear of the encampment of General Cuvier Grover and that of General Godfrey Weitzel. They reached the far side of General Weitzel's encampment: their destination: Brigadier General William Dwight's encampment lay beyond Weitzel's.

Nathaniel tightened his upper lip. "We're closer to General Dwight than I want to be," he said. "Whoever assigned the locations of the encampments didn't do General Dwight any favors. His camp is located almost to the Mississippi River, behind a swampy backwater marooned by the river in the last spring flood."

"You seem to want to stay away from Dwight. Is General Dwight some kind of problem?" William asked.

"The man is a hard drinker and considered the most unpleasant officer in the entire Department of the Gulf. His own men dislike him."

"Then, so why does General Banks keep him around? Seems to me we have generals to spare in this army. General Banks could pick up another one for a commander right here at Port Hudson."

Nathaniel raised his eyebrows, looking wise. "The rumor back in Boston is that General Banks is deep in personal debt to General Dwight's father. Whether that's true or not, clearly General Banks enjoys surrounding himself with a lot of rank who must do his bidding."

William sighed and wagged his head from side to side. "Where do you learn about such things?"

"Company commanders gossip more than any women I've ever run across."

~~~

Nathaniel reported to the guard on duty at General Weitzel's camp; the guard directed the regiment toward the troughs to water their horses and await the arrival of the supply wagons. They dismounted.

"We're fortunate, you know," Nathaniel remarked to William. "If I could select a commander to lead us into battle, I would choose General Weitzel. He trained at West Point and is professional to the core."

"Good, but something is digging a furrow between your brows. What's bothering you?"

"The challenge presented by the location of Port Hudson itself. A defensive genius chose and equipped the location on a bluff forty feet straight up from the water, and just after a sharp turn in the river, increases the velocity of the water flow. The heights are well equipped with a canon that can be turned and repositioned to address any threat. Now I understand the challenge Admiral Farragut had getting past the guns of Port Hudson and on to Vicksburg last spring. Maybe sending us up to Port Hudson from Baton Rouge just to be backup for that operation was a wise precaution."

"I've had second thoughts about that experience as well," said William. "We were naïve to think we could storm Port Hudson by ourselves. The march we just completed around the arc shows us the entire Union position. The terrain appears less daunting on this north side, but the encampments are even farther from the fort. The fortification is so far it is barely visible from here, nor can we see what lies between here and there. There will be a heavy price to pay for staging an assault over that difficult terrain."

A smile crept over Nathaniel's face, and William reacted.

"Nat, what the devil do you find amusing about the challenge? It looks daunting to me."

"There is a possibility we won't be needing to make an assault."

"What are you saying? No assault?" William asked.

"With our ships controlling the Mississippi River from above the turn toward Port Hudson all the way down to Springfield Landing below the fortifications, and our land forces camped on the other three sides, we could just cut off all supplies to the Rebels. Food is already in short supply. With nothing coming in, they can't last long. Eventually, they'll have to capitulate."

William's eyes opened wide. "Are you saying we could just wait?"

"Yes. But there are two big obstacles to adopting plan B."

"Which are?"

"First, General Gardner is tightly tucked up in the fortification in dreadful conditions, but his forces are loyalty beyond reason."

"You mean they wouldn't leave him?"

"Right."

"And the second obstacle?"

"General Banks is obsessed with making assaults. He's just cleaning up after the latest one and is already planning another as soon as possible."

"Why on earth does he love assaults?"

"Because, my friend, he wants heroic tales to tell."

"What do you mean? Are you saying starving out the enemy doesn't fit his narrative?"

"That's the way I read it."

William squeezed his eyes shut for a moment. He sighed.

"So, we keep up attacks even though they are costly in human lives and not really necessary?"

"If we are ordered to do so, yes."

"Nathaniel, I'm as anxious as anyone to finish our mission and go home, but—"

The mule-driven wagons of equipment clattering around the rear of General Glover's encampment and reaching General Weitzel's encampment interrupted their conversation. Col. Greenleaf greeted the quartermaster of the Fifty-second Regiment at the head of the parade. The quartermaster gave William his assignment: find General Weitzel's duty guard and get the men started unloading the tents and setting up our encampment where and how he directs you to do so.

"Save a spot for the Chaplain's large tent," Col. Greenleaf instructed. "He'll be here from New Orleans soon. I'm taking Lieutenant Bradford to headquarters with me to report our arrival to General Banks. I expect we'll bring back the next orders for the regiment."

William set to work organizing the camp.

~~~

The Chaplain arrived from his furlough in New Orleans ahead of schedule. He looked no less portly than he did before but had much better color after the rest and good healthy food prepared by an old friend. William complimented him on his bloom.

"I thoroughly enjoyed my period of poor health, my friends. I slept on a feather bed under a real roof. For six nights, I had a case of dysentery to list as one of the *good* things to be thankful for when I said my evening prayers."

"You don't have to lie and say we look good also," William told him. "Our uniforms are in tatters. We're as thin as scarecrows. My head of hair is as shaggy as a black pony, and I think I see more grey hairs. Grooming is not worth the physical effort even to think about. Under a calculation most favorable to the Union brass, our nine-month commitment expires in less than two weeks. They tell us they'll clean us up for the trip home so we don't frighten our families. Why worry about fixing up when we think we're about to engage in another assault? But what about our replacements, Chaplain? We've heard nothing about them. Have you heard who will replace us?"

"Not a word."

William pinched his lips together, arched his eyebrows, and shook his head slowly."

The Chaplain brought William a long letter from Elizabeth. She began with a drawing of a smiling whale shooting water out of a hole in his head. Under the sketch, she had written her name: *Elizabeth*. She said she couldn't get out of her own way or turn over in bed without help but she felt well. Pierre's Marie rarely left her side. Dr. Thomas came by for another visit. He told her the baby was a big one and could come any day.

Elizabeth had one bit of news about Aaron that was good news. He was now eighteen but hadn't rushed off to enlist. He was back at work on the Wells farm. Unfortunately, he still ran around with his friend Henry Arnold at night and on weekends. Then came the next kicker. He and his friend Henry still wanted to be carpet baggers!! They had located an abandoned plantation in St. Martin Parish and were working on getting investors lined up. They were counting on William to find reliable freed slaves to run the plantation and mill. They were telling everyone his brother had made friends of freed slaves who knew about running sugar farms.

Will was furious. And he was even madder when he opened a letter from his mother begging him to help "poor Aaron."

William told the Chaplain the news about Aaron. As usual, the Chaplain had good counsel.

"Your father can't prevent Aaron from volunteering for the service or from doing whatever he might decide to do. But you know more about what is involved in taking over a plantation than anyone back home. You have every right to refuse to be involved. Aaron is a disaster waiting to happen. Please write to your mother often to be with her in her pain. I hear these carpetbagger schemes are having trouble finding investors. Surely two kids won't garner many backers."

"I'm glad you've returned to us, Chaplain."

Nat wasn't as sanguine. He let go with words Will had never heard from his mouth.

That night, Will turned his mind round and round, trying to figure out if Aaron could borrow money against his share of the farm. He hoped that would not be possible.

The Chaplain also brought a bit of news for William from sources he would not disclose. Col. Greenleaf would receive an expedited communication when William's baby arrived.

Representative Davis must have found another string to pull!

~~~

While Nathaniel was away with the Colonel, General Grover's men gave the Fifty-second Regiment help organizing their encampment between that of General Grover and Brigadier General Dwight. William heard many versions of what had occurred at Port Hudson in the assault two days prior to their arrival. General Weitzel's duty officer, the rank and file, and even the cooks and orderlies wanted to tell the newcomers the "true" story behind the failure of the assault of May 27th.

The operation had been disastrous, everyone agrees. When the attack began, the spirits of the Union troops had never been higher. They had overwhelming force and ample munitions and armament. They expected to end the day with a decisive military triumph. Alas, at day's end, their spirits had never been lower. The forces of each of the five generals who led advances had been soundly repulsed. Union casualties far exceeded those of the Rebels. The fortification stood unharmed on the bluff, mocking them with its invulnerability. Quite naturally, the search for scapegoats followed.

Controversy swirled around one engagement in the assault: the first battle in which negro troops in the Department of the Gulf had been engaged in combat. William was all too familiar with the conflicting opinions about whether men of color had the courage and skill to fight, particularly if they were led by a commander of color. Even in his own Fifty-second Regiment, especially in the officer corps, many doubted negroes could be relied on in battle. They sought to limit black troops to fatigue duty and manual labor in support of white fighters.

The negro troops themselves made their wishes clear. They wanted to serve to earn respect and the postwar rights and privileges of any soldier. Question of the day: did the conduct of the Native Guards in the assault of May 27th prove their detractors wrong?

First reports enthusiastically answered the question in the affirmative. General Banks himself extolled the bravery of the Native Guards in letters home and official reports. The northern press went wild in praise. Clearly, there was some exaggeration. One account gave detailed plaudits for a unit on duty at Ship Island at the time!

Disparagement of the conduct of the Native Guard began almost immediately and seeped into the conversations like river water through a leak in a levee. General Grover's duty guard told William the negro troops weren't all that good. Others claimed they personally saw two of them panic and run. He heard the familiar refrain: *I was there, so I should know.*

Not necessarily! In the fluid confusion of battle, no one can see it all.

One of General Weitzel's officers gave William a blatantly impossible assessment of the engagement: the cowardice of the Native Guard was the reason the assaults of *all five generals* failed! He offered as evidence that at one point, the first Native Guard unit fell back. General Banks backed off from his initial over-the-top praise.

Casualties in the assault had been heavy. General Banks did not treat the Native Guard survivors as the heroes he first claimed they had been, nor did he order a truce to retrieve their dead. The black bodies were left in the sun to rot. One of those bodies was that of Captain André Cailloux, a member of a prominent free black family in New Orleans who led the First Regiment of the Louisiana Native Guard.

A sergeant who was present at Captain Cailloux's advance told William that the captain was a true hero who had been sorely used by Brigadier General Dwight.

William listened with care to all the explanations for the defeat of the assault. He wanted to remember so he could discuss them with Nathaniel when he came back from the General's headquarters.

~~~

"I wish you could have seen the Ryder place," Nathaniel said when he and Col. Greenleaf returned from reporting to General Banks. "A negro groom took our horses. He directed us down a long hall to what must have been the dining room of the plantation. Three massive bouquets of fresh garden flowers sat on an embroidered runner down the center of a comically extended banquet table. The twenty chairs had matching cushions. Can you imagine an embroidered garden scene on a dining table in an army headquarters? General Banks leaned back in the one chair with arms, chewing on a cigar. Our privates in attendance on the General wore clean, intact Union uniforms. Except for privates, the scene looked a hell of lot like it must have in the high days of the Ryder Plantation!"

William shook his head. "General Banks slips easily into the life of the privileged. He probably wouldn't have answered the privates if they'd addressed him as *Massa Banks!*"

"Right. I learned nothing of a new assault Col. Greenleaf hadn't already told us, but I did pick up something of interest. I asked the groom who brought back my horse if there were any negro soldiers, other than the Native Guards, stationed at Port Hudson. He said there were members of the Corps d'Afrique attached to the Fifty-fourth

Massachusetts Infantry."

"What? The Fifty-fourth Massachusetts? I'll be damned. Blind hog found another acorn, as the Chaplain would say. The Fifty-fourth Massachusetts is under the command of General Grover. He's our neighbor, camped right on the other side of General Weitzel. We had no way to trace our friends since we didn't even know their new names, but JeanLouis and Alphonse may have fallen right into our hands. I'll find a free hour to see if I can find them."

"I'll come with you if I can manage," said Nathaniel.

Col. Greenleaf assembled the company commanders and read the new orders they had just received from General Banks.

Relying on more "information and experience" and the advice of newly arrived siege experts sent from Washington, General Banks ordered every regiment to prepare for a new assault using a double strategy. They would continue the siege but at the same time plan and execute an assault designed to take advantage of the opportunities presented by the unusual terrain around the fortifications. Adjustments to that terrain would begin the following morning.

"The siege experts will instruct our troops in the process of deepening the ravines between here and the fortifications," the Colonel reported. "When each ravine is complete, we will physically move into it. Staging through the ravines and smaller, connecting tunnels, we will get closer and closer to the fortifications. Meanwhile, no supplies will be permitted to reach the Rebel stronghold—no food, no fresh water, no medicine, no armaments. Sooner rather than later, we will launch another assault."

Everyone responded, "Yes, sir!"

When William and Nathaniel returned to their tent a short time later, William exploded into a rant.

"Damn it! Another assault, even though the previous one failed? I'm more anxious than anybody to get the Rebels turned out of Port Hudson so we can go home. I don't know the casualty count from May 27th, but I hear there was a steady stream of wounded men going to the hospital set up back on the railroad. I've heard the Union ended up with three to four times as many casualties as the Rebels. I'm thankful we weren't here. How many casualties will it take if we fail again—or even if we succeed? And what's the point?"

William took a couple of deep breaths and continued. "Deserters have reported that fevers and various other sicknesses are rampant inside the fortification. They are slaughtering and roasting their own animals. Did you know mule tastes better than horse? Those poor devils know it now—if they're lucky. How about roasted rat? Ever eaten that? Things are getting worse every day. The defenders cannot last long. Since they grabbed the supplies from our storehouse at Springfield Landing three weeks ago, they've received no shipments of food—none. We've taken possession of their mill on Cemetery Hill, so they cannot produce flour to make bread. All we could do is just wait."

"Nathaniel, do you honestly think siege and assault can be done at the same time? How can we wait and not wait? Don't you think we're more likely to have success if we choose one strategy rather than dissipate our strength on two at the same time?"

"The strategy is not for me to determine. Maybe one day…"

William would not stop his tirade.

"What's the point of risking lives on another assault? General Banks knows the price. He's having Col. Greenleaf construct an extension to the cemetery behind the encampments. How's that for optimism? We may have twice as many men serving with us as the Rebels, but that doesn't mean General Banks should send them out to die. Why? Tell me why?"

Nathaniel hung his head. "Politics. Politics determines strategy in this army."

William snapped up his head. "What? What's politics got to do with it?"

"Everything."

"How is that?"

Nathaniel spoke with the reluctance of a father explaining to his son one of life's hard lessons, right up there with the fact there is no Santa Claus and life isn't always fair.

"When the Union controls the Mississippi River, the Confederacy will be cut in two. Our ships will run freely from the north to New Orleans. We will then prevent any Rebel presence below the Red River from receiving supplies from the west. The wavering border states will forget about seceding to keep their slaves. The Confederacy will collapse. The commander who brings about that outcome will be a hero. Do you agree?"

"Yes, yes. Of course. We've all known that since we came south."

Nathaniel continued. "Two fortifications stand in the way: Vicksburg and Port Hudson. General Grant is assigned to bring down Vicksburg; General Banks is assigned to occupy Port Hudson. When one fortification falls, the other will receive the full fury of two armies and will fall as well. The war will come to an end. Do you agree with that prediction?"

"Sure, sure. Of course."

"Each general wants to achieve his mission first."

"Why does one have to be the one to succeed first?"

"Ah! There's the key to the strategy. To ride his military victory to political success."

"What are you saying?"

"As savior of the Union, the man who captures his goal first will be a hero—and ride that status to be elected the next President of the United States."

William staggered as if his best friend had delivered the statement with a blow to the gut.

"What? What are you saying? Are you telling me each one will base a decision that means life or death for so many on the effect it will have on his political career?"

"Yes, I am."

"Damn! And President Lincoln will allow that to happen?"

"Our President does not make military decisions. He hires and fires but lets his proud generals duke it out."

"Damn, again!"

"Are you so sure?"

"Here's my proof. General Grant refuses to help General Banks take Port Hudson. General Banks will not help General Grant at Vicksburg. The President is silent. I rest my case."

William squeezed his eyes shut. He took long, deep breaths. A minute passed before he spoke. His voice cracked.

"Nat, are you really going to sign up for another nine months? Haven't you had enough of this madness?"

"I believe one day I can make a difference, Will. To do so, I need the credibility I will earn for having served. Think of the variety of strategies we have seen! Meanwhile, I will do my duty to obey the orders of my superiors." Will was silent for a few minutes. Then he sighed.

"And I will do mine. I was convinced before that preserving the Union was worth the sacrifice. Now, we've added the end of slavery as the goal of our effort. That goal is also worth sacrifice. I pray the sacrifice is not our lives. I don't know how the powers will work out all the problems of emancipation, but our President will lead that cause, and you will be there to help him, Nat." William clasped his lifelong friend around the shoulders. "You're a better man than I am, Nathaniel. I've always known that to be true. May we both survive to see this phase through."

~~~

Two days later, William and Nathaniel found a free hour to see if JeanLouis could be at General Grover's encampment. They checked in with the guard on duty.

"We have two members of the Corps d'Afrique cooking for us," the guard responded to their inquiry. "The others are out on work detail. Our mess is way back there, beyond the tents, at the edge of the woods. A couple of cooks are fixing dinner right now. I'll take you to them. I can't help you with talking to them. The Frenchies don't speak much English, but they sure can cook! Stale beans taste great with seasoning and cured pork. We eat much better since they came."

"Not to worry. We know we can talk with them if they're the ones we're looking for."

The guard led them through the camp. They passed into a clearing in the rear. Next to the woods, a black man with grizzled hair wearing an apron perched on a high stool slowly stirred a pot over a low flame.

"Wow! Looks like JeanLouis to me!" Nathaniel exclaimed as they emerged from the area of the tents.

They walked across the open space and saw a younger black man expertly chopping vegetables on a table to the side. The lieutenants heard chatter in French as they approached. Sweat beaded up on both ebony faces. Onion tears dripped from the eyes of the younger man. At the sight of them, the older cook stood up and smiled widely. He slapped his thigh with his free hand.

"*Mais, coupe mon cou! Bonjour Lieutenant Guillaume et ton ami. C'est moi, JeanLouis.*"

"Cut my neck? I never heard that expression back home." William rolled back on his heels and laughed.

"You can teach your Pierre something new. I can't believe you found me, Lieutenants."

"And I can't believe we found you. We left Brashear City without even knowing if you had a new name. We just now heard there were men in the Corps d'Afrique attached to General Grover. We camp close by."

"They're calling us the Colored Infantry now. *C'est dommage.* I kind of liked being Corps d'Afrique." JeanLouis introduced his friend. *"Mon ami,* Bernard. He speaks English too."

"You're very good with that knife, Bernard. I bet you can do more with it than chopping vegetables," said William. Bernard started a shy smile.

"JeanLouis teach me English," he said. He let his smile open to display a pirate's chest of ivory doubloons. "Now, he teach me cooking. Chop onions, green pepper, and celery—*on dit La Trinité de la Cuisine.*"

Nathaniel raised his chin and sniffed. "I'm catching the aroma of browning flour. Now, you're teaching your friend how to make a roux! I wish I could stick around for the finished product. Chicken stew? Maybe a gumbo? We haven't had food that began with a roux since we left the bayou country."

"Smothered chicken. I wish I could show proper respect and stop stirring while we talk, but you know I can't do that. The roux would burn." JeanLouis looked over the edge of the pot and frowned. "You'll need another hour to get the good color."

"So, JeanLouis, did you get to pick your new last name?" William asked.

JeanLouis' complexion turned a shade darker, if that were possible. *"Mais, non.* They give me one. Just the one I didn't want!"

"Not Broussard!"

"Oui. Je m'appelle John Broussard."

He told the story William and Nathaniel had heard before. When the recruiter at Brashear City asked for his second name, JeanLouis said he didn't have one. The recruiter asked the name of his master.

"I had to tell him. He said that's my name now. I said no. My name is JeanLouis. Not anymore, the Yankee said. Now you're John Broussard."

"How about Alphonse? Is he here, too?"

"Oui, Lieutenant. He's here. He works on the bridges. His second name is Wiley. He came from the Walet farm, but the recruiter didn't hear it right."

JeanLouis told them the Union kept their deal. He's cooking, and he has extra work helping with the French speakers. His wife is getting her allotment. His English got a lot better.

"It certainly has," said Nathaniel. "I understand everything you say in English or French."

"See," JeanLouis said, pointing proudly at his feet. "I still got them

Rebel boots you found me. They're better than the boots they gave me with the uniform. Now, Bernard asked the quartermaster to get him a pair."

"Tell me about your son Louis," William asked.

"Louis went back to the plantation, but he didn't stay. The master wanted both him and Maman to come work for wages, but he wasn't going to pay them by the week or even by the month. Only if Louis stayed through grinding and managed the crew to the master's *satisfaction* would they get their pay. And there would be deducts for food and use of a cabin. He said then he'd give Louis some land to work on shares."

"Louis didn't like that?"

"Too many ways a master could wiggle out. Louis heard that was happening to sugar workers all over. And the Union army was trying to hire him to run plantations for their carpet bagger friends. He won't do that either."

William kept quiet.

Bernard got into the conversation. "Land is going for cheap now, especially what needs some draining. Several of us who served want to find land together. There's some available near what they call the *Marais*."

"I bet you have to drain any land called *un Marais,* a swamp."

"So, where's Louis now?" William asked.

"Louis makes out okay doing odd jobs in New Orleans, but his mind stays fixed on gettin' his own land. He thinks in another month he might have a better offer of work, get real wages, and be able to save money. Getting help for the cane season isn't easy for planters. They know Louis can do the work and manage men to work for him."

JeanLouis scowled. "But first, he's got to get Maman out of Brashear City. It's not good for her there."

"Really? You said she's getting her check."

"She's getting it—after a few weeks delay. But she's not safe in that place, Lieutenant."

"Really? They told us they were all set up for the refugees," said William.

"Harrumph! The Union soldiers were *all set up for the refugees,* all right—waiting for the young and pretty ones," said JeanLouis. "Bad things happen. It's a dreadful place for the old ones, too." Again, JeanLouis had a dark face. "Maman had a friend die, and they just tossed her body in an open pit back of the lake."

William shook his head. "I hear General Mouton and the Rebels are headed back there."

"Louis thinks he can get Maman to New Orleans next week." He shook the topic out of his head. "But tell me, Lieutenant, you've got *un bébé?*"

"Not yet. My wife is past due. You'd have heard already if I had!"

JeanLouis had a scowl again when they said goodbye. He had a warning for William and Nathaniel.

"*Bonne chance, mes amis. La fortification, c'est formidable.* How you say that in English? It's a real bitch!"

William sputtered out laughter. "Shame on you, JeanLouis. I didn't teach you words like that!"

They shook hands all around—the first time Nathaniel had ever shaken the hand of a man of color. Walking back, William said there was no way JeanLouis, and his family should be someone's property.

"I know all slaves aren't like them. But who knows what they all could be? Slavery is just plain wrong."

The area of Union encampments filled up with even more resources. New regiments arrived. Additional field guns rolled in daily. More Union warships found berth across the river from the fortified bluff. Training by the Union forces continued non-stop. Col. Greenleaf told them the same activity took place upriver at Vicksburg.

CHAPTER SIXTEEN

Nathaniel barely kept his footing when the siege experts sent by General Banks delivered the new assignments for the Fifty-second Regiment. General Banks appointed Col. Greenleaf to be General of the Trenches, commander of the project to refashion and extend the ravines on the north approach to Port Hudson. The next assault was to be launched from the protection of these ravines. General Banks ordered Col. Greenleaf to select three companies of the Fifty-second Regiment for initial training by the General's experts. Nathaniel's company would be one of the three. They, in turn, would train the next cohort, who would train the next.

"Colonel, sir," said Nathaniel. "I hope General Banks doesn't think we know anything about earthworks. We do not. What we saw on the south side of the fort was completed well before we arrived. And those traps are not a good model. They were constructed to prevent assaults on the fortifications. Our goal will be the reverse: to facilitate forward movement, not defense."

Col. Greenleaf answered. "General Banks has great faith in your abilities and in mine, Lieutenant Bradford."

"As to me, more faith than understanding, I fear."

Earthwork training began the following morning. The siege experts introduced themselves and explained they were going to train everyone in the process of deepening and extending the natural ravines into safe passageways. They would begin by training a small number of men, then *each one teach one* would be the plan.

The men were incredulous when the siege experts described what lay ahead. They peppered their trainers with questions.

"Are you saying we're going to live in the ravines day and night as we *refashion* them? Day and night? We will never stand up straight?"

"Only when it's dark. We will train a special crew to supply everything you will need."

"How long are we going to exist like moles in their holes?"

"As long as necessary to get to the area ready to make a full-scale attack."

"Straight through? Without a break?"

"If necessary, yes."

"And we will launch an attack lying on our bellies?"

"The conditions for the attacks will depend on what the terrain for the assault requires. We will not have the plan until we know exactly where to launch. Exigencies of the moment will determine."

The training team first tackled the existing ravines within approximately thirty yards of the Union encampments. They brought in negroes for the heavy digging. The siege experts trained both the soldiers of the first three companies and the negroes in the laborious process. They piled up the extracted dirt to raise the sides of the cuts. They trained the companies in how to train others—and pitch in where needed.

The following day, the advisors extended the training field farther away from home base and worked on connecting one ravine to the next. They called the connectors "saps." Most importantly, everyone received extensive instruction in accomplishing all the tasks of the project while keeping themselves low in the cuts and unexposed to the sightlines of crack-shot Rebel sharpshooters who might be watching from heights: tall trees and the fortifications themselves.

When the trainers believed an area of ravines had been refashioned to their satisfaction, and the original three companies were sufficiently trained in the process, they moved on to another area. The trainers chose those members of the first team they felt were the best teachers and sent them to other companies as well. When all the men in a cohort had been trained in the process, they took on another cohort, leaving the first on their own with only occasional guidance: *each one teach one* until they would all know how to reach a safe point from which to launch the next assault on the fortifications on the bluff.

The original companies were reconstituted in less than two weeks. The trainers withdrew, and the training morphed into the duty of doing the job of extending and linking the ravines with trenches—tough work.

Later on, every man in the regiment pronounced what they endured during trench duty to have been the worst conditions of their entire military service, harder than the non-stop nausea of the Atlantic storms on the high seas, worse than the incredible rain and muddy slog from Port Hudson back to Baton Rouge, even worse than climbing on the bloody fallen at Irish Bend to look into the eyes of the Rebels as they sent them deadly fire. Crouched underground, with a few hired negroes to do the heaviest work, they dug passages all day long, hollowing out the ravines and creating connector saps six feet wide and six to eight feet deep. One of the most dedicated workers was Pvt. Harbor. Col. Greenleaf had taken him off discipline for his failure to handle the battle at Irish Bend, and he was determined to make the Colonel glad he had done so.

Not everyone in the Fifty-second Regiment accomplished the work safely. Every few nights, a lad went back to base camp on a stretcher.

The men created tents with their rubber blankets to protect themselves from the heat and brutal sun during the day. Unless rain actually fell, the blankets went under their bodies at night as a barrier against seeping dampness. Dig anywhere in Louisiana, and you hit water. In addition to old acquaintances, they met some new Louisiana residents—snapping beetles. The men stuffed their ear canals with cotton to keep the bugs from making cozy, night-time beds inside.

"My God, I believe there are millions more bugs than people living in the State of Louisiana."

Their meals, such as they were, came in, and their waste went out after dark. They had only stale water to drink.

Often the diggers encountered something truly foul, like an area once used to dump dead animals or detritus from a prior occupation. They gagged on the odor of each other and what they dug into. William was only half serious when he had asked the trainer the better course to follow: to throw up in place and bury the product or attempt to crawl back to a spot designated for such waste and risk not making it in time. Or worse, lifting a head a few inches too high. No matter what the men experienced, they were never to let any task cause them to expose an inch of themselves or each other to a Rebel sharpshooter.

Nathaniel commended William on the return of his energy.

"You seem to be throwing aside your malaise with every shovelful of dirt. Your spunk is back."

"I noticed the same. Apparently, what I have a hard time handling is idleness. When I have a specific project, I can launch myself into doing what I must—and maintain the belief that someone more experienced than I am knows the purpose of it all."

"Now, that's a soldier!" said Nat.

Gradually, the reformed tunnels made a tighter and tighter ring around the fortifications.

One afternoon, a private working in a ravine not fifteen feet away from Company D lost concentration, yawned, and stretched out his back. He failed to notice a sharpshooter perched in a tall tree way up and to his right raise his rifle and take aim. William saw the sharpshooter and spread the alarm to his men to take cover. They dove to safety in the depths of the ravine. The unfortunate private in the neighboring ravine did not. A bullet blew his head apart. William used the last of the day's allotment of water to wipe the private's brain matter from his face. That night, the dinner crew carried a headless body out with the dinner plates. Back at base camp, the Chaplain performed another burial service in the new cemetery. They didn't have all the body to put into the grave.

For the most part, the men acclimated to their duty. Not all of them. One night, William stayed up with a Corporal who lay on his blanket unable to control his shaking. Fear or fever? Either was a problem. Almost dawn, William crawled to find Nathaniel asleep in another cut. He asked permission to send the poor lad back to Doc Sawyer. Nathaniel agreed. Once a man cracked, it was better to put him in the hospital than risk a weak section in an advancing force. They couldn't keep anyone on duty who hadn't made a special chamber in his brain to lock the horrors of war.

During this period there were no major battles. General Banks ordered minor skirmishes, and Rebel snipers continued to take a toll along the arc of the Union positions. From the parapets and tall trees, they took deadly aim at any part of a Yankee body that showed itself above the sides of the saps. The Union troops fashioned cotton barriers at the head of the trenches to gain a few additional inches of protection for the forward digging teams.

One afternoon, a young private saw an opportunity to breach a strip of ground and connect the burrow of D Company to a natural trench closer to the fortifications. He raised his head a few inches as he crawled forward. William spotted a Rebel sharpshooter on a high bluff moving into a position to take aim. William called to Nathaniel that he was going out to pull the private to safety. Nathaniel ordered William to halt. William called out that he had plenty time to get the lad; the sniper had to cross a ravine to reach a position from which to fire. Nathaniel repeated his order. William argued against the order again.

Nathaniel scrambled along the base of the trench to reach William just before he moved out in pursuit of the lad. Nathaniel grabbed William's boot and pulled him down into the trench. He wrapped his arms around his friend and struggled until he could pin him in the bottom of the trench. After a few moments that seemed an eternity, Nathaniel loosened his hold on William. Nat crawled out quickly, grabbed the lad's ankle, and pulled him to safety just in time.

William's face had turned scarlet with rage.

"Damn it, Nathaniel. It was safe when I first went out there to get the kid. It was not safe when you went. The delay could have been fatal for both of you. I could not live with myself If you'd been picked off."

Nathaniel steamed as well. "You disobeyed my direct order, William. I'd never have forgiven myself if Elizabeth's baby had no father."

When he cooled down, William wrote Elizabeth that if Nat gave them permission to do so, they could do no better than name their baby after their brave friend. William still had concerns Nathaniel might one day want the name for a son of his own. He put off asking Nathaniel for permission, but he would do so once the baby arrived—if the baby were a boy. The birth should be soon.

The Union continued to receive reports from Rebel deserters that General Gardner's force had but a few days' supply of corn meal and that malaria and dysentery ran rampant. General Banks sent General Gardner a demand for capitulation. *I desire to avoid unnecessary deaths,* he wrote. General Gardner refused to give up. His return note read: *My duty requires me to defend this position, and therefore I decline to surrender."*

~~~

"Nevertheless, I sense a change," Nathaniel said two days later. "The Rebels are firing the canons less frequently. They might be running short of powder or conserving ammunition because they think an assault is imminent."

"Col. Greenleaf must have had a similar thought. He sent the negro support workers back to base camp. I bet the Rebels who still have strength are watching us dig closer with trepidation," Nat observed.

On June 13th, General Banks issued a general order for another grand assault. Generals Augur, Weitzel, and Dwight were each ordered to attack the following morning as early as possible. Nathaniel drew Col. Greenleaf aside and spoke up more boldly than he usually did.

"Sir, *as early as possible?* Perhaps I have no right to comment on our strategy. I was not here on May 27th, but it appears to me a major reason the Rebel defense was successful that day was because our attacks were not launched simultaneously. The Rebels cannot defend every point at once. They have to move their men and cannons from one location to another to meet the Union threats. Couldn't the order be more precise as to time to give them that problem?"

"I'm ahead of you on this one. I discussed with General Banks the advantage of more precision. General Banks believes we don't have the ability to communicate between separated forces. Everyone has ears to hear. He said he informed his generals that when any one of them heard the sound of an attack, the other two should respond and attack also. He declined to change the wording of his original order. End of discussion."

[1]Early on the morning of June 12th, the Fifty-second Regiment assembled battle-ready with the forces of General Godfrey Weitzel. They tied branches to themselves to be less visible. Before dawn, when snipers would have the hardest time taking a bead on their targets, they began moving forward. The Fifty-second Regiment entered the ravines on the farthest right. The main body of Wetzel's command occupied the ravines immediately to their left. As the sky lightened, William and Nathaniel looked at each other and exchanged a thumbs up. They all dropped down into the tunnels and began to crawl.

"It sure feels different to be down here with a rifle and not a shovel," William whispered. "I'm grateful for every inch of dirt we dug out."

Midmorning, Col. Greenleaf passed a new order to his regiment. "We will detach from General Weitzel's assaulting force and move to flank his right column. When the General begins the assault, we stay and cover General Weitzel. Then follow me."

Col. Greenleaf led the regiment out of the trenches. When the men started to fall into their usual marching order, he commanded a full march to the right. He led them in a sharp turn up a wooded hill to a high, partially cleared terraced field. Once there, he summoned the men of three companies, including Company D, to turn left and advance head-on to the fortification. The larger body of men remained in the field.

The startled Rebels in the fortification reacted slowly to the approach of the three companies, but react they did. "Serpentine! Serpentine!" Col. Greenleaf commanded as bullets whirred over their heads like wasps in

---

[1] For encampments of generals at Port Hudson, see map on page 171.

springtime.

Next to William, two men fell. "Advance! Maintain the advance!" the Colonel commanded. "We will get the men tonight." William forced himself to obey.

The attackers did not slacken the pace until each one struck the rise of the ground at the fortified bluff. Col. Greenleaf and Nathaniel dropped their rifles, pulled out their pistols, and aimed to pick off the defenders on the parapets above them. Everyone did the same. In a few minutes, Rebel fire from the north rampart went silent. The pounding in William's chest slowed.

~~~

Down below and to the left, the sound of the exchange of fire between General Weitzel's assaulting team and the fortification diminished around noon. Col. Greenleaf sent a scout to determine the status of General Weitzel's assault. He returned with a report that General Weitzel had withdrawn his men in the face of withering fire. They were now digging rifle pits, rolling up logs, and otherwise protecting themselves from further losses.

Night came. Not knowing the fate of the others, everyone stayed in place. The forward companies and Col. Greenleaf remained beneath the bluff. The remainder on the terrace found what shelter they could among the disorder of the stumps and tangled brush on the high field. Under cover of darkness, they sent medics to retrieve the officer and two men who were casualties of the dash to the bluff.

In the early morning, the adjutant-general arrived from General Weitzel with new orders. The forward companies under the bluff, spelled as needed by replacements from the men remaining in the field of felled trees, were to hold their position beneath the fortifications. General Weitzel ordered Col. Greenleaf to move the "headquarters" of the Fifty-second Regiment farther to the rear of the high terrace, sheltered by the felled trees and brush. From there, communication with home base could be maintained without threat to life and limb. In truth, the "headquarters" of the regiment consisted of nothing but the Colonel himself!

Wagons came to the field from home base with supplies to set up camp. They reestablished meal service from the mess. By the end of the day, Col. Greenleaf had "settled in" both portions of his command.

Word passed that all three Union generals in the main assault had been repulsed with loss of over a thousand fighting men.

William found Nathaniel. They embraced.

"There's got to be a word for refining a strategy that already failed and expecting a different result," William observed.

"There is, and you know the word."

General Banks had few takers when he called for volunteers to make a new assault on Port Hudson the following day. The Native Guards volunteered, but he turned them down.

Inexplicably, General Banks delayed asking for a truce to retrieve the wounded and bury those who died in the assault. Bodies lay in the sun for three days—until the Rebels, who could no longer stand the odor, asked for a truce themselves. They helped deliver bodies to the Union base camp under a white flag of truce. Horses were not buried but left where they fell. The putrid odor of the battlefield increased.

General Banks planned yet another assault; he ordered trench living to continue, adding to the misery from the summer heat. William and Nathaniel were grateful to be on the foreword detail beneath the bluff.

"Not the finest accommodations, but I'll take them over the trenches any time," said Nathaniel.

"Ditto. I'm getting accustomed to dining by moonlight."

~~~

On July 3rd, Col. Greenleaf received a message for William that his wife had safely delivered a fine baby boy. Mother and child were well. With the Colonel's blessing, Nathaniel left the forward station in the woods and returned to base camp. He visited the encampment of every general in search of a celebratory beverage for his friend. He struck gold at the camp of General Dwight. The General invited Nathaniel to come with him to visit his full bar.

"Take a whole bottle, two if you'd like," said General Dwight. Give Lieutenant Wells my congratulations."

Nathaniel got back to his unit before dawn. He vowed never to say another disparaging word about General Dwight.

CHAPTER SEVENTEEN

Nathaniel returned from a meeting at Col. Greenleaf's tent and shared with William a rumor: Vicksburg had surrendered to General Grant on the 4th of July.

"Col. Greenleaf made clear that he had no official notice; no one should pass on the rumor. All prior orders were to remain in place until official notification of change."

"A good plan. General Gardner is going to have to face reality, and he will, but we don't want one more accidental casualty. There'll be a few Rebels who either don't get the word or choose to ignore it."

"William, I'm leaving you in charge of the foreword group under the fortification. I'm going back to headquarters. We won't return to base camp until we receive an order to do so."

"Someone else is going to have to face reality," said William. "General Banks can kiss his dreams of another assault goodbye—and a few other dreams as well."

Early on the morning of the 7th of July, a Union gunboat arrived from upriver, bringing confirmation of the report of Grant's victory three days before. A gunboat in Admiral Farragut's fleet moored below the fortifications received the news first. For some unknown reason, his signal system to Union headquarters at base camp did not function. A member of General Grant's staff did not reach General Banks until noon. Banks wrote a note with the news and had it delivered to Col. Greenleaf in his capacity as General of the Trenches. He added instructions to Col. Greenleaf. "Find a stone; if there is no stone, find a clod of clay. Wrap the note securely around the stone and toss it into the fortification."

Col. Greenleaf kept the confidence requested, but like the first cool breeze after a hot summer, the good news spread on the smiles from one trench to another without the need for a single spoken word. A scout

brought the news to the forces on the high terrace. They passed it on with
real words to the forward companies under the fortification. By mid-
afternoon, the location of every Union force hummed with patriotic
music and flew the Union colors.

Within the fortification, General Gardner attempted to keep the news
secret until he could receive verification from Vicksburg. He wanted the
status quo until the unconditional surrender became official. Alas, such
news could not be contained by either party. The Rebels saw the flags
and heard the song. They absorbed the news with incredulity, denial, and
then acceptance. By nightfall, the sentiment of most in Confederate gray
accepted the relief the ordeal had ended.

That evening, General Gardner gathered his commanders. Shortly
after midnight a messenger with a small escort, bearing a lantern on a
long pole with a white handkerchief hanging beneath to serve as a flag of
truce, reached Union headquarters at the Ryder farm. General Gardner
asked for verification of the report from Vicksburg and asked for a truce
to consider terms. General Banks responded with the few additional
details he could provide as verification but refused a truce. He demanded
unconditional surrender.

An hour later, General Gardner sent a new communication: *Having
defended this position as long as I deem my duty requires, I will surrender to you.*
He ordered a cessation of hostilities and requested a meeting of
representatives of both sides the following morning.

By 2:30 on the afternoon of July 8th, both General Banks and General
Gardner had signed the document entitled ARTICLES OF
CAPITULATION. Article IV set the time of 7:00 a.m. July 9 for Union
occupation of the fortifications of Port Hudson and receipt of its garrison
as prisoners of war. Only then did the Fifty-second Regiment receive an
official order to return to their encampment at the base—and another
reminder to steer clear of the woods.

Back at the encampment, William stayed up late writing a long letter
to Elizabeth and his week-old baby. Soon, my love, he wrote. We are in
line to leave for home.

~~~

While the Fifty-second Regiment was totally absorbed in the siege of
Port Hudson, Rebel General Richard Taylor recovered from being
chased to Opelousas after the battles of Bisland and Irish Bend. He came
back down the Bayou Teche, recaptured Brashear City, and headed east
to LaFourche. For months, General Banks had refused pleas from his

commanders in other parts of South Louisiana to share some of the close to 30,000 troops he had amassed for the capture of Port Hudson. Now, General Banks agreed to send help. General Weitzel and those in his command whose service time had not expired, departed for Donaldsonville to shore up the defenses of the Union position.

By any calculation, the nine-month commitment of the Fifty-second Regiment had expired, as had the terms of commitment of several other regiments. The Fifty-second continued to perform their duties without complaint. The reaction of many other forces ranged from grumbling to insubordination. As a result, the commanders selected the Fifty-second Regiment to receive the first available steamer going north as a reward for their commitment to the cause.

William sought out his friend Nathaniel.

"I know my first duty is to assist in the mission of our company, but if you could spare me for an hour, I'd like to go back to General Grover's encampment to see if JeanLouis is still there. I particularly want to know if Louis got his mother out of Brashear City before the Rebels arrived. And I want to say goodbye."

Nathaniel slapped his forehead. "The family totally slipped my mind."

"Mine too, until this morning. I don't know whether General Taylor took back Brashear City a month ago or just last week."

"We've had a few other concerns—like whether we'd live another twenty-four hours! I'll cover our assignments. Give JeanLouis and Bernard my best wishes."

William turned to look back at Nathaniel before he left the boundary of their encampment. When he did so, he saw Nathaniel looking at him. They waved at each other with the same thought. After over nine months, when their lives could have been extinguished at any moment, the possibility of being a casualty of the war had passed. Thanks be to God!

The departures thinned the encampments on the northern arm of the arc of Union forces. A few goats on long ropes enjoyed finishing off the cleanup of General Weitzel's encampment. There were not many tents left in General Grover's encampment either. They must have gone to occupy the fortification in the first wave. William asked the duty guard at the rump encampment about the cooks.

"They're still right here. We're keeping the mess down below for now." He wrinkled his nose and tossed his head in the direction of the heights. "It may be a while before the men want to eat food prepared up there. I sure don't. I'd rather go back to hard tack."

William found JeanLouis in his usual spot working next to a hot fire. They raised their arms in greeting to each other when they were still twenty feet apart.

"*Mon ami. Comment ça va?*"

"*Trés bien,* Lieutenant. I'm most happy to see you unharmed."

William explained to JeanLouis that their nine-month commitment had expired. They would leave for home whenever there was transportation available. "I hope that will be soon, so I wanted to check on you and your family before we left. Did Marie Adele get out of Brashear City?"

"*Mais, oui.* The Union moved all the contrabands out of Camp Ullman at Brashear City before the Rebels arrived. She is at a new camp outside of New Orleans. It is some better, and Louis can check on her often. He promises he can have her come to New Orleans in a matter of days."

"I worried she would be in Brashear City when the Rebels reoccupied the place."

"*Non.* Long gone."

"And Alphonse?"

"He's still down here. It was touch and go for a while when they were looking for strong backs to work at cleaning up the fortification, but it didn't take much to convince them cooking was more important than burning garbage. Right now, he's gathering some supplies General Weitzel left behind. *Mais, dites moi, Lieutenant Guillaume. Vous avez un bébé?*"

"I do! He's over a week old. He and Elizabeth are doing fine."

JeanLouis threw his head back. "*Felicitations! Un garçon!*" His smile was the broadest William had yet seen.

While they were visiting, an officer came to ask JeanLouis to help explain something to a few French-speaking former slaves who just arrived.

"*Bien sûr.* 'Do you want to send them to me, or should I come? I can leave my pots."

"I'll send them. They don't know what's going on. We've signed them up for the lessons."

"While you're here, sir, let me introduce Lieutenant William Wells. He's a friend of mine."

William asked the officer if he knew who the commander at Port

Hudson would be after the Union troops left. The officer said he heard Captain Franklin Nelson of the Fifty-second Regiment, Massachusetts Volunteers, was going to sign up again, get a promotion to colonel, and be in charge.

"Wow! That's very good news, JeanLouis. Not my company, but he's from my part of Massachusetts. I'll be able to keep in touch with your family and know how you're getting along."

"And I'll hear about your *bébé*. What name have you given him?"

"None yet. Elizabeth says she can wait until I get home. Maybe—. No, I better not say."

William looked up at the woods.

"When the goats are finished cleaning up the campsite, *mon ami*, you should ask your commander to let you move back to where the tents were. As I told my company, we're in the Rebels' corral. Port Hudson has surrendered, but the war isn't over. Keep watch and be careful. *Au'voir, mes amis*. Nathaniel says the same."

~~~

When General Gardner surrendered Fort Hudson, the priority for General Banks had been to send in a supply of beef and hard tack to the fortification, welcome indeed for those who had been reduced to eating roasted rats, horses, and mules, but hard duty for the Union trench dwellers who had not seen decent meat in weeks. The return of the Rebels to South Louisiana had severed the Union supply route from New Orleans. During the past two weeks, the rations for the Union men had been worse than at any time before. Sickness and deaths had increased. In fact, if transportation home was long delayed, Doc Sawyer feared many men of the Fifty-second Regiment would not live to see New England skies.

The second occupation priority for General Banks was to service the Rebel officers who were to be paroled, highest ranking officers first. The Union set up tents on the bluff, moved the officers in, and supplied them with rations. William didn't like the assignment.

"You mean we've got to send them what we haven't had for ourselves?"

"Those are the rules of war. The victorious do without to feed the vanquished—officers, that is. Ships to take them away are arriving daily. They'll be gone soon.

"Good riddance."

"We've got a shipment of food coming from Springfield Landing.

That should help us." And it did.

The Fifty-second Regiment entered the fortification with the second wave three days after the surrender. They cleared out the garrison and proceeded to organize for departure the Rebels without rank. Although the Fifty-second Regiment was late to the site, they did not avoid what they would forever call "the stench of the siege of Port Hudson." They pitched their tents on the grounds, trying to get as far as they could from the main structures and catch every fresh breeze.

General Gardner warned them the fortification was full of disease. Malaria was the worst illness and the most transmissible. A good number suffered from fevers neither Rebel nor Union doctors could identify.

"A lot of people lived up here during the Forty-nine days of the siege. Whatever do you think they did with their waste? For that matter, a lot died. After we cut off their communication with the outside world, what did they do with the bodies?" William asked.

"Look over that precipice. It's forty feet straight down to within one foot of the river. Thanks be to God for the current. Even realizing who and what went in there for the past few months, at day's end, I can't wait to join everyone else in the moving water. A rag and a bucket can't make any headway against the filth of my own body."

Hundreds of swimmers, Rebels and Feds, mostly naked, bobbed up and down in the river. They scrubbed their clothing before they put them back on. No one thought they could ever remove all trace of Port Hudson.

The Fifty-second Regiment placed the seriously sick Rebel prisoners on stretchers and littered them down to Union ships waiting to take them to hospitals in New Orleans. They helped the walking wounded maneuver their way to the exits. A pile of refuse burned day and night in the corner of the bluff. As each area of the fortifications emptied, the Union dismantled and burned not only the bedding but the wooden structures that had served as shelter. Only fire and relentless weather had a hope of ridding the heights of the evidence of the horrors that had occurred there.

The work let up a bit after the first week they had occupation of the bluff. They had a few afternoons off. Nathaniel, for one, was sorry to see General Dwight pull out his force. A few evenings, come five o'clock, he and William had joined General Dwight at his well-stocked bar.

"All the better that the other generals shun him as if he had malaria!"

William said.

The generals floated a plan for a celebration to mark the accomplishment of liberating the fortification. The men had no interest. Perhaps if the generals had made the same suggestion before they entered, the men might have approved. Too late. Now, they had no stomach to gloat over an enemy that had been eating rats and mules to forestall death from starvation.

CHAPTER EIGHTEEN

All ashore who're going ashore! We sail in fifteen minutes."
Captain Conner's cry on the megaphone struck William like
a body blow. He tightened his grip on the end poles of a
stretcher he helped carry up the ramp to the dock. A question
stunned his brain. Where is Nathaniel? William realized he
hadn't seen his good friend this morning.

William and Nathaniel spent the previous day with the sick and
wounded of the Fifty-second Regiment. In the morning, they supervised
Company D as the men under their command turned the largest and
most comfortable portion of the steamer *Chouteau* into a sickbay. At
noon, they accompanied Doc Sawyer and George Clark, the hospital
steward, on rounds of the patients in the building the Union had
appropriated for a hospital—the old railroad depot behind Port Hudson
the Rebels had used to store sugar and cotton. During the week before, a
steamer gathered all the convalescents of the Fifty-second Regiment who
were scattered in the hospitals in Baton Rouge and New Orleans to
determine if they were well enough to take the trip home.

Doc Sawyer decided which men of the Fifty-second Regiment were
now well enough to be transferred to the *Chocteau* for the trip north and
which had to remain in Louisiana for continued recovery before they
were strong enough for the trip.

During the heat of the afternoon, William and Nathaniel supervised
the transfer of the fortunate ones onto the *Chouteau*. William, Nathaniel,
Doc Sawyer, George Clark, and the Chaplain, who followed behind
them, gave words of encouragement to each patient. By the end of the
day, sweat beaded the dust on their lined faces.

Satisfied with a job well done, they parted company at dark.

Nathaniel said he'd see William at the dock in the morning, an hour before it was time to sail. Nathaniel said he had to clean up to meet with the generals at General Banks' headquarters at Ryder's Plantation to finalize plans for his re-enlistment.

The dock buzzed with activity when William arrived on the morning of the sailing day. A couple of dozen horses stomped and whinnied as Company C urged them onto the ramp of the steamer's deck. William felt a pang not to see his faithful mount Excalibur among them. Did he have second thoughts? Should he have accepted the quartermaster's offer to let him take his horse north? No. Excalibur had served him well. Why put him through the stress of the arduous trip by steamer and railway when the Wells farm had an ample supply of horses? Having a mount Pierre hadn't trained would probably hurt his ranch manager's feelings. And hurt Madeleine's feelings as well.

William paused to check on a few of the sickest members of his company. Then came another diversion; Doc Sawyer pressed William into offloading the body of an unfortunate private who had passed away on the steamship during the night.

Stunned at the call to sail in fifteen minutes, William ran through the steamer. "Had anyone seen Lt. Nathaniel Bradford?" he called. Negative. He found the ship's captain on the foredeck, still holding the megaphone.

"Captain, sir. I can't find Lt. Bradford. He said he'd meet me at the dock this morning. Something must have happened to him!"

"And?"

"I need to find him, sir."

"You heard my order, Lt. Wells. We sail at 0900 hours."

"Nathaniel would have told me if he weren't coming, sir. He had an appointment for a meeting with General Banks last night. Perhaps the meeting continued this morning."

"No, Lt. Wells. General Banks dismissed me at headquarters at 07:00 hours this morning. I know for a fact that no meeting was taking place then. You are aware, I am sure, that Lt. Bradford has been recommended for a commendation. He plans to re-enlist after a thirty-day leave. He probably decided to wait for a later ship going north."

"Perhaps, Captain, but I can be back in less than half an hour. I fear Lt. Bradford may have caught a fever from one of the men we handled yesterday."

Capt. Conner turned full-face to William. "And if he caught a fever, what can we do? The engineer says the boilers are primed and ready. You can disembark, but the *Chouteau* will not delay departure."

"Fifteen minutes at the most, Captain. I'll run the whole way there and back. I beg you, sir."

Captain Conner lowered his eyelids to half-mast. He took a deep breath and let the megaphone hang down from the strap on his wrist.

"I should not have to explain myself to you, Lieutenant, but I respect your service to the Union. Pressure in the boilers builds up while we are stationary. When the engineer says it is time to go, safety requires that we do so. That is the rule. There is a good reason for the rule. Explosions are not an uncommon event on these steamers."

"But Captain Conner, sir. Just fifteen minutes."

Captain Conner drew in a big breath and let it out again.

"Do you see the ship hanging out in the middle of the river? If we do not sail when the engineer signals us, our escort vessels will take that ship wherever they want to go. Your regiment earned the first up-river departure for never complaining about serving past the last day of their nine-month commitment. If you forfeit the preferential place for the regiment, ten days or more may pass before we obtain another escort of specially trained armed scouts. You jeopardize the advantage for some seven hundred men. A few more may pass away without ever again seeing New England skies and those they love."

"But—"

Captain Conner turned his back on Lt. Wells, raised his megaphone, and repeated his order for departure.

William sought out Col. Greenleaf. He pressed his case. The Colonel refused to intervene.

"We are no longer on land, Lt. Wells. On the water, the captain of the ship is in command."

The sidewheels creaked and came alive. Accompanied by wheezing blasts from the tall stacks, slow rotations began. William watched the crew loosen the mooring ropes and pull up the anchor. The passengers cheered. The *Chouteau* pulled away from the dock and steamed into the middle of the river to meet the gunboats.

The heat steaming in William's chest could have provided all the power the *Chouteau* would have needed to move.

The initial day on the steamer was not without other delays, the first within hours of leaving Port Hudson. Mid-afternoon Capt. Conner ordered the steamer to the east riverbank and drop anchor. Two of the escort ships pulled up behind, leaving the third on guard. Casually dressed armed scouts jumped to the shore and vanished into the thicket to check out a rumor of Rebels lurking in the vicinity. The war had ended for William. Not all Rebels felt the same. A Rebel might jump at the opportunity to strike a blow against the enemy from his own back woods. Those scouts are real soldiers, William thought. I'd be useless hunting rebels in the woods.

Capt. Conner spotted William on the starboard deck scanning the riverbank.

"Lt. Wells, don't even think about sending a courier back down to Port Hudson to look for Lt. Bradford. My orders are to deliver to the Union post at Cairo, Illinois, every man of the Fifty-second Regiment who is alive when we arrive there. From Cairo, those Doc Sawyer pronounces able to travel will continue to Massachusetts by railway. If you leave my ship any time before I complete my assignment, you face a charge of insubordination. The punishment for that offense is confinement at Ship Island until the end of the war. Now get yourself down into the river with everyone else, take a wash, and put out the fire in your belly."

Several more days passed before the sight of Captain Conner did not reignite that fire.

<center>~~~</center>

The following morning, Doc Sawyer's assistant, the hospital steward, found William to report that a company member had disappeared from sickbay.

"Disappeared? A person can't disappear on a ship. Who? Tell me!"

"Cpl. Hawkes, sir. His buddies report he was as usual last night. He made rounds, shaking the hands of his companions in arms. He spread his blanket on his pallet and settled down to sleep. This morning, the pallet lay empty. We have searched the entire vessel. The Corporal is nowhere on the ship."

"Impossible! Except perhaps—"

"It was a beautiful evening, sir. A sliver of a new moon hung in the western sky. The Corporal's companions surmised he woke in the night and took a walk on deck to enjoy the air. Depleted from fever and three weeks in the trenches, perhaps delirious as well, he could have missed his step in the dark and fallen overboard."

Already haunted by how he would explain to Nathaniel's father and Abigail how he could have left Port Hudson without Nathaniel. William made a vow. At the moment, he could do nothing for Nathaniel or Cpl. Hawkes, but he could do his best by those on the *Chouteau* still under his command. He resolved to monitor every company member for the rest of the journey. He asked Doc Sawyer if he had any suggestions for how he could help those in sickbay.

"I do have a suggestion, Lieutenant. When I volunteered for service, we received training in amputation and wound care. What I needed most for this assignment was instruction in treating fevers, dysentery, and depression of spirit. I've learned quite a bit from the experience of the last nine months. We're having more recoveries now that we're on the water. Those with fever who lie closest to fresh air do better than those crammed into airless corners. Those with dysentery are doing better also. We have little fresh food, but we can provide a more healthful bland diet now that we have bread that isn't crawling with worms!"

"So, we're doing all we can?"

"To a point. The men are discouraged. They've watched many of their numbers sicken and pass away. Everybody needs family when times are tough. I believe you can help your company by sharing your companionship and facilitating their companionship with one another."

"I have been visiting…

"The men tell me so, and they appreciate your attention. I suggest you move all the men of your company to an area where the breeze reaches their pallets. Encourage them to visit with one another. Tell them if someone wants to take a walk, he must find another person to go with him."

William put the suggestion into practice.

~~~

The following day, the *Chouteau* pulled up to the dock at Vicksburg. While they took on supplies, Capt. Conner offered a few hours ashore for anyone interested in taking a tour of the fortification. Curious to compare Vicksburg with Port Hudson, William, and a half dozen others stepped forward. One who joined them was Captain Franklin Nelson from Greenfield.

"I'm surprised to see you on board, Capt. Nelson. Are you going home on leave before returning to take over the command at Port Hudson?"

"You haven't heard? I've changed my mind about signing up again. The mountain breezes of western Massachusetts are calling me home. Every day we waited for transportation diminished my enthusiasm for remaining any longer in the oven of the Louisiana summer. I don't believe Greenfield ever had one day as hot as every day we spent at Port Hudson."

"I'm sorry to hear you won't be the one in command there. Do you know who will be? I want to keep track of the French-speaking former slaves I befriended."

"I remember your interest. The command at Port Hudson is still under discussion. I've heard General Andrews is the leading contender, but there's some complication. I suggest you contact General Weitzel. He's taken an interest in the Colored Infantry, that's the new name of the Corps d'Afrique that will be headquartered there. I believe you told me the former slaves enlisted in that unit, one as a cook."

The exchange ended when a veteran of the Vicksburg siege came onto the dock and announced he would be their leader for the tour. He had the same tattered clothing and hollow eyes as William, Capt. Nelson, and the other veterans of the battle at Port Hudson who waited for his guide services.

Like Port Hudson, Vicksburg could be found at a sharp bend in the Mississippi River. But unlike Port Hudson, Vicksburg did not crown a high bluff. A thriving city before the war, Vicksburg was physically accessible from the river as well as from the surrounding plains. As General Ulysses S. Grant and his forces approached from the north, the civilian inhabitants of the city fled to the hills, leaving the buildings to be used as defensive shelters. Varying the timing, type, and location of his assaults, General Grant was able to exercise his strategic skills.

By contrast, the fortifications at Port Hudson crowned a bluff high above the river. Before the war, they did not support a significant civilian population. A honeycomb of crevasses and ravines created by centuries of changes in the course of the Mississippi River left access to the stronghold a challenge. The fortified heights were, therefore, inaccessible from the water and difficult to assault from land. Approaches were disguised.

Assaults on both strongholds failed. Both went under siege.

Union forces could keep supplies from reaching both strongholds. Both suffered dreadfully from deprivations, but three weeks living in the approaches to the fortifications on the high bluff of Port Hudson had been a deadly nightmare for the Union soldiers under General Banks, Commander of the Department of the Gulf. Little wonder Union losses were proportionately higher at Port Hudson than those at Vicksburg.

General Grant's forces broke into Vicksburg first.

The smell clinging to the walls of the Vicksburg fortifications and everything the guide described brought back memories William wanted to forget. He returned to the steamer anxious to turn the page on the siege experience. He had no desire to leave the ship again.

"Capt. Nelson, I have an invitation for you. You might care to join me on the upper starboard deck tonight after dark. Last night, I enjoyed a display of stars, a new moon, and the coolest breeze I've found on this steamer."

"As sweet as fresh air in the Berkshires?"

"Well, not quite. But close."

"I accept your offer."

~~~

William took two chairs out onto the upper deck and settled in one of them. He tipped up his chin and gaped at the display above him. Magnificent! He hadn't been enjoying the sight for many minutes when, to the accompaniment of gasps and grunts, Capt. Nelson's head poked up in the hatch.

"Damn! I'm barking my shins on every rung of this medieval instrument of torture."

"Easy does it, Captain. I know it feels like you're going to pitch off backward, but you won't. Just slow down until your feet trust what your mind is telling them to do. You'll get the hang of it. I promise you the view is worth the trouble. This night is even clearer than last."

Capt. Nelson stumbled out of the hole and straightened up.

"By God, it's black as pitch up here!"

"Head down and snuff out your candle, Captain—sir. We don't know who might be watching. You'll be able to see where you're going when your eyes get accustomed to the dark."

Franklin dropped onto the chair next to William.

"You're not a sailor, Lt. Wells. How did you learn to climb a ship's ladder?"

"In the barn, sir. My ranch manager Pierre and I have been scampering up to the hayloft and down again since we were toddlers."

"Maybe it would help if I were taller or younger."

Capt. Nelson settled in the chair with a deep sigh. When he raised his eyes to the sky, the display stunned him to silence. Within a minute, a soft purr accompanied each exhale.

"Worth the climb?" William whispered a question.

"Damn right. If my arms were just a little longer, I think I could touch those stars. The magic canopy looks no farther away from us than the ceiling of the capitol in Boston."

After a while, William heard a chuckle.

"What's amusing you, sir?" William asked.

"You know, probably since man first walked the earth, humans have gazed at the night sky with wonder. The Greeks and Romans made all those stars into Gods and Goddesses whose antics controlled the earthly world. I don't believe the stars have such powers, but there is something about star gazing that turns us all into philosophers."

"Agreed. I believe the thoughts I have up here are wise. Here's an example. It appears the moon is moving and not the earth. What lesson do I get from that observation? I learn that what you see with your own eyes is not necessarily true. What are you thinking, Captain?"

"The sky surrounds a whole earth full of people and maybe even life somewhere else. How can we think each one of us is so damn important?"

William laughed. "Right, Captain. The night sky puts us in our proper places."

They sat in silence.

Franklin Nelson spoke again next. "You seem to know Chaplain Moors well, Lt. Wells. May I call you William?"

"Please do. Or call me Will."

"And please call me Franklin or Frank. I think the Chaplain is wise— and not just star-gazing-wise. I made good use of the tip he gave us to keep up our spirits. He suggested that we review the events of the day every night and think of three circumstances to put on the plus side of the scale."

"He gave me the same technique. When I sank into despair about the brutality of battle, wanton looting, man's cruelty to other men, and just plain loneliness, the acts of bravery I saw gave me hope for us all. I concentrated on them.

Capt. Nelson sat up in his chair.

"Right now, I'm wrestling with a problem about which you and the Chaplain might have an opinion."

"And what is that?"

"I have a request from the Editor of the *Greenfield Gazette* to do some writing for the newspaper. I could tell you about it, but it's kind of complicated, and…

William's breathing slowed. He spoke the next words with unusual measure. "Let's get a professional on the job, Franklin. This is just the kind of personal issue the Chaplain likes to consider. I think I can tear him away from his nightly letter to his wife to join us." He hesitated. "There is one delicate issue, however. The climb!"

"I'll give him climbing lessons! No, I'm joking."

"It may be a tight squeeze fitting him through the hatch!"

Eventually, William and Captain Nelson were sleepy enough to go to bed. When each ran through the Chaplain's exercise of weighing the events of the day, both put their new companionship on the plus side of the scale.

CHAPTER NINETEEN

The Chaplain accepted William's invitation to join them for an evening visit on the top starboard deck. By the time the Chaplain stepped on the straight ladder's second rung in the hatch and his bald pate appeared in the opening, William knew they had a problem. The Chaplain's girth filled the entire space of the hatch! He twisted his back like a contortionist but still could not find a crack of space to peer down to his own feet groping for the next rung. "Hm-m," William said. "Let's see if I can help you. I was hoping that a dividend from the meager rations of the past months would have been the loss of a few inches of his girth."

William crawled over the deck and lay down on his stomach behind the Chaplain, who began to giggle. "Does anybody have a very large shoehorn? Or a boot hook?"

Using his imagination, William coached the Chaplain as best he could to where and when to place his feet. Eventually, laughter helped the Chaplain wiggle loose. William pulled him the last couple of feet and led him to the largest of the deck chairs they had on deck. William and Franklin promised him they would not tell anyone about the expletives that accompanied his ascent to the upper starboard deck of the *Chouteau*.

Before engaging in the contemplation of the eternal verities that stargazing seemed to inspire, Chaplain Moors threw out a question to William and Capt. Nelson.

"My friends, where are we anyway? Does anyone know?"

"I couldn't tell you," Capt. Nelson responded. "Still on the Mississippi River, of course, but both right and left banks have shown us nothing distinguishing since we pulled away from the dock at Vicksburg. There are so many twists in the river I am relieved each time the North

Star reappears and reassures me we're headed in the right direction."

"Now that I've recovered from the terror of the climb, I have an unusual occurrence to report to you, my friends. Maybe one of you will be able to explain it. Was anyone else awake at dawn this morning?"

A snort from Franklin Nelson. "Awake at dawn? Surely, you jest! Not I."

"Nor I," said William, punctuating his denial with a toss of his head to uncover his eyes from his long forelock, even longer now. "The food on this ship isn't going to restore any weight we've lost, but the sleeping is glorious. I'm taking full advantage."

"My dear young friends," said the Chaplain. "I envy you. Some day, you will find sound sleeping, like climbing ladders, is more difficult with each passing decade. William, you scamper up and down from one deck to another like one of those bushy-tailed squirrels we've seen so often over the past months. Franklin, you scamper also, although your scamper is not quite as quick. Me? I whack my shins on every rung on the ladders, and nothing happens in the night I don't know all about. I'm still surprised that young fella went overboard without my knowledge on our first night out of Port Hudson. You'd think for once I could have put my sleep issues to some good use and heard the splash. But I digress. I woke at dawn this morning when I sensed our ship had stopped moving."

"Nothing singular about that," said Franklin. "We probably pause at least once a day for our escorts to chase down a rumor of Rebel activity in the woods."

"This morning, the noises penetrating my mind fog seemed unusual. The sound of scraping, perhaps. I opened an eye and rose to peer through my porthole. I saw only pine trees. I sat up on my cot, looked straight down, and spied a gangplank protruding from our lowest deck. Glancing back to the shore, barely visible in the morning fog, I made out a narrow path cut through the thicket. Mooring ropes secured the gangplank to a couple of sturdy tree trunks. I saw no people."

Capt. Nelson raised his eyebrows. "If the mooring ropes were tied, someone made the knots, most likely a sailor."

"Good observation! But why?" the Chaplain asked. "I saw no buildings, no sign of human habitation. My cabinmate didn't break the rhythm of his snores. I let him sleep."

A guffaw from Capt. Nelson. "Your cabinmate is Col. Greenleaf, right? I'm thankful you didn't disturb him. I think there's something in the rule book that says you don't wake the commanding officer of the regiment unless you're confronting a matter of life or death."

"As the early morning fog lifted," Capt. Nelson continued, "I made out the figures of five negro men in ill-fitting cottonade work clothes coming down the path. Each one pushed a handcart of cut wood. Approximately four-foot lengths, I'd say. When they reached the shore, the men mounted the gangplank. They stepped on the bottom deck of the steamer, and everything disappeared inside the hold: the men, the wagons, and the wood."

Captain Nelson stroked his chin. The Chaplain continued.

"After a few minutes, the men emerged, descended the gangplank, and climbed up the path into the woods, pushing their empty carts. Each man returned with another load of wood. They came five more times; six cartloads each in total. Then the five men assembled on the gangplank, slouched really. Not military men, for sure."

The Chaplain had the full attention of his friends.

"Captain Conner came out of the lower deck and handed an envelope to one of the negroes. They went back up the path and vanished into the woods. Captain Conner and the gangplank disappeared into the lower deck of the *Chouteau*. Accompanied by a few blasts from the stacks, our paddle wheels creaked and began to turn. The *Chouteau* pulled away from the dock, and we resumed our trip upstream, minus one of the three gunboats that had accompanied us from Port Hudson. That gunboat steamed down the river and vanished around a curve."

"Curious. What was that all about?" William asked.

"Additional fuel for the steamer, I suppose," said the Chaplain. "Boilers burn up a lot of wood, especially on this twisting course. I hope we aren't running short."

Franklin Nelson stroked his chin again. "We'd know if we'd passed Memphis. The west bank here is rural; we must still be in the State of Arkansas, the Confederacy. A Rebel State. You'd think Captain Conner would start us off with enough fuel to get us to friendly territory."

William had a question for the Chaplain. "Did you ask Captain Conner about what you saw?"

The Chaplain threw back his head. "William! And risk being given a tongue-lashing like Captain Conner gave you?"

William covered his ears. "I can't fault you for that. I'd sure as hell rather take a trip straight down to the underworld than disturb Captain

Conner in his cabin!"

A deep belly laugh came from the Chaplain. "Dear William. I don't think the existence of the underworld is at all *certain*, or that we will find it in one location. But whatever hell there is, Captain Conner may already be headed in that direction."

"Really? Then you agree with me about that man?"

"I'm thinking about what I witnessed this morning."

"Oh? Have you figured it out?"

"I believe I have. I think I saw Captain Conner's side hustle."

"Side hustle? What is it?" asked Franklin Nelson.

"I think he has engaged some runaway slaves to steal timber for him."

"Why would he do that?"

"The same reason most people take what isn't theirs." The Chaplain rubbed his fingers together. "Either he sells the wood, or he uses it and pockets the money the owner of the *Chouteau,* or the Union, gives him to buy fuel."

"Pretty blatant criminal behavior, wouldn't you say?" asked Franklin.

"Who is there to do anything about it? I wish schemes for making a profit off this war were not a common occurrence up and down the line from the lowliest private up to the Generals, and many a civilian as well."

Franklin nodded slowly. "Well, I'll be damned. Makes me hope those runaway slaves made him pay them in Union greenbacks. Confederate money is about as valuable as those miserable fleas we called by the same name: graybacks."

William tipped up his head and moaned. "Oh, God! Don't remind me of the curse of our accommodations in the South: myriads of crawlers!"

When William opened his eyes to the stars, his arm shot up. He pointed straight overhead and called out.

"What's that, my friends? Did you see a bright light streak across the sky? Do stars move like that?"

"I saw it," said Franklin. "Perhaps we're being attacked by some creatures that live on one of those celestial bodies."

William grabbed both sides of his head. "Oh, my God! Please don't tell me we're being invaded while we're on the river. If we are, I'll have to follow all Captain Conner's commands. I'm sure he knows nothing about fighting. Fury at him will make me worthless again!"

His friends had a laugh over that.

"As you can tell, I've reached the point where I make a joke about my temper. That's progress."

"Indeed, it is," said Franklin. "We talked about the problem you had with Captain Conner before the Chaplain joined us. Do you want to run the situation by him to see what he thinks?"

"I'd like that. Nine months together taught me the Chaplain has wise council."

The other two encouraged William to tell his story.

"Chaplain, I was furious when Captain Conner refused to delay our departure for me to find my friend Nathaniel Bradford. The ship's captain had some very good reasons why we had to sail on time, but I wouldn't listen to them. In fact, I was in such a rage I couldn't function for days. When I realized I was miserable, and the person I thought had wronged me—Captain Conner—wasn't suffering at all, I got even madder."

"I watched you running through the ship that morning, my young friend. Can you now think why you were so mad? You admit the captain of the ship is in command, and Captain Conner had good reasons why we had to sail on time."

"After a few days, I realized I should have felt guilty for being distracted and not noticing Nathaniel's absence earlier. Or I could have been aggravated at Nathaniel for not sending word he wouldn't be there."

"Good thinking. Looking for someone to blame is a common human reaction. I'm glad you see you might have been doing just that."

"But here's what does worry me. For nine months, I followed without question every command from anyone who outranked me. March here, turn around, march back. Have your men pitch the tents right there even though you see dark clouds on the horizon and know the creek will rise. Ignore the action on the left; that's someone else's assignment. Even that ill-fated last assault on Port Hudson. I had a strong opinion about that and said nothing."

"But this time, you couldn't just follow the orders of someone in command?"

"No, I couldn't. Was it perhaps because I didn't respect anyone who hadn't been through what we had? Did I feel I'm able to make my own decisions because I am *a veteran of the Union Army*? Maybe the sin of pride?"

A kindly smile widened the Chaplain's face.

"My dear William. You have every reason to be proud of what you have done. You have served your country in a noble cause. You are also wise to worry you might carry your pride too far. You might feel distanced or even superior to those who do not know what you've endured. Yes, you will be different, but you will not be better or worse than any of God's creatures. If you get to feeling you are somehow more important, a bit of time spent gazing at the enormity of the universe will restore perspective."

"And a bit of time with Nathaniel is also good medicine. I wish he were here right now."

"Of course, but for what reason in particular?"

"In these past nine months, Nathaniel also obeyed every order given to him, without fail, even though he knew some of them made no sense at all. He is quite knowledgeable about military strategy, you know. He played with toy soldiers when the rest of the boys along the foothills of the Hoosac Mountains were more interested in learning how to cast our lines in the rivers. Stories of military exploits were his favorite books. He has thoughts of an appointment to West Point. How can he obey unwise orders without complaint?"

The Chaplain nodded his head. "He does so because he's a fine soldier. Unquestioned obedience is necessary during military service. The Army teaches that lesson very well. Unfortunately, the Army does little about preparing soldiers for when service days are over."

Franklin and William nodded. The Chaplain continued.

"My friends, I think you will find the home front has changed over the past nine months as well. No one would now be taking a picnic basket to watch the battlefield like they did at Bull Run! I hope I can stay in touch with the Fifty-second Regiment, and we can talk about the return to civilian life. I think we could help each other."

"I'm going to see to that," said William.

"Equally important, William, I think you've learned that when you get blinded by anger, you are the one who's miserable. The person you're mad at goes on with his life unaffected. You suffer; he doesn't. You might as well get over your anger."

"Yes. I have to put my fury at Captain Conner into a corner of my brain where he can't poison my equanimity. We'll be finished with him soon."

"Let me say, William, your mother's unreasonable request, which no one here knows about, annoyed you, but you kept your cool, gave her the respect a mother deserves, and moved on. Congratulations."

William smiled and nodded his thanks.

~~~

Franklin Nelson shifted his chair a few inches back from the edge of the deck. William thought he would next hear from Franklin about his invitation to write for the Greenfield newspaper.

"Chaplain, I'd like to thank you for giving us a technique for helping us through dark days during the past nine months."

"How did I do that?"

"To keep us from obsessing about dreadful experiences, you suggested every night we review the events of the day to find three circumstances to put on the plus side of the scale."

"Simple enough. I'm glad you found the technique useful."

"I did as well," said William. "We earned the first trip home because we never complained about having to serve beyond our nine-month commitment. Nathaniel told me he thought you are the reason he has a promotion and a commendation coming his way."

"I don't think that's true."

"He told me he took over leadership of the pursuit of General Taylor after the Battle of Irish Bend because you inspired him."

The Chaplain smiled. "Nathaniel is a natural leader of men. When he saw the troops floundering, he moved his company to the head of the column, including the color guard. I admit I gave his actions a thumbs up. Nathaniel dug in his spurs, and his mount flew up the road. The others followed."

"See there, my friends. The Chaplain may not be a sharpshooter, but I could give you many more instances when he inspired our service. I'll look at the stars on any beautiful evening but take guidance from the Chaplain both day and night."

Even in the starlight, William could see color brush the Chaplain's cheeks.

"How about a commendation for my faithful mount, Dolly? I could not have stayed with you if Dolly hadn't mastered her task of taking me to the edge of the action and then marking time until my next command." He paused. "I hated to leave Dolly behind. Perhaps the commendation should be for you, William, for trading in that wild-eyed monster they assigned me and finding one appropriate for my ability."

"And girth," William said under his breath.

Franklin had not the heart to insert his problem into their pleasant evening. He returned to reminiscing about their experiences.

"I was surprised I found brave deeds to celebrate in the worst of situations," he said. "But I was also surprised how many times I put on the plus side of the scale some fascinating natural phenomenon in this unusual area of the country we were fortunate enough to come to. That moon up there—and the sun as well—shine on Massachusetts and Louisiana—but they are very different places. Until I had to endure three weeks of summer heat, I was going to sign up for another nine months just so I could learn more about Louisiana!"

William added to this idea.

"I will not soon forget waking up to a spring shower of colorful little birds decorating the bushes like Christmas ornaments: birds of every color of the rainbow and some who had feathers with the entire palette on the same little bird! Or the sun breaking through after a rain to make every leaf luminesce with a green glow. There's an intensity about the light in Louisiana."

"Unfortunately, I missed the bird fall. I wasn't on the side trip through St Martinsville," said Franklin. "But I also saw many wondrous sights. Chaplain, were you on the march between LaFourche and Brashear City? Those alligators look like prehistoric beasts. Did you see them opening wide to snap up a bunch of egret chicks walking too slowly along the levee? Or the powerful surge of the Mississippi River churning around a sharp bend? Not just the light is intense; everything about Louisiana is extreme."

"The sun and the rain, for sure," said the Chaplain. "And the night sounds. I can close my eyes and remember the crickets starting the symphony as soon as the sun sets. I think Massachusetts animals are like you, William; they like their sleep. I wish we could have had more opportunity to spend time with people here. We would disagree about slavery, I suppose, but what about everything else? Do you think we're different in other ways?"

"My regret as well," said William. "And I had more interactions than most. I've told you about the days I spent talking with the doctor in New Iberia. And I befriended a family of slaves who opened up to me because I spoke their language. Did I tell you all that Nathaniel and I met up with the father of the family again at Port Hudson? He enlisted with the USCT and is a cook attached to the 54th Massachusetts. *Le cuisinier*, he calls himself," Franklin said he had told him.

The Chaplain responded. "You didn't tell me. I'm interested you were able to find him again."

"A couple of times. As soon as we had a break after the siege ended, Nathaniel and I went on a search and found the mess behind General Weitzel's camp. There he was, stirring a roux for a chicken stew. When I first met him, he called himself JeanLouis. When he enlisted, they gave him the name John Broussard."

"Was he in the Louisiana Native Guard?"

"No. The Native Guards are from New Orleans. USCT is a regular colored infantry unit."

"Was he happy to see you?"

"Indeed. His face cracked open with a huge smile. He said the Union had kept their promises to him. He had his work as a cook, and his wife gets her allotment. He also helps the command at Port Hudson with the language problem. His English has improved. Two others who enlisted with him are fine with their duty as well. None of them bears arms. His son Louis did not enlist but keeps in touch. Louis is another you call a *natural leader,* Chaplain. He was a Godsend when we had to organize those runaway slaves who didn't speak a word of English. Nathaniel and I were the only ones who could explain to them what was going on."

"No wonder they were glad you befriended them."

"I had no such experiences," said Franklin.

Maybe you didn't try, William thought.

"I had the idea Elizabeth and I would come back here one day. Now, I have doubts Louisiana would ever want to see us again. We're leaving wreckage behind. Not all of it is our doing, but who would care to sort through the details to divide up the blame?"

The Chaplain stood. "My friends, I hate to break up this pleasant evening. If I stay here any longer, I'll be too tired for the dangerous descent. I'll have to locate a knapsack to put my head on and curl up on the deck. One skill I learned over the past nine months is the ability to fall asleep anywhere. But I try to write detailed letters home every night—two birds with one stone. My wife saves my letters, and I end up with a contemporary record of our adventures. I'm a bit behind. I'd best get to work."

"Hold onto that practice, Chaplain. A lot of men are keeping journals. There's a good project for you when we're home. No one person can see the entire picture. You could gather other letters and put together a fine record of the Fifty-second Regiment in Louisiana. You're a writer. I know from your sermons. If I wrote anything, I'd ask you to read it."

The Chaplain walked over to the open hatch and peered down at the challenge.

"What's your advice, my friends? Should I face the ladder or give it my backside?"

William squeezed his eyelids together. "Please, please face the ladder! You are wise, but you don't have super-human power to grab hold of air!"

"I wasn't thinking. Wish me luck, my friends."

"I'll come take my position behind you to "coach" you down."

"I thank the Good Lord that the Massachusetts Volunteers didn't draw duty in the Navy. I would not have survived climbing ladders all day long!"

When the Chaplain's head disappeared below deck, William got up off the deck and put his hand on Franklin's shoulder. "We'll talk about your issue tomorrow night, Franklin. Tonight, we celebrated our Chaplain."

"I had the same thought. Tomorrow will be time enough. We have days more on the river."

Before he fell asleep, a new worry pricked William's brain. The Chaplain thinks we'll be different because of our experiences during the past nine months. I can be on guard not to think I'm somehow better than those who haven't served, but will Elizabeth find me different in other ways?

For that matter, will I find Elizabeth different now that she's a mother? We have both faced a transformative time without the other.

CHAPTER TWENTY

A rainstorm washed out the next meeting of the stargazers. To be certain he didn't miss his opportunity to hear the Chaplain's council, the following evening, Franklin wasted no time putting the problem on the table.

He spoke up as soon as he and William finished congratulating the Chaplain on his progress with the climb.

"Chaplain Moors, may I run a request by you? I've been wrestling with it ever since we pulled away from the dock at Port Hudson. Having been the beneficiary of your thoughts during this whole experience, I thought you might have a bit more wisdom to share before we part."

"Of course, you may—my privilege. If I have any thoughts, I will share them. Whether they are wise or not is another matter. I'm pleased you found a Chaplain useful for something other than praying over the fallen. There are those who would happily trade their noncombatant Chaplain for a sharpshooter."

"The mail, the mail! Bringing us letters made you the most popular person in our regiment!" said William, who was the third person on the deck that night.

"Yes, popular with those who had someone at home who wrote letters. I did a bit of praying for the poor souls who did not."

William thought but did not express another complaint he had heard about the Chaplains. Grey-haired men put them in place to salve their conscience. They could turn their backs on the toll combat and disease took on the young men they sent into harm's way.

"Here is my problem," Franklin said. He had finally obtained the opportunity to lay out his problem. "I have an offer from the Editor of *The Greenfield Gazette,* which you know is the most widely circulated newspaper in Western Massachusetts. He has asked me to write a column in his paper about our experiences in the Fifty-second Regiment."

The Chaplain's eyes popped open, but not as wide as William's.

"My congratulations to you, Franklin!" the Chaplain said. The Editor has paid you a compliment. I had no idea you were a writer."

William pinched his lips together. His next few breaths took in only half as much air as usual.

Franklin continued. "Sir, I have no training or experience with the press. I've never written one word for public consumption. The Editor knew me in school, but that wasn't yesterday."

The Chaplain raised his eyebrows.

"Apparently, you did not reject the Editor's request out of hand."

"No, I did not."

"And why is that? Does the idea appeal to you?" the Chaplain asked.

"In some ways, yes."

"In what ways? Can you tell me?"

"To be frank, I'm trying to figure out what I want to do with the rest of my life. I've decided against re-enlisting. I've seen enough blood. Unlike our friend William here, I don't have a family farm to go back to. My father has a successful store in Greenfield and hopes I will join him, but I do not look forward to spending my days indoors behind a counter."

"So, you think writing a newspaper column is an opportunity to try something different?"

"Yes, and to expose myself to new possibilities. I've kept a diary these past months, so I believe I have material. If it turns out I don't enjoy reporting, or if I do not satisfy the Editor, at least people will know who I am."

"I've heard you might run for public office."

Franklin smiled. "I won't deny I've thought of it."

William's chair creaked. He sat up straighter. The Chaplain turned to him quickly—a wordless plea. Let me handle this, William. William sat back.

"Do you know the Editor well?" the Chaplain asked.

Franklin answered. "Not well, but we have corresponded for the past few months."

"Is there any subject he is interested in having you write about?"

Franklin smiled and dipped his head. "You've put your finger on the very concern I have, Chaplain. The Editor repeatedly asks about my impression of the negroes who are serving in the army."

"Why do you suppose that is?"

"I do not know."

"William, you are puffing like the engines of the *Chouteau* building up steam! In just a minute, I'd like to hear what you have to say on this subject, but not quite yet."

"Certainly, sir. I didn't mean to interfere."

The Chaplain turned back to Franklin.

"Tell me, how did the Editor bring up the topic of the negro soldiers?"

"When he first wrote to me, which must have been about six months ago, he asked whether I thought negroes should be permitted to bear arms or just be in support roles in the services. At that time, there was a lot of talk about the men of the Union making sacrifices to free people of color, while negroes, the beneficiaries, played no part. We had to do all our own fatigue work—hauling, digging, building bridges. There was growing objection to the policy of returning runaway slaves only to have them turn right around and work against us. We shed blood while freemen in the North did not."

"Did you give the Editor your opinion about negroes bearing arms?"

"No. I said my answer would depend on their training."

"But he wasn't put off? He asked further?"

"Most certainly. One way or another, he brought up the subject in every letter he wrote to me from then on. Then, I received a firm request from him right after the May 27 assault on Port Hudson. He said the people in Western Massachusetts were interested in knowing how the 1st and 3rd Louisiana Native Guards performed in the assault. He said there appeared to be a full range of opinions, from proof positive the negro would fight to those who said they were cowards whose conduct caused the entire operation to fail! And some said one thing at one time and another after a while."

"What did you tell him?"

"I said I couldn't answer his request. Our regiment had not yet come to Port Hudson at the time of the assault. I thought that would be the end of it."

"But it was not?"

"No. He said I was at Port Hudson now and could talk to all the parties involved. I could get to the bottom of what happened."

"Did you make any effort to do what he asked?"

"I did ask a few questions, but I immediately ran into difficulty. There is no general agreement about anything that happened that day! I know battles can be confusing. Nobody sees everything. What's the expression? Where you sit is where you stand. Somehow, the opinions about this assault are the most confusing I've ever heard. And the opinions change. They are still changing. Case in point: initially, General Banks sent rave reports of the conduct of the Louisiana Native Guard in his official reports, but now he disparages their performance."

"And the Editor hasn't stopped asking your opinion?"

"No. Even if I don't write a column, now he wants me to give the paper a report on the assault. Give both sides, he says, and handle the comments and questions that come in."

"I gather you haven't told him if you will or will not write the column. You have just temporized."

"That's about it. I know he will ask again as soon as we return to Greenfield. And praise the Lord, that will be in just a matter of days!"

The Chaplain turned to William. "Okay, my friend. I think you are ready to join this conversation."

"Indeed I am. If it is agreeable with you, Franklin."

"Yes, it is. I need all the help I can get. The deadline is looming."

As he did when about to launch into a difficult subject, William slowed his breath and his words.

"I have to tell you that I have a very strong opinion about whether you should write a column for *The Greenfield Gazette*."

"And what is that opinion?" the Chaplain asked.

"I beg you. Do not get anywhere near a newspaper column."

A smile cracked open the Chaplain's face. "You do have a strong opinion, William. And your reason?"

"My reason has two parts. First, I don't fault the Editor for asking you. His job is to sell papers. For years, the big city presses have increased their readership by printing controversial columns on the decisions of the President and his Generals. Now that we are again needing troops to replenish our forces, the columnists are talking about recruiting negroes. The opinions are flying. Do they have the will to fight? What tasks should they be asked to perform? Should they bear arms or only be in support? Should they command? How much should they be paid? The columnists and those who comment to the papers get twisted into knots because the answers to these questions all get back to opinions about the negro race. Controversy is good for circulation. The Editor would love to put the *Greenfield Gazette* in the company of *The Boston Globe* and *The New York Tribune*. You, my friend Franklin, do not need to dance to his music."

"And your reason has another part?" the Chaplain asked William.

"Yes. Nothing that is printed in the newspaper is ever lost."

"Is that a bad thing?"

"Indeed. Especially for someone who might want to go into politics. Think back a few years ago when the winds of war first began to freshen. At that time, did you think the slaves should be set free? Did you think their owners should be compensated for the loss of their *property*? Did you think freed slaves should be sent somewhere, like the West or back to Africa? Did you think they could be worked into the white world? Or were you certain that we had to save the Union but had not thought deeply about any of the problems that would follow?"

"The last is true. I hadn't really thought about the problems. I guess I thought the Rebels would have to solve them, not the North. Now I know that if we are a Union, any problem is everyone's problem."

"Consider this, my friend. If you had written your thoughts down in a newspaper column at that time, you might well have expressed ideas that have now changed."

Franklin rubbed his hands over his eyes.

"I understand what you are saying. My words would come back to haunt me."

The Chaplain pushed back his chair.

"My friends, the Editor is not alone in his desire to know about the conduct of the Native Guards at Port Hudson. I do, as well. William, do you have an opinion about the quality of the service of the Native Guards?"

William turned his chair to face his two companions.

"I also tried to learn about the conduct of the troops and the command of the Louisiana Native Guard. I concluded that there was no way to make an accurate assessment."

"And why is that? You also had access to those who served in the assault, and you had the advice of a knowledgeable expert, Nathaniel Bradford, to evaluate what they had to say."

"I did not talk to Nathaniel about the assault at first. I had no idea he was studying it in detail. I asked a few questions of participants but could not have any confidence in any conclusions they drew."

"Why was that?"

"For two reasons. First: no opinions being expressed about the service of negro soldiers could accurately describe the entirety of their conduct. The opinions reflected, rather, the sliver of the action the individual person observed. Second: perhaps more important, the opinions seemed to be a better reflection of the pre-existing attitudes about the negro race held by the observers than of what happened that day."

"Could you know that? How could you know their attitudes.?"

"There were a few whom I personally knew who believed negroes were in no way equal to white men. They said they received reports of poor conduct. Others I knew to believed negroes could fight well if they were well led. They said their information was to the contrary. I had no confidence in any conclusion I could come up with. I gave up. Then, I became very busy preparing for another assault. I saw no point worrying about the past."

"But you changed your mind?"

"Nathaniel changed my mind. After the June 15th assault, which also failed, I learned that Nathaniel had been studying the conduct of the Native Guard since the day we arrived in Port Hudson. He studied the strategy of the assault. He spoke at length with anyone who had an opinion about the conduct of the Native Guard. He came to some conclusions. Most importantly, he devised a brilliant system to test the conclusions he did come to."

"And he told you his conclusions?"

"For the three weeks, we waited for transportation home, Nathaniel and I talked about little else. I wish he were here to explain what he concluded. I will be happy to do my best, but it will take some time."

"I'd like to hear what Nathaniel had to say. What about you, Franklin?"

"I would as well."

Chaplain Moors tipped his head back and looked up at the display above him. "Oh, stars in the sky! We are going to need all the wisdom you have to send to us tonight."

The Chaplain stood up. He rubbed his hands over his eyes.

"My friends, before we hear from William, I need to stretch a bit. While I do so, may I tell you a fable in which you might find a kernel of wisdom to guide us? I promise you my tale is many times shorter than any sermon I ever delivered."

~~~

The Chaplain made a deep bow to his companions.

"In ancient days, five blind men who lived in what is now India heard that a strange animal called an elephant had come to their town. If they wished, said the Maharajah, the blind men could go into the town to examine the animal to learn what an elephant might be like. The blind men did so.

"The first blind man reached out his arm. His hand encountered the elephant's trunk swaying toward him. He grabbed the trunk and stroked it. *Ah, ha*, he exclaimed. *This being called elephant is like a thick snake.*

"The second blind man approached the elephant, reached out his hand, and felt a floppy ear. *No,* he said. *This animal is not like a thick snake. This animal is like a fan.*

"The third blind man approached the animal, reached out his hand, and encountered the animal's leg. *Ah, ha,* he said. *This animal is not like a thick snake. He is not like a fan. He is a pillar like a tree trunk.*

"The fourth man placed his hand on the animal's side. This animal is not like a thick snake. He is not like a fan. He is not a pillar like a tree trunk. This animal is like a wall.

"The fifth man felt the animal's tusk. You are all wrong. This animal, called elephant, is hard and smooth like a spear.

"My friends, I do not know of an issue about which there are as many shades of opinion as the conduct of the negroes at war. A poetic man named Saxe has written a poem about the blind men and the elephant that points up the influence of what a man brings to his observation. The poem concludes:

"And so, these men of Indostan disputed loud and long, each in his own opinion, exceeding stiff and strong.

"Each was partly in the right, and all were in the wrong."

Franklin and William applauded the Chaplain's performance.

~~~

When the friends were again seated, Chaplain Moors brought William directly back to the question on the table.

"I believe you have told us that you found the evaluation of the conduct of negro troops on May 27th impossible for two reasons: all opinions are limited by the portion of the battle observed, and in this case, preconceived attitudes about negroes seemed to affect every value judgment on their performance. Is that right?"

"Yes."

"But you say Nathaniel persuaded you that knowing the strategy planned for the May 27 assault enabled him to make an evaluation of the role played by the Louisiana Native Guard. And he also persuaded you that it was possible, but a bit more difficult, to pick up how preconceived attitudes about negroes affected the judgment of the observers."

"Yes."

"That second idea may take some time to explore. Could we start with an analysis of the May 27 assault?"

"A good plan. Once we touch the subject of slavery, we may not exhaust the subject until the *Chouteau* reaches Cairo, Illinois!"

William took a deep breath.

[2]"As I have told you, Nathaniel began his study of the May 27 assault as soon as we arrived at Port Hudson on May 28. His analysis of the assault may not be definitive but, I believe, is the most thorough I have heard. He didn't inform me he was making the study until June, when we were knocking on the door of the fortifications. He and I talked about his studies then and almost nothing else during the last weeks of waiting for transportation home.

"First, the basics of the May 27th assault. As you know, General Nathanial Banks is the Commander of the Department of the Gulf. He had at his disposal for the assault on Port Hudson the forces of five generals: Brigadier-General Dwight and full Generals Weitzel, Grover, Augur, and Sherman. In preparation for the assault, the generals set up in an arc, twelve to five o'clock, north and east of the fortification. Let me demonstrate."[3]

William stood up in front of and with his back to his friends.

"Consider that my body is the fortification of Port Hudson. My left side faces west, toward the Mississippi River. I am looking north, upriver."

He lifted his right arm above his head. "The forces of Brigadier General Dwight were above me at twelve o'clock. Actually, he was subordinate to General Weitzel, who was next at twelve-fifteen." He moved his arm fifteen degrees right, opening and closing his fist.

"The forces of the other generals—Grover, Augur, and Sherman—

---

[2] For encampments of generals at Port Hudson, see map on page 171.

continued around, ending at about five o'clock." William drew the arc in the air with his right hand, pausing as he indicated the location of the forces of Generals. He then returned his hand to twelve o'clock.

"Now here at twelve o'clock, included in the forces of Brig. General Dwight were the 1st and 3rd Louisiana Native Guard. They were not designated to be a first striking force but were, rather, held in reserve. Do you have the picture of how the Union forces were arrayed for battle?"

They told him they did.

"General Banks' strategy was to have the forces of the four full generals engage one after the other, *seriatim as* they say in Latin, from 8 A.M. until 2:30 P.M., in the following order: Weitzel's—including Dwight's Louisiana Native Guards if needed—then Grover's, Sherman's, and last of all, Augur's.

"Brig. General Dwight had bragged that the physical location of his forces was the ideal entrance to overcome the defenses of Port Hudson. Not true! He could not have conducted a personal reconnaissance because that path was, in fact, the worst: a backwater marsh well exposed to Rebel fire.

"General Weitzel engaged his force first. Brig. General Dwight sent in his strike force next. His force was also repulsed. He then ordered the 1st Louisiana Native Guards under the command of Captain André Cailloux, a *gens de couleur libre* from New Orleans, into the fray. This force had been building a pontoon bridge and was not in an ideal striking position.

"Here come the only statements that Nathaniel thought universally accepted as true. Shouting commands in French and English, Capt. Cailloux charged; the men followed. They threw themselves into the battle with great spirit and courage."

William stopped and took a deep breath before he continued.

"In a short while, Rebel fire and the treacherous terrain of the backwater marsh combined to make the position of the Guard untenable. Capt. Cailloux took a bullet in his left arm. With his arm hanging lifeless, he obeyed General Dwight's order to continue to fire—a vain effort because of their location. Rebel sharpshooters now occupied a ridge and rained fire. Captain Cailloux suffered a mortal blow. The 1st Louisiana Native Guard fell back onto the 3rd Native Guards which had been sent in support.

The remaining generals engaged their forces and were unsuccessful as well. By dusk, the Union withdrew. Later reports indicate that General

Dwight was drunk and engaged in a personal squabble with General Banks that day."

The Chaplain asked the next question. "So, no force succeeded."

"That is correct."

"What did Nathaniel think was the reason for the failure of the entire assault? Did he come to a conclusion?"

"Yes, he did. For two reasons: the failure of the generals to attack simultaneously and poor communication between the Generals."

"Those would be flaws in the overall plan or strategy, would they not?"

"Yes."

"And that means General Banks is responsible for the failure?"

"That was Nathaniel's view."

"Did General Banks learn his lesson for the June 15th assault?"

"He did not. However, General Weitzel pressed him to make the later attacks simultaneous, which Nathaniel knew because he was talking to General Weitzel those days about his reenlistment. His order to his generals was to attack "as soon as they were able.""

A chuckle rumbled in the Chaplain's throat.

"Out with it, Chaplain," said Franklin.

"Remember the *bon mot* that made the rounds of the armchair strategists in the press? General Nathaniel Banks moves in mysterious ways, his blunders to perform."

A welcome break in the intensity.

"So," the Chaplain asked, "the failure of May 27 cannot be attributed to the negro troops?"

"They were not perfect, but no troops were. There are credible reports of a range of conduct by the negro and white rank and file, as well as negro and white officers. The important conclusion, according to Nathaniel, is that defects of neither white nor black troops were relevant to the outcome."

They sat quietly, absorbing what William had told them, and tipped back their heads to be soothed by the canopy of stars.

"Are we ready to move on to Nathaniel's second conclusion: why the reports he received are unreliable?"

"Let us proceed," said the Chaplain.

"The second point Nathaniel feels strongly about is that the observers' conclusions depend on which part of the battle the person observed. Remember the Elephant! Even more important, he believed the opinions of all observers were strongly affected by their pre-conceived attitudes. He can prove this conclusion."

"How on earth could he do that?"

"Franklin, here we have an example of why I expect one day Nathaniel will be in charge of the army. Each time Nathaniel talked with someone about the battle, he slipped in an extra question or two. He gave me many examples, but it seemed to me the key question was this: *what do you think will be the role of the freed slaves after abolition?*"

The Chaplain and Franklin were on the edges of their chairs but had puzzled expressions.

"The answers varied tremendously, of course, but could be divided into two rough categories. The first category, accomplishing assimilation, presented challenges, but the challenges could and would be solved. Second category: the problems were insurmountable. When Nathaniel correlated the responses, he found there was a remarkable correlation between those who thought the negroes fought well with those who thought the assimilation would be difficult but possible and a similar correlation between those who thought the Native Guard failed to fight well with those who thought assimilation impossible. The first group praised them. The second blamed them for the sins of the world."

"As simple as that?" the Chaplain asked.

"It's not simple at all. Nathaniel said sometimes it took a while to get through the observer's insistence that he saw something or had information directly from someone who did. But still, the correlation between those who thought the negro was not capable of ever being equal to a white man with those who disparaged their ability to fight was remarkable."

After a period, William had a question for the Chaplain.

"I don't mean to put you on the spot, but I really would like your wisdom. How would you answer the question? What should the role of negroes be after abolition?"

"My friends, that is a fair question. I've fielded many comments about how slavery is fine because there are slaves depicted in the Bible. Nonsense! Two thousand years ago, culture was entirely different. I am persuaded that owning another human being is morally wrong. You would have to believe those with skin of another color are a different sort of human being to endorse it. I do not. I do recognize the significant problems that abolition will present. If we could create a unique form of government, a Republic, and preserve it, we can solve these problems as well, with God's help."

"You sound exactly like my wife, Elizabeth," said William. "We have a wise President. I hope we will all support him as he undertakes the hard work of bringing us to the place where we live comfortably with abolition." Franklin scratched his head. "Do you think if we grew up with slavery, never knew anything different, if slavery was the economic foundation of our whole economy, we'd have the courage to overthrow it? I would hope we would see the evil. I cannot be sure."

"Nor I," said William. "I enlisted for the preservation of the Union. When the war began, our President wouldn't get into discussing slavery. He thought the problems insurmountable. He changed. He still believes tremendous problems lie ahead, but we must have faith that men of good will be able to solve them. Prejudices run deep and not only in the south."

"Thank you, my friends," Franklin said after a bit. "My newspaper career will not happen. I think I would be in over my head before my first column hit the newsstand."

CHAPTER TWENTY-ONE

The *Chouteau* left the scorching heat and the Confederacy behind. The days remained warm, but the nights became cooler. For the next three nights, the friends and a few more officers who joined them pondered eternal questions from their chairs on the deck. When the conversation veered toward the subject of slavery or commanders of color, William changed the subject. He purposely turned his mind to drift forward to what awaited him at the end of this interminable voyage: the arms of his beloved wife, Elizabeth, and the sight of his month-old son.

Mid-morning on the seventh day after the steamer *Chouteau* left Port Hudson, Captain Conner took his megaphone to the foredeck and announced the sighting of the Stars and Strips flying over the landing dock at Cairo, Illinois. Cheers rose from the steamer, from the two gunboats that had safely escorted her up the Mississippi River, and from the Union soldiers keeping watch on shore. By the time the steamer worked her way alongside the dock and the hands secured the mooring ropes to the stanchions, General Buford, commander of the Post, had assembled a welcoming party. The Fifty-second Regiment disembarked to rousing music and cheers of welcome from the troops in formation. After the brief concert, the band led the Fifty-second Regiment to the Union camp a short march away.

Their worn threads and emaciated bodies presented a painful contrast to the splendid uniforms and full faces of the resident troops. The regiment had caught up on sleep aboard the steamer, but even Col. Greenleaf had sunken cheeks and eggplant-hued puffiness like the eyes of every private. General Buford sent the quartermaster to them to offer what replacement parts of uniforms he could supply to replenish their rags. Almost all items of clothing they needed were several sizes smaller than those they dropped on the tent floor.

"You are a challenge, Lieutenant," he told William. "I have nothing tall enough for your body. But I have someone who sews well. He can add inches to the bottom of the legs of a pair of pants and the length of a jacket within the day—if he gets started right now. Come with me."

At Port Hudson, William had turned down a uniform stripped from a casualty. Now that he had a look at himself in a mirror at the quartermaster's tent, he was less squeamish. He wanted to present Elizabeth with the best version of himself he possibly could.

"Scarecrows in a cornfield, that's what we look like!"

A hot bath and a night on a feather mattress would have been welcome, but not a man suggested there be any delay in finding seats on the first railway car headed north. They showered, cut each other's hair, and trimmed their beards. They enjoyed a sumptuous breakfast, a fine early afternoon meal, and awaited the train. The regiment boarded in the early afternoon.

But not every man. Eighteen men of the Fifty-second Regiment were thought too frail to endure the trip by rail. They took transport to a hospital in Mound City, Illinois. Their families were to be notified.

The days in the railway cars seemed interminable. Soot and steam replaced the clear, fresh breezes on the river. Only the highest-ranking officers had more than a single seat. As the train traveled through towns in Illinois, Indiana, Ohio, and Pennsylvania, people streamed to the stations to load them with provisions. The men had a good rest on the *Harry Chouteau,* but the ship's fare had not put on any weight. Home-cooked meals brought to the train began to fill in a few of the wrinkles on their drawn faces. But Greenleaf insisted they show proper appreciation by joining the people at groaning picnic tables and returning thanks.

"Gentlemen, we do not eat and run."

The train stopped again at Syracuse and Utica, but then mechanical problems brought them to a six-hour delay for repairs to the coupling on one of the cars. Not knowing when the trip might be repaired kept them close at hand and irritable beyond belief. Men who took enemy fire with equanimity let go with unbelievable language! Eventually, the train made a brief stop at Albany, New York, and finally crossed into Massachusetts at the little town of Hinsdale. They pulled into the Springfield station where flags, a twenty-piece band, and a crowd of at least a hundred waited to greet them.

As soon as the train crossed the state line, William wished he had Excalibur or even Madeleine at hand. On any mount, he could have been home in Deerfield within the day. Col. Greenleaf denied him permission to dispatch a courier to Pierre to send him a horse from the farm.

"You are under my command until I deliver you to the station appearing on your orders, 2nd Lieutenant Wells. The same rules apply to everyone. But first, the people of Springfield have prepared a feast and celebration worthy of your valor."

Did Col. Greenleaf have no one waiting for him? He allowed the mayor to review a welcome parade that must have included every person in Springfield from school children carrying miniature stars and stripes to grey-haired veterans of the frontier wars. The Colonel presided over the groaning table of food, rising to acknowledge the donor of every dish.

Enough! The Chaplain closed his eyes and mumbled words that so rarely had crossed his lips. Col. Greenleaf used a cartful of adjectives as he developed more and more facility with flowery language. "I guess that's how you get a promotion to colonel," William grumbled.

"Get a grip, Lt. Wells. Good manners require the able-bodied to show proper appreciation."

"We're stopping in Deerfield?" William asked Col. Greenfield when the train was slower. "How awkward! We don't have a station in town."

"You do now. Built just for this occasion."

And there they were: his wife, Elizabeth, holding a baby in a blanket. Behind her, he saw Pierre and his parents. William thought he would faint.

Ten minutes seemed like an hour as Col. Greenleaf presented papers to each standing soldier. Duffle bags and knapsacks flew from the baggage cars onto the quay. The door opened. A stool appeared beneath. William stepped from the railcar. The arms of his wife encircled him and his baby boy. His parents, the flags, the band, and the table of food were all a blur.

~~~

Later that evening, William and Elizabeth, the baby in a cradle at their feet, sat on the back porch of their cottage.

"I hope everyone will forgive me. I realize people mean well, but I couldn't hold myself together for another minute. I had to get home and wash up as soon as I could. I hope I didn't turn over your stomach and that the baby is too young to remember what his father smelled like when he returned. I felt too dirty to touch either of you, and I wanted to hold you both forever."

"My love, my love. You can do no wrong. You promised to go to the farm tomorrow. They will be waiting. Do you feel better now?"

"I can't stop looking at your two faces. You are both the most beautiful sights I have ever seen. You described the baby, but I had no idea how incredibly marvelous he would be."

"I think we can give the baby his name now."

"And what will the name be?"

"Nathaniel, of course."

"We must ask Nathaniel. I haven't done it yet. I was going to ask him on the trip home, but—."

Elizabeth swallowed hard and cut him off.

"You don't know?"

"Know what?"

Elizabeth slid tight against William and put her head on his chest.

"Mr. Bradford received the telegram last week."

"What? What telegram?" A sick feeling rose in William's stomach. Elizabeth continued, speaking quietly.

"Nathaniel lost his life the day your regiment sailed out of Port Hudson."

The words stabbed William's chest, opening for sobs to escape. He took a few rasping breaths between the sobs moving through his body.

"How could that be possible? The fighting was over, and…"

How long Elizabeth held him, he could not say—a long time passed before he asked her if she knew any more about what happened.

"Mr. Bradford has a letter from General Banks. He'll show it to you. Early in the morning on sailing day, Nathaniel left headquarters to go to the dock. He passed behind General Grover's encampment. That's where one of the cooks found him lying next to another cook named Bernard, the blood of the two men pooling together. Nat was dressed up for sailing, and the cook was in his apron stirring the beans for lunch for General Grover's men. A Rebel in the woods must have shot him along with Bernard, who was cooking breakfast. Another cook in the Colored Infantry said he saw the two bodies as one, their blood flowing together. He went for help, which came too late.

ACKNOWLEDGMENTS

When my late husband, Jerry Simon, brought me to South Louisiana a half-century ago, I fell in love with the beauty and the easy humor of the colorful characters who live here. From the start, I noticed almost anyone with whom I enjoyed a more than casual conversation had the pages of a "book in progress" tied in string tucked in a box in the attic, a collection of poems in a notebook on a high shelf in the bedroom closet, or several journals they hoped one day to mine for characters to bring life to a play. However, I had no idea the area would become an incubation for literary flowering that I could join when I retired from the judicial bench.

I thank my "more than a daughter-in-law," Margaret Simon, and the late Deacon Diane Moore, who first gave me the courage to write. This work exists only because of the encouragement and patient guidance of my friend of sixty years, Ann B. Dobie.

As always, I am thankful for the patience and support of my family, particularly my daughter Claire, who came to visit at the end to help pull this book together.

Recently, I was delighted to find Rose Anne Raphael and Kate Ferry, two daughters of old friends and now my new friends, who have grown up to be skilled artists. They were willing to handle the artistic needs of this book, for which I thank them. I thank my publisher, Dr. Victoria Sullivan, and Border Press Books.

And, of course, I thank Dr. Phebe Hayes, President of the Iberia African American Historical Society, for sharing with me the story of her ancestors that inspired this story.

BIBLIOGRAPHY

Baum, Dale, *The Civil War Party System, The Case of Massachusetts 1848-1876,* Chapel Hill and London, University of North Carolina Press, 1984.

Dobak, William A., *Freedom by the Sword, U. S. Colored Troops, 1862-1867*, Washington, D.C., Center of Military History, U.S. Army.

Edmonds, Edward C., *Yankee Autumn in Acadiana, A Narrative of the Great Texas Overland Exhibition through Southwestern Louisiana October-December 1863*, Lafayette, LA, The Acadiana Press. 1979.

Feldman, Noah, *Lincoln, Slavery and the Refounding of America,* Farrar, New York, N. Y., Straus and Giroux, 2021.

Flinn, Frank M., *Campaigning with Banks in Louisiana, '63 and '64*, Lynn Mass., Thos. F. Nichols Press, 1887.

Irwin, Richard B., *History of the Nineteenth Army Corps,* Coppell, TX, Civil War Classic Library, 2020.

Johnson, Ludwell H., *Red River Campaign: Politics and Cotton in the Civil War.* Kent, Ohio, Kent State Univ. Press. 1993.

Moors, J. F., *History of the Fifty-second Massachusetts Volunteers,* Boston, Press of George H. Ellis, 1893.

Ouchley, Kelby, *Flora and Fauna of the Civil War, An Environmental Reference Guide*, Baton Rouge, Louisiana State University

Press, 2010.

Rodrigue, John, *Reconstruction in the Cane Fields,* Baton Rouge, La., LSU Press, 2001.

Schouler, William, *A History of Massachusetts in the Civil War*, Miami, Hard Press, 2017,

Strait, Fatima, *Economy Hall: The Hidden History of a Free Black Brotherhood,* The Historic New Orleans Collection, New Orleans, 2021.

Tanner, Lynette Ater, Ed., *Chained to the Land, Voices of Cotton and Cane Plantations,* Winston Salem, John F. Blair Pub, 2014.

Taylor, Richard, *Destruction and Reconstruction*, Coppell, TX, Pyrrhus Press, 2020.

Wade, Michael G., *Sugar Dynasty: M. A. Patout & Son, Ltd. 1791-1993,* Lafayette, Louisiana: LA Center for Louisiana Studies, University of Southwestern Louisiana, 1995.

Weaver, C. P., ed., *Thank God My Regiment an African One; The Civil War Diary of Colonel Nathan Daniels*, Baton Rouge, LSU Press. 1998.

Wilson, Keith P. *Campfires of Freedom; The Camp Life of Black Soldiers during the Civil War.* Kent, Ohio: Kent State Univ. Press. 2002.